T0379175

WASEEM

A NOVEL

LILAS TAHA

Arcade Publishing • New York

Arcade Publishing books may be purchased in bulk at special discounts for sales promotion, corporate gifts, fund-raising, or educational purposes. Special editions can also be created to specifications. For details, contact the Special Sales Department, Arcade Publishing, 307 West 36th Street, 11th Floor, New York, NY 10018 or arcade@skyhorsepublishing.com.

First Edition

Arcade Publishing® is a registered trademark of Skyhorse Publishing, Inc.®, a Delaware corporation.

Visit our website at www.arcadepub.com.

10 9 8 7 6 5 4 3 2 1

Library of Congress Cataloging-in-Publication Data is available on file.

Cover design by David Ter-Avanesyan
Cover photo credit Getty Images

Print ISBN: 978-1-64821-127-0
Ebook ISBN: 978-1-64821-128-7

Printed in the United States of America

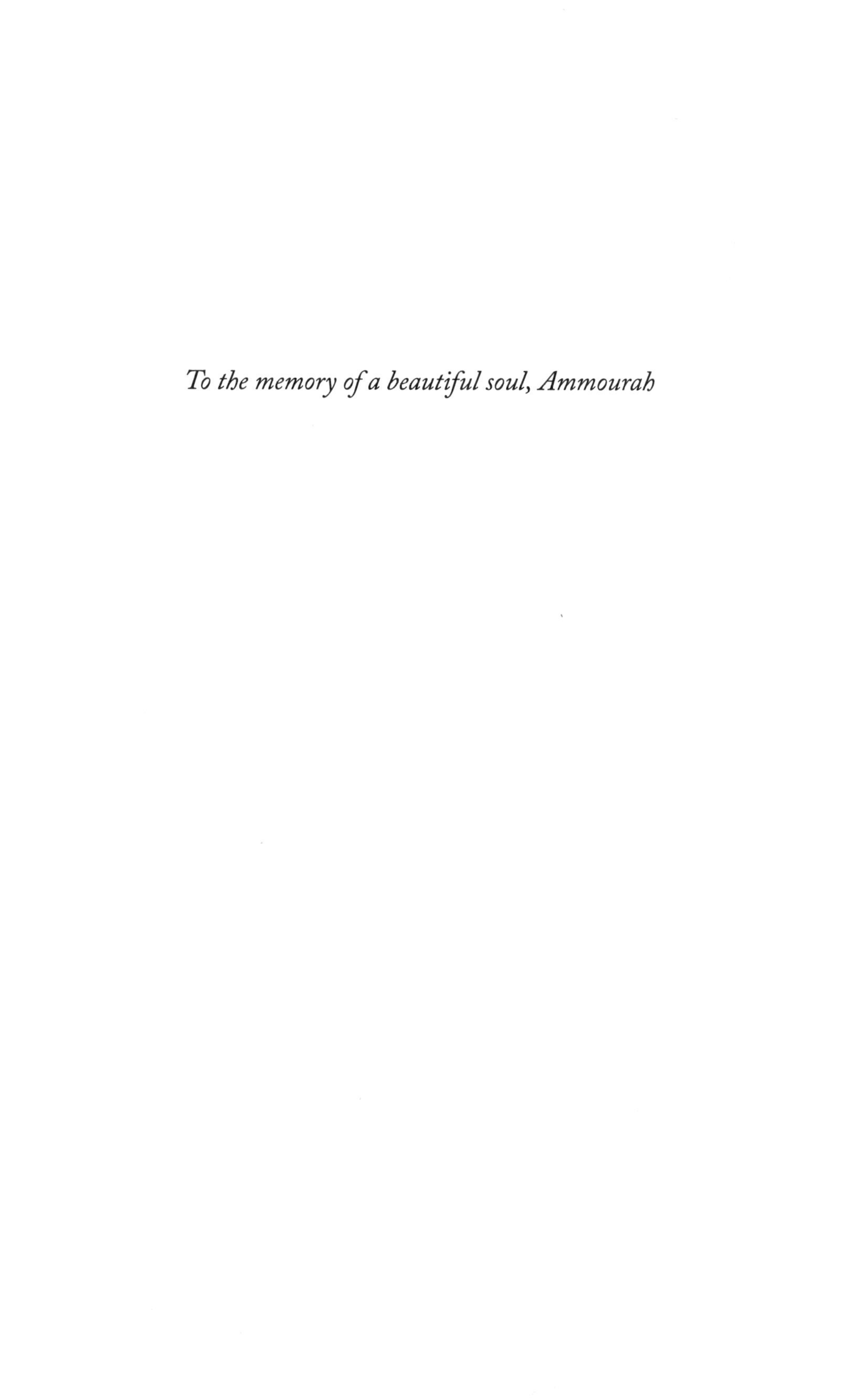

To the memory of a beautiful soul, Ammourah

CHAPTER ONE

I shall tell you lies. You are going to believe them, and in the end, you will thank me for them.

I heard the sole reason God created humans is to worship Him. I say "heard" because that's what I picked up from conversations around me. No one told me. And no one taught me how to go about the worshipping process. In fact, no one took the time to teach me anything at all.

Except her.

Ameena taught me how to make a killer knot in my necktie.

This God I'm supposed to worship must have been in a foul mood when He created me, bestowing onto my body a number of handicaps. I can't move my tongue to articulate words. I express myself through limited verbal expressions and a combination of grunts and sounds. My mother understands everything I attempt to convey, my two sisters manage to catch most, my three brothers discern a few, and my father grasps barely any.

My brothers compensate for their poor comprehension by carrying me around on their backs since I can't walk on my own. If they take me to a paved road, I'm able to push an UNRWA-issued walker with great difficulty until the pain in my lower back forces me to stop. My knees rub against each other, my ankles turn inward. As for my hands, I can't do anything useful other than gripping a spoon or a shoe and flipping the finger when the mood strikes. And sometimes when I become too excited, muscle spasms take over my entire body.

But God gifted me twenty-twenty vision—though I am cross-eyed—and fine-tuned hearing, albeit my pointy ears sit high on my unnaturally-elongated skull, so my head resembles that of a fox. Add on jagged teeth to complete the image. God also granted me a strong immune system. I rarely fall ill.

In short, I look like a hairless fox, healthy and smart in a neat tie.

Should I tell you my name? It's Waseem. A first-born son, I should have been named Saleem, after my paternal grandfather as tradition dictates. Saleem literally means "physically healthy" in Arabic. The kindhearted neighborhood midwife wanted to spare me ridicule and suggested my parents choose another name. They decided on Waseem. It means "handsome."

Did I forget to tell you my parents had a strange sense of humor?

My brothers and sisters received special hugs from my mother at the door every morning before they went to school, leaving me behind. Often, to the point of a predictable habit, my second brother, Wael, returned home hours before school let out, claiming a headache or an ailment of some sort, which my mother never accepted nor investigated. She would take him by the hand, the collar of his shirt, or a fistful of hair and drag him back. But not before she used me to admonish his foolish efforts to abandon education. She would point at me while yelling at my brother that he should be grateful for the privilege of attending school. I, in turn, would fake convulsions and howl to enhance my mother's sermon with special effects. Sometimes, I would help her dislodge his firm grip off the door by throwing shoes at him. I never aimed at his head.

I spent most of my childhood on a stack of long cushions under our east window and watched the world unfurl. I followed my siblings' schooling when they did their homework around me and picked up the written language on my own. I read anything that came to me.

A mechanic, my father returned home at the end of each day with stacks of newspapers. He smoked cigarettes and read the news aloud, and I listened to each word he uttered. My mother spread the papers on the floor to protect our faded rug when we ate. I read around plates and cups and pored over every leaf she didn't use. I licked my entire palm to manage turning the flimsy pages.

I learned everything by observing, listening, interpreting body language, searching for clues in shifting tones, feeling my way through this wretched life God handed me.

Yes, I say wretched and will add unfair, and I'm not going to apologize for it either.

I find life to be hideous. Unattractive. Like death. It's an ugly business expelling the last breath. I've witnessed such turmoil—limbs twitch, lungs gurgle, lips contort, eyes bulge. And life is messy as soon as it begins. I've seen the agony and the disgusting production that accompanies a baby into the world. Both events took place in our home—actually one by my feet. The death when I was sixteen, and the birth when I was twenty-one. Why didn't I leave the room, you ask?

Wedged between two other units in a two-story structure, our home sat in the heart of a Palestinian refugee camp in Southern Lebanon. One room was our entire home. To free up precious space, my mother often parked my walker outside the door. Those death and birth incidents landed in the dead of winter five years apart. I preferred not to crawl out to the wet, biting cold. So, I huddled in one corner, tried to make my useless body as small as possible, and followed the gruesome happenings.

No one objected.

I doubt they even took notice.

But that's not where I begin this story. I shall start with the story of noble Ameena, the girl who brought me gifts in her panties.

CHAPTER TWO

During the day, Ameena's head tilted slightly to the skies when she walked—a sunflower immersed in worship of the morning star. She shielded her eyes with her palm when the glare turned harsh. Her trim body pulsed with vitality from her daylong prayer. Tan skin glimmered, dark eyes sparkled, neck veins thumped with the beat of life.

The moon ebbed Ameena's mood. Subdued, she slowed down, became quieter, easier for me to understand and interpret her moves. I could talk to Ameena all night and never fall asleep.

If only I could talk.

Every Friday, my father took my brothers to communal noon prayers at the mosque. He left me out of the procession. I didn't mind, for that was when she came over to study with my sisters.

Established by the International Committee of the Red Cross in 1948 to accommodate Palestinian refugees, our camp expanded over seven decades through haphazardly constructed shelters and dwellings. My mother's parents were forced to flee from *Yaffa* under heavy bombardment, carrying the keys to their homes tucked with whatever belongings they could load onto a beaten truck until they reached Lebanon. With little money in their possession, and like more than the hundred thousand others with them, they sheltered in the camp. Their stay was supposed to be temporary—two to three weeks—as mother remembered from her parents' painful recounts of the *Nakba*. The day to return to Palestine never came, and she was born a refugee in this camp. As was my father.

Our particular crowded area balanced on a hilly incline. My home overlooked a busy alley at a considerable elevation. I often stretched down my arm out the window in an attempt to tap the heads of passersby, but I never managed to touch anyone.

Ameena lived in the structure across the alley. Born on the same day, but two years my junior, she was an only child, which was an oddity among Palestinian families in the camp. She spent a lot of time with my sisters. Two years apart, Maryam and Fayzeh sandwiched Ameena. But unlike them, she paid attention, listened with her heart—a kindred heart enlightened by the golden sun.

One Friday, the girls huddled in their corner on the rug. Fayzeh sprawled on her abdomen meticulously inscribing letters in a notebook. Maryam and Ameena worked on a reading assignment about a boy and a stray dog. Heads together, they spent more time whispering than reading through the story. I crawled to their spot and grabbed one of their books. Maryam snatched it out of my hands. Fayzeh hugged her notebook to her chest. They ran into the bathroom whining to my mother, who was buried knee-deep in laundry.

And what did Ameena do?

She snuggled next to me, slowly flipped pages and let me read the rest of the story. At age seven, she understood I wanted more. She knew my need, fed my hunger. Ameena leapt onto the tattered stage of my life and executed a graceful pirouette.

From my window, I watched her perform her special dance one late Thursday afternoon. Just as the owner of the small bookshop at the corner of her building prepared to close for the week, Ameena ran in. The owner continued collecting unsold newspapers and magazines from the stand outside the door. He ushered dejected Ameena out of his store and dropped down the aluminum shutters. She walked home fast, head bowed, hands flat over a small bulge on her belly.

At noon the next day, she waited until my father and brothers left to attend Friday prayers before she joined my sisters for their study circle. Mother disappeared in the bathroom with the weekly wash. While Maryam and Fayzeh set up UNRWA-issued stationery in their designated area, Ameena slipped a book from under her dress and stuffed it under my cushions. She pressed her index finger to my lips and winked.

Late at night after everyone went to sleep, I read Ameena's offering cover-to-cover using the streetlight outside my window and the wide sill to prop up the dog-eared paperback book. Too excited, I ignored the fact that she chose her first gift to be an Arabic translation of *Beauty and the Beast.* I suspect the bookkeeper never learned of the theft. No businesses opened on Friday. Come Saturday morning, Ameena was the first of his patrons. She returned the book while he was busy setting up the newsstand.

After that weekend, Ameena rarely came over empty-handed. One of the problems with her daring dance was the size of her panties. She only brought me material that would fit under her colorful dresses—mostly Ghassan Kanafani's resistance literature and Agatha Christie's translated mysteries. Ameena couldn't snatch long comic books or thick novels—Naguib Mahfouz's *Cairo Trilogy* and Tolstoy's *War and Peace* drew the attention of the bookshop owner, and I couldn't possibly finish reading them in time.

The other problem was that Ameena grew up. The year she turned eleven, her regular visits abated, her offerings dwindled. She started wearing long trousers under her mid-thigh dresses. Along with her childhood, Ameena left the unauthorized borrowing behind.

~

One particular spring day, Ameena bolted out of her home. Below my extended hand, her dark hair glistened a healthy sheen under the sun. The thick curly strands must tingle when fingers run through them.

I would love to put my theory to the test.

Ameena rushed into our home, shook off her shoes and popped her head behind the curtain concealing the kitchen to greet my mother with her usual, "*Salam, khalto.*"

When Mother cooked, she always kept the front door open to circulate air and let the neighbors know what was on the menu. A seasoned manager of limited resources, she stretched our UNRWA food basket rations to concoct mouthwatering meals. It was a special day. I smelled roasted chicken. I ran my tongue over my teeth. My family would have to share the single chicken without one of the drumsticks. Mother would make sure I am served first today.

"How come no one is back from school?" Ameena asked.

"The girls should walk in any minute now," my mother said. "The boys are helping their father close the shop early today."

"I ran out of school the instant the bell rang, dropped my bag at home, and came over as soon as I could." Ameena joined me at the window. She produced a yellowish lollipop from her pocket and unwrapped it. "Happy birthday, Waseem."

I opened my mouth, and she centered the oval-shaped lollipop on my tongue. I wanted to smile, but my entire body jerked from the intense sourness.

"It's lemon and grapefruit," she said through a tentative smile. "You like it?"

I nodded. How could I not? I turned fourteen that day, Ameena twelve. Sweet Ameena always celebrated our birthdays with lollipops. My mother marked the day with a roasted chicken.

Ameena rose onto her knees to look out the window. "I'm so bored, Waseem," she mumbled. "I think I'll go crazy here."

I rested my arms on the windowsill and made an effort to gesture at people down below, bustling to and fro.

"Gaaaaa . . . mmmm?" I could have enunciated the word a tad clearer had the citrusy candy not been watering my mouth. But Ameena understood. She understood me even when I sat still and silent.

"What sort of game do you want to play?" she asked.

I curled my palm over the lollipop stick and pulled it out of my mouth. I eyed a man about to pass under the window, swirled my tongue and spit. Ameena gasped. My saliva landed at the man's feet. He looked up. Ameena jerked me back, and we tumbled onto the cushions, me in a heap of tangled stiff limbs, she in a poised crouch.

She slapped my shoulder. "I can't believe you did that."

I howled with laughter and wiggled my eyebrows. "Gaaaammme!"

"Dare to hit? Is that your game?"

I nodded. I failed to mention I inherited my parents' perverse humor.

Ameena scrambled to her feet. "I'll get a glass of water." She went into the kitchen and returned before I was able to sit properly. She held my arm and helped me regain my position by the window.

"No more spitting," she whispered, "use water."

We held the glass together, her hand on top of mine to keep it steady. We tried to time it right for water to land on an unfortunate soul. We spared women and children and only aimed at men—Ameena's requirement to play along. It took us several tries to score a bullseye upon a shiny bald head. We ducked under the window and Ameena's hand clasped over my mouth to stifle my triumphant hoot.

Something flew through the window, hit the opposite wall, and struck a ceramic tile hanging above the television. My mother hurried out of the kitchen. Her sole possession of her family's home in Palestine passed on by my grandmother scattered into colorful, sharp pieces on the floor. She knelt down and collected the shattered square tile.

"Our home in *Yaffa*," she said, wiping away tears. "Who did this?"

Ameena stumbled to her side. "Someone . . . uh . . . threw a rock into the window."

"*Allah yila'an salsafeel abooh*," my mother spit her curse against the man's father and grandfathers. She clutched the shards of tile to her bosom and disappeared behind the kitchen curtain.

Ameena turned to me, eyes wide, lips tight in a straight line, anger and regret screamed from her beautiful face. "We did that," she whispered.

I opened my mouth, but only abrasive sounds emanated. Ameena stormed out. I wished I could will my vocal cords to tell her, "No, I did that. I destroyed my mother's prized memento of her family's stolen house and a homeland long gone."

To the best of her ability, my mother glued together her precious geometrically designed tile and mounted it back on the wall. "Your grandmother told me how she used to play *haileh* on the tiled living room when she was a little girl. Just imagine, Waseem, a room big enough for a girl to skip after a rock." She stepped back to admire the hanging art piece. "*Allah yirhamha*, your grandmother was snatched out of this world too early. She never even met your father. I wish you knew her. She had a special gift for recounting details. To remember her description of the splendid taste of *Yaffa* oranges alone waters my mouth." Mother turned to me with a determined smile. "We will take this tile with us when we return home. You will see how beautiful the floor of our big house is and taste oranges grown in the blessed, rich soil of Palestine."

That day, I learned something new. For some people hope never dies.

I resent that notion. To know that my mother still held on to the dream of returning to reclaim her family's artfully tiled home in Palestine, after spending her entire life in this refugee camp, angers me. It explained her persistence to keep having babies after my arrival. She harbored hope, not despair.

Why would anyone have lofty aspirations to escape the life they were handed, when I have none whatsoever? I am forever trapped in this hell of a body—my mind's designated refugee shack. Entertaining the slightest optimism is futile, a barren waste of time. What is the use of desiring something that you knew would never pass? Hope is for what is possible. I have no hope. And I have no regrets.

After that day, Ameena stopped coming to our house. A month stretched without a reprieve. I thirsted for her sporadic gifts, longed for the feel of a book in my hands, and craved our nonverbal conversations. But most of all, I missed her delicate voice caressing my soul. I yearned for her invigorating energy to enliven my days and rouse my nights. She visited only once to consult with my sisters on a piece of clothing her seamstress mother made. Ameena avoided looking at me. I never took my eyes off her. The sun charged Ameena's spirit, and Ameena nurtured mine. If she meant to punish me for the tile incident, she had very well accomplished her goal. To ease her conscience about what we had done, I let her simmer in anger and disappointment, then vowed to put an end to her evasion the next time she made an appearance.

Three weeks passed. She came over to study with my sisters for an exam. I could take her shunning no longer, nor her struggle with the simple math problem she was working out loud. I wiggled in my corner and groaned to force Ameena's eyes to me.

Everyone acknowledged my effort to communicate. Father lowered his newspaper, Mother stopped peeling oranges, my youngest brother laughed, the others told me to be quiet, my sisters sat to attention, and Ameena finally looked up from her math book.

"*Abooh*," I said.

Ameena blushed and shook her head.

"*Abooh*," I repeated and pointed in the direction of the hanging tile.

"It's fine, Waseem," my mother sighed, knowing what I referred to. "We can't do anything about it now."

"*Abooooooh*," I screeched.

"What is he talking about?" my father asked.

"The broken tile." Mother handed him a peeled orange. "I told you a draft knocked it down, remember?" She sampled a slice of the fruit and spit it out. "These are tasteless. Nothing comes close to the juicy oranges from our neighborhood's grove in *Yaffa*."

I cringed at my mother's mantra. Whenever she wanted to express displeasure or change a subject, she would bring up *Yaffa*'s unparalleled oranges as if she were the one who grew up accustomed to their splendid taste, not her mother. The fact that she never enjoyed the special citrus didn't deter her from using it in her arguments. My grandmother had influenced her daughter's logic with exceptional depictions of the fruit, and my mother, in turn, twisted ours. We all knew how upset she was whenever she mentioned the scrumptious *Yaffa* oranges.

Father rolled his eyes and returned to his paper.

I chewed the inside of my cheek. So, Mother lied about what happened. The tile was that important. Did she think my father would go looking for that audacious man? How could he find him? Ameena and I were the sole witnesses who could identify him.

I yelled at the top of my lungs, lunged off the cushions and crawled toward the girls in the opposite corner. "*Abooooh*!" I bellowed.

Yasser, the oldest of my brothers, held me under the armpits and lifted me back to my spot, but not before I connected eyes with Ameena.

She smiled and mouthed silently, "I will find him."

And so, our pact began.

CHAPTER THREE

We searched for our stone-thrower for days. A hawk with clipped wings, I perched at my vantage point and relied on Ameena to comb the neighborhood after school. One afternoon, Yasser came home earlier than usual and carried me to the alley. I pushed my walker up and down, meandering a path around potholes and chunks of aluminum sheets—remnants of the only roofing material allowed into the camp by Lebanese authority. Vegetable stands, fruit crates, and cheap plastic household items spilled out of shops onto the narrow strip of pavement, the only surface forgiving enough for my walker.

Children followed me like flies. If I wanted to make them go away, I could have stopped, bared my teeth and yelped like the fox they expected. But I didn't do that. I like children.

Women averted their gazes as if the sight of me hurt their delicate nature. Those who visited with my mother were far from genteel. They sipped pots of Arabic coffee and talked of topics no boy had any business learning. They pitied my sisters. I saw the sorrow in their resentful eyes, confident that men would not marry my sisters for fear of spawning children like me. I hated those women.

I passed under a collection of hanging beach balls. Who in their right mind would buy a thing like that? Leaving the camp to reach the seashore required a special permit to pass through the soldiers at the gates. People went through the trouble for needed medical treatment, or to chase essential government and education documents, but certainly not to have fun at the beach.

I wondered what vast stretches of blue water look like. Would I abandon the restraints of my body if immersed, weightless, and free? No walker to push, no rigid knees and elbows to unlock. When mother bathed me on the chipped floor of our tub-less bathroom, before my father took over the chore, she used to soak my feet in a bucket as she scrubbed me clean. I could wiggle my toes freely in the warm water. It felt good, liberating.

Do sea waves sound like cooing doves when they wash the pier and grace the shore? They must, for those who venture out and make it to *Saida* harbor return seemingly revived. Reading about these occurrences leaves me wanting. The curse of education plagues my imprisoned mind.

Ameena's father left the camp on a regular basis. I didn't know why a baker was granted so much access, but he had promised Ameena to take her with him someday. I hoped she would remember every detail so she could relate the experience to me. How else would I be able to smell the saltiness of a sea breeze, if not in Ameena's hair?

My walker took me as far as the butcher's shop. The pavement lapsed into rubble beyond that point, and I needed to relieve my back by then. Wearing his stinking, blood-soaked leather apron, Abu Ali plopped a tattered plastic chair outside his shop and invited me to sit. I gestured for him to move the chair away from the carcass hanging from a hook by the door. He laughed and nudged the chair with his foot.

I took my seat and parked my walker to the side. I shooed buzzing flies in the direction of the boys following me. The children dispersed. The flies returned. I lifted two fingers to my mouth and puffed.

Abu Ali tapped out a cigarette from a newly opened pack of Camels, inserted it between my lips, and lit it with a matchstick struck against his leather apron. Tobacco smoke kept the flies away and smelled better than gutted lamb. I puffed along, pretending to listen to the butcher while I scanned the crowds for a bald head.

Abu Ali talked nonstop. Men did that around me. They spoke about events in the camp, politics, actions of competing factions, and who had it in for whom. They reasoned since I couldn't talk, I couldn't expose their views. They considered me safe and unburdened their souls. I allowed them the comfort of disclosure—even led them on. A grin at the right moment opened dams of knowledge.

"Done?" Abu Ali flicked the butt end of his cigarette to the side, landing it in a dirt hole.

I tossed mine after his but missed. The still burning stub rolled toward his feet.

"I need your help." Abu Ali crushed my discarded cigarette with the tip of his shoe and fished a rolled pita bread from a plastic bag hanging on the door behind him. He tore the sandwich and held the larger portion out for me. "My wife insists on sending sandwiches every day, but I already ate." He grabbed my right hand and wrapped my stiff fingers around his offering. "Hummus. I can't go home with it uneaten. Um Ali scares me." He rumbled out with a loud laugh. "She insists I buy her fresh bread from Abu Nidal's bakery every morning. Something about the flour he uses. Exceptional quality, she says." He took a big bite that left but a morsel of his portion and motioned with his head for me to do the same. "Abu Nidal is more than a baker, you know."

I wasn't hungry but bit into the moist sandwich to keep him talking and flipped my left wrist in question.

Abu Ali looked over his shoulder and leaned closer to whisper, "He is *connected*."

I stomped my foot several times.

"Someone powerful outside the camp. I can't tell you who, so don't ask."

I growled in objection, pushed back his sandwich. He refused to take it or elaborate.

"If you really want to know, talk to *El Sabbak*."

So, I would have to find out from the plumber, whose name I never learned since everyone in the neighborhood referred to him as *El Sabbak*, which literally means "the plumber." I ate my sandwich and contemplated my next steps. Fishing for information would require coming up with a convincing reason to justify a trip to the plumber's shop on the main road. I'd need to bribe Yasser for that job. Swallowing the last bite, I pointed at Abu Ali's cigarette packet.

"You want another one?" Abu Ali asked.

I nodded.

He stuck two Camels between his lips, lit them then handed me one.

I patted the breast pocket of my shirt.

"Another? For later?"

I nodded again.

"Promise me you won't tell your mother where you got it from if she finds it, okay?"

I kissed my index finger and touched it to my forehead to seal the vow.

He tucked a cigarette in my pocket.

I cracked a smile without revealing my teeth. That was easy. I secured payment for Yasser's transportation services.

From a distance, I spotted Ameena in a striped blue and white dress. No matter how big a crowd Ameena walked in, my eyes found her. She saw me and waved. Before I could wave back, she ducked behind the barbershop. I tossed my spent cigarette butt to the dirt, tried to crush it under my shoe, and waited.

Where was Ameena? There was no passageway behind that shop, just a dead end filled with cat urine and rancid smell. My heart slammed against my chest. What could she be doing there? I grabbed my walker and pulled myself to my feet.

"Wait." Abu Ali returned to me. "I have something for you." He went into his shop and came back with a plastic bag. "Excellent shoulder cut." He dropped it in the cloth sack tied to my walker and winked. "To appease your mother in case she finds out about the smoking."

Too distracted by Ameena's disappearance, I let the butcher's charity dangle from my walker and voiced no objection to his generous offering. I never accept hand-outs from anyone. Sharing a sandwich to encourage a flow of information didn't count. I saw straight through Abu Ali's not-so-subtle effort to save my dignity with the ridiculous story about his scary wife, but the good man did try. And for Ameena's sake, I could forget to be proud just this once. I would have to lie to my mother about the meat's source. Another thing I take great pains not to do. I could say I had arrived at the right moment to witness Abu Ali butcher a fresh *thabeeha*. Father came home once with a similar bounty and gave the same excuse. He had cited the common practice of distributing portions of a sacrifice to those who observe its slaughter.

Ameena dashed out from her hiding spot. The collar of her dress flipped, hair loose from its braids, cheeks streaked with tears.

"Ammmmee . . . nnaaaa!" I screamed.

Abu Ali turned and caught running Ameena in his arms. "What happened to you, girl?"

"He hit me. He . . . he said I . . . stole a toothbrush. I didn't, *a'mmoh.*" She kissed her index finger and tapped it to her forehead three times. "I swear. I didn't steal anything."

"Who hit you?"

"A man in the pharmacy." Ameena pointed down the alley. "There, that one . . . in the black shirt. I don't want my father to know, *a'mmoh*. Please!"

A couple of men from neighboring shops surrounded us. Lead by the butcher, they marched toward the man in black, got in his face and shoved his shoulders. Fists swinging, they gave the bald man a solid beating.

Ameena ran her fingers through her hair and fixed her collar. She touched my hand and winked. "I got him for you, Waseem."

From that day onward, Ameena wasn't just the girl next door, the goddess I worshiped. Ameena became my vixen.

CHAPTER FOUR

Within minutes, news spread that the pharmacy supplier from outside the camp received street justice, but no one knew why. The butcher and his comrades never spoke of Ameena, kept the accusation and her identity hidden. Reasons behind the beating mattered little. Brawls were a common occurrence in the overpopulated camp. An outsider learned not to mess with camp folk. That was sufficient gossip to pass around.

The butcher returned to his shop. He patted Ameena's head. "Go to your mother, girl."

"*Shukran, a'mmoh.*" She flicked her restored braid over her shoulder and sauntered away.

He pointed at the bag dangling from my walker. "You should go home, too. Before the meat spoils," then wagged his finger at me, "you will not speak of this to anyone." Dropping into his chair, he flicked his hand. "You know what I mean. If word reaches her father . . . no telling what he will do to the *dactor* and his stupid delivery man."

I don't know why everyone referred to the pharmacist as the doctor. If he had a medical degree, he would open a clinic—not a pharmacy—and frame his diploma on the wall next to a still missing pharmaceutical commercial license. Most pharmacists in the camp didn't hold proper accreditation and got away with almost anything. The number of *real* pharmacists who insisted on a doctor's prescription could be counted on two hands, but family stores selling any medicine under the sun marred every corner.

Once, one of those obnoxious women who visited with my mother spilled coffee onto her lap, eager to show the medicine package she'd acquired for her epileptic son at an affordable price. "So what if it expired last year?" She had shrugged, and my mother, ignoring my loud protests, elaborated that the only reason they print those dates was to pass UN regulation and border control. "Only a formality," she had claimed.

Expired medications were in ample supply in a lawless world such as ours, outside the Lebanese Health Department's reach with its guidelines and restrictions. It explained why people from surrounding cities ventured into our camp in search of good deals. It also explained why that woman's son never got better.

Before I could push out of the butcher's shop, the pharmacist hobbled toward us. His legs supported his heavy frame by bowing outward. Gray hair covered his thick arms. He took the chair I had occupied minutes earlier, ignoring me. "I need to know who to watch out for, Abu Ali. What did my foolish delivery man do?"

Abu Ali tilted his head in my direction. "He taunted Waseem and his friend."

Interesting. I stiffened in my spot. The butcher lied.

The pharmacist's flabby cheeks blanched. "The girl who just left here . . . Abu Nidal's daughter, right?"

"She's too smart, *dactor*. Won't open her mouth to her father. The other men know what's good for them." Abu Ali tapped his chest. "I guarantee their silence." He lifted his eyes to mine. "As you well know, Waseem can keep a secret."

I gave a confirming nod. The pharmacist's dismissive look irked me. In his mind, I didn't count.

He looked over his shoulders and whispered, "I can't afford to get tangled with Abu Nidal. The baker has many friends. Can easily cause trouble for someone like me."

"I'd find another supplier, if I were you," Abu Ali said.

"Yes, I have to." The pharmacist scooted forward, resting his bulging belly on his thighs. "Be honest with me. Do you think Abu Nidal is sending me a message? A warning?"

"For what? What did you do?"

"Nothing," the pharmacist said, a knee-jerk answer. His wide forehead gleamed with sweat. "I serve all factions, no matter where loyalties lie. You know that."

Abu Ali drew a long breath and narrowed his eyes. Did he believe the pharmacist was really unbiased? Did he approve or disapprove of his professed neutrality? And with whom did the butcher align his allegiance? With Abu Nidal and his powerful friends? Or with the competing groups controlling northern and southern areas of the camp? The very notion that a delivery man accused Abu Nidal's daughter of stealing, even an alleged petty theft of a measly toothbrush, alarmed the mighty butcher enough to doubt the pharmacist bordered on amusement. I hid a smile behind my closed fist. This was a simple testament to just how powerful Ameena's father was.

"Your delivery man made a stupid mistake, *dactor.* He will not dare show his face here again. I made sure of that." Abu Ali rose. "Go back to work and try not to worry." He turned to me, tucked two more cigarettes into my shirt pocket. "You too. Go on. Forget this ever happened."

I managed the slow walk down the alley. Yasser spotted me and signaled he needed a couple of minutes before he caught up for the lift home. I chose a spot in the shade, leaned against a wall covered with soot and graffiti and weighed what transpired. Without realizing it, Ameena's clever scheming provided me with a fortunate opportunity. Not only did we punish the stone thrower—a skewed measure of justice, I admit—but now I also had something on the self-proclaimed, so-called neutralist. The *dactor* did *not* stand on the sidelines, and he wanted his partiality hidden. Holding secrets is a weapon in our camp.

It took me years to decide how to wield it.

CHAPTER FIVE

The year I turned sixteen, my father passed away. He lasted few minutes after a massive heart attack, long enough for my mother and sisters to scream and alert the neighbors, but not long enough for my brothers to hurry back from their after-school jobs. My father's life ended in an ugly manner, in our dank home at the center of our decrepit refugee camp.

On that early afternoon, the winter sun hid behind heavy clouds. Practicing his ritual of reading newspapers full of depressing news, my father paused several times to rub his chest or flex his left arm. Winces and burps interrupted his narration, and his voice abandoned its monotone and kept disappearing mid-sentence.

I caught him eyeing the forgotten book in my hand, Gibran's potent poetry fables, *The Prophet*.

"What is he reading?" Father directed his question to my mother. He did that when he wasn't sure if he should be pleased or incensed. He avoided addressing me.

"It's about the prophet Mohammad's life. Isn't that right, Waseem?"

I nodded and returned my gaze to the pages. What was the point in correcting her if I couldn't begin to explain what the book was about? She hit the mark on one thing: the spiritual content.

My father responded with a groan combined with a burp.

"Hot chamomile tea. What you need to soothe your upset stomach," Mother declared before she went into the kitchen. "Maryam, Fayzeh, how many times have I told you to put away all the pots after we eat? Come, now!"

My sisters scurried after her.

I had to re-start the same poem several times as my mind remained with my father's uncharacteristic digestive struggle. Once he resumed a somewhat normal reading pace, I focused on one line: *For thought is a bird of space, that in a cage of words may indeed unfold its wings but cannot fly.*

I scratched my head. My mind's agitated tongue talked non-stop. Perhaps that was the reason I was deprived of the ability to cage my thoughts within a spoken language. Multiple folds of confinement corralled my lips, body, and entire existence. In the permanently combative state I languished in, the words I wished to set free would not come out eloquent nor unfurl with smooth feathers. My thoughts would start wars.

A sharp gasp snapped my eyes off the page. My father slowly leaned to his right until his head hit the rug. His face drained of color and glistened with sweat. I yelled. My mother came running, dropped to her knees, lifted his head onto her lap. He gurgled and gasped. She cried. My sisters screamed. I crawled over, wanting to pry his jaw open and blow into his mouth to force more air into his lungs. Neighbors barged through our door before I could.

Over everyone's shrieks and shoves, I detected my father's last breath as it brushed the back of my hand.

His demise forced my sisters to grow up overnight and prompted the end of my brothers' education. To make ends meet, the three boys left school—Wael too willing to forgo the agony of forced education. I resented the folly, his squandering of golden opportunities all those years. I still do.

The shop owner who employed our father took in Wael and our youngest brother, Nabil, to train as mechanics and continue our father's trade. Yasser found employment with Ameena's father—not in the bakery, mind you. When my mother asked him about his duties, he shrugged an answer, "Whatever *ma'almi* Abu Nidal asks me to do." From then on, Yasser referred to his employer as his mentor, and plump chickens graced the meager spread of our birthday celebrations.

As for me, I remained imprisoned, inept in my body, on long cushions by the window. I watched my mother wither away under the burden of harsh life, eyeing Yasser skeptically whenever he brought home an unexpected bushel of apples, or a spotless hand of bananas, or a full crate of oranges. She would shoot down his efforts to gain her favor by declaring his apples tart, or the bananas too ripe to last more than a couple of days. When she wanted to express strong displeasure at his evasive activities, she would stress the inferiority of his dry oranges to the ones from *Yaffa*.

As for Ameena . . .

What of beautiful, cunning Ameena?

Ameena blossomed into a stunning creature, the woman she was destined to become.

Year after year, I followed Ameena's delicate transformation with adoration and yearning. I am not a dreamer, and I'm all too aware of the impossibility of a normal life with her. I don't need to be reminded of my shortcomings. I know. I comprehend. I accept what I cannot change. I don't ignore my reality. I have no misconceptions, no hope, remember? So, I settled early on for any kind of life with Ameena, in any shape or form: neighborly concern, condescending mentorship, distorted friendship, even charitable pity, as long as it kept her under my focused lens of admiration and wonderment. I challenge anyone to find fault in that.

But I never imagined what she set out to do with me.

CHAPTER SIX

Of all my siblings, Nabil is the kindest. His gentle nature stood out in contrast to Fayzeh's, which manifested in her complete distaste toward me. My youngest sister showed her repulsion by endeavoring not to touch me, which was a hard feat to accomplish given our compact, always-in-your-face living conditions. Resourceful and mean, she managed the aversion well, finding urgent things to dash to whenever we came too close. Somehow, she ran late on her five daily prayers almost every day before the time window for each lapsed and bolted to perform her godly duty as soon as I came within her vicinity. She beat Maryam in volunteering to fetch whatever Mother needed from the vegetable cart or the market with a laughable frequency. My proximity triggered her small bladder or reminded her of neglected homework. I found her not-so-clever schemes close to amusing.

Once our father died, my brothers took over the chore of bathing me, though Yasser didn't do it for long. I suspect he considered the task beneath his self-proclaimed importance as Abu Nidal's apprentice, though he never said anything to that effect. Mother would never have forgiven him if he had, and Yasser sought her approval above all else. He believed his success in life was tied to her appreciation of him as an honorable man. Like many, he accepted that God's favor was linked to a mother's level of contentment with her children. I found this idea strange, for bounties from a supposedly supreme power should be individually earned, unaided nor augmented. As for us mortals, true love should maintain independence and govern hearts entirely free of conditions.

Wael scrubbed hard when he bathed me, sometimes too hard, to the point where my skin tingled for a long time afterward, especially in the winter. My youngest brother, Nabil, started bathing duties when he turned thirteen. He was always gentle. He took his time to lather me, sang songs, told stories, and recited poetry—some his own. If he had the chance to continue with his schooling, I believe he would have turned out a great literature scholar. It pained me to see his sensitive, poetic soul shrivel between car parts and motor oil, but such was his life—our destiny—as Mother would say every now and then, accompanied by a sigh as heavy as a fully-loaded vegetable cart creaking down alleys in the early hours of the morning.

I looked forward to my Friday baths when it was Nabil's turn, even though he neglected to dry between my toes sometimes, which made my feet itch and stink. Fayzeh complained all the time and berated Nabil for doing a poor job, and Mother made her prepare a saltwater bath for my feet to atone for his oversight—or perhaps to put an end to her discontent. I luxuriated in this remedy and the doting of my sister, however forced. I wonder if Nabil knew that and did it on purpose. I like to think that he did.

I imagine if I were physically sound, I would have taught him how to ride a bicycle or control a ball between his feet to score goals, or whatever it is big brothers do for younger ones. I cheered on enough fights, where boys and young men jumped in to defend their kin without hesitation, not bothering to figure out who was in the wrong. I never had the chance to be the big brother protector. Reveling in the guaranteed guardianship of my younger brothers, I was always on the receiving end of such blind devotion. Though I rarely needed to put their armament to the test as I basked in Ameena's royal favor. No one dared hurt me for fear of unleashing her father's wrath. Besides, I had an added shield; a crooked body no one wanted to go near, touch, or deal with.

Among the many other things I could not do for my siblings centered around Eid. My father never had enough to give us money or buy us new clothes on Eid, so our celebrations had always dwindled to a kiss on the forehead and a meal my mother put extra effort into. As the eldest, it should have fallen onto my shoulders to take on the obligation after Father died, but I had no means to earn a living. So, it came down to poor Yasser. He strived to hand us modest amounts of money every Eid morning no matter how small the number of bills were. But he dropped the kissing routine—that essential act was left up to me. I inflicted wet kisses on everyone, even on Fayzeh as she wiggled and screamed while our mother held her down.

Ameena literally saved my life the day I turned seventeen and Ameena fifteen. I wanted to beat her to our birthday gifting routine for a change, so I asked Nabil to take me down to the alley that morning, and made my way to the market in search of the perfect lollipop. I had some money saved from Yasser's Eid present and could afford to buy her a modest gift, a beaded necklace or bracelet, but I balked for fear of my brothers and sisters teasing me if they knew. So, I adhered to our birthday celebration ritual with candy on a stick. I chose a watermelon flavor, easy on the pallet, soothing and comforting like her effect on my soul. I was in a poetic mood that day.

Anxious for the time to go by until Ameena came over, I lingered on a plastic chair outside Nabil's auto shop and watched him and Wael work on—well, mostly under—various vehicles. The shop next door was being renovated. Busy workers transported piles on a creaky wheelbarrow and dumped them a couple of steps from me. Wael shouted at them to watch out, and they shouted back obscenities. I hissed and spit at them a couple of times to keep them at a distance. It worked. When the call for afternoon prayer resonated from minarets, my brothers and the other men headed to the mosque, yet I lingered behind as usual. The alley emptied fast, except for a couple of mothers who went around the corner with toddlers in tow.

Nabil once told me during our bath time that he thought women were lucky to not be required to attend communal prayers at the mosque. He had confessed that, sometimes, he wished he were born female. I remember the expression on his face then. Nabil seemed serious, his kind, dark eyes sad with a wistful expression. A heartbeat after he had uttered his confession, he dumped water over my head and laughed. I closed my eyes, but the sound of his laughter remained with me—a nervous, embarrassed, forced chuckle.

After that day, his casual following of professional wrestling matches broadcast on television spiraled into an obnoxious obsession. He idolized a particular Irish champion, Devlin, and talked about the tough man's attributes and accomplishments in the ring to our brothers and sisters, his friends, our neighbors, and anyone who would listen. Never directly to me, though. I memorized the name of the wrestler not out of interest but because of hearing it uttered so many damn times.

I couldn't reconcile Nabil's professed sport fascination with his sensitive, quiet nature. It felt as if he worked extra hard to broadcast his captivation and shield his true, tender self from unforgiving camp eyes. But I never revealed my suspicions to him or anyone else. My intuitive brother must have detected my misgivings and excluded me from his zealous ramblings to avoid what he could have wrongly imagined an uncomfortable conversation. We shared no dialogue about his escalating fixation. Allowing Nabil to conceal his kind heart behind the rugged mask he created with meticulous efforts was the only thing I could do for him. I, myself, am a master of camouflage. If I failed to detect my brother's need for disguise, who would? Our grim world left no room for men presumed vulnerable.

A cat grazed my leg and interrupted my musings. It moseyed into the shop and leapt over a propane cylinder to flop down upon a bundle of rags. The scrawny feline winked at me before it closed its eyes. I checked my watch. Schools would let out soon. If I were lucky, I would spot Ameena on her way home if she came up this alley and could surprise her with my gift. Sometimes she walked a different route if she was with friends. Too anxious to sit still, I went into the empty shop, edging my walker around a dented car and an injured motorcycle lying on its side.

A rat scurried across the grimy floor and climbed onto the propped-up hood of the ugly car. Twitching long whiskers, the rodent stared at me. I stared back, repulsed by its stocky, gray-brown body. In a split second, the cat pounced, kicking the propane cylinder. The rat escaped. The propane cylinder wobbled and hit the floor, knocking down a shelf full of metal junk. Car parts and tires flew by my feet and around my walker. The metal edge of the propane cylinder hit a pile of car batteries. Black acid oozed out. An acrid, sulfuric odor stung my eyes. I tried to lift my walker over a metal chain that blocked my way but couldn't keep my balance. I looked around in search of an escape and quickly realized I was trapped behind the car. The only way out was to jump over a stack of tires. I yelled, hoping someone on the street would hear me.

There was no one. A pool of acid surrounded me until it ate up the rubber of my walker's wheels and the soles of my shoes. My legs spasmed, my body shook. I tried to lift myself up onto the car's bumper, but my useless hands couldn't get enough of a grip to support my weight.

I screamed louder, out of fear, of pain, I couldn't tell the difference.

"Waseem?" Ameena's voice called from outside. "What's that smell?"

"Stay away!" I yelled, but only savage noises came out. Horrified, I saw her running toward me, pushing something before her. I couldn't see what it was, but it was big enough to shove aside everything in her path, creating a loud raucous.

"Hurry. Drop in." She stopped before me with the creaky wheelbarrel from the construction site. I threw myself in, landing on my side with the walker on top of me. Ameena struggled to pull back but managed to wheel me out of the shop. Crying and screaming for help, she grabbed the hem of her shirt and attempted to remove my melting shoes. I howled in pain, as if she were ripping my feet off my ankles. People came running from all corners. I passed out before they reached us.

~

For nearly two months after that incident, my feet remained bandaged. I could only crawl around our room if I needed to move, and I barely wanted to. Nabil fastened new wheels to my walker—mismatched and clunky-looking, but functional. Ameena visited every day after school, bringing a book or a magazine. She implored Wael to paint my walker and wheels all in one color to lessen the ugliness. He chose metallic green, which glowed in the dark.

One Monday was particularly difficult. Depressed and suffering an unusual bout of pain, I almost wished she hadn't stopped by. After repeated attempts to draw me out of my misery, Ameena pointed at my mother's tile on the wall, wiggled her eyebrows and whispered, "*Aboob*!"

That simple word invoked the pleasant memory of our covert pact and carried the weight of our unique relationship. *Aboob* became our private signal, our secret tunnel to a better state of mind. At that desolate point in time, it extracted a smile out of me.

Ameena stared into the space separating us for a long moment. Her lips came together in a soft pucker as if she were about to kiss an invisible entity. The expression in her eyes, not distant nor placid, but severe, intense, a look that enhanced her dark irises.

"I will!" she said then flinched as if surprised to hear her voice.

I flipped my palm. "Wwha . . . aatt?"

"Go to Palestine! Someday, Waseem. Someday, I will."

I tapped my chest.

"I know," she whispered. "You long to go, too."

I slammed my chest harder, in part to stress my never before expressed desire, and to keep my heart from escaping its rib cage. Ameena had infiltrated my skin and wriggled her way into the folds of my brain. She knew my hidden thoughts, the ones I hadn't trapped into words in my head.

She reached for my hand and cradled it within the softness of hers. "We . . . you and I, Waseem. We are different from everyone here."

I nodded with my entire body. We *were* different. She, a heavenly creature far, far superior to the distorted human residing in me.

"I know everybody speaks of returning to Palestine, but you know what?" She winked. "We are the ones who will."

She left me with that impossibility, worrying how she would cope with the unfulfilled dream. In our people's refugee permanence of the past seventy-some years, her fantasy was predestined to remain as such, unreal and unattainable. When the time came to prove her wrong, how would she take it? I was accustomed to damage, I knew how to handle disappointment, but could she?

Mother changed my bandages and applied ointment every other day. Black shriveled skin covered my soles. The doctor at the hospital said I was fortunate that Ameena acted so fast, that if it weren't for her quick thinking, the acid would have eaten through my flesh and entered my bloodstream in higher amounts. I was lucky that she came by. She saved my life, he declared in a lofty tone, as if delivering a heavenly revelation.

But I already knew that I received deliverance the day Ameena was born.

~

As soon as Ameena finished school, her father secured for her a clerical job with the *Saida* office of the United Nations High Commissioner for Refugees, UNHCR. She also enrolled in a two-year afternoon program at a private international university, which raised plenty of eyebrows in the community.

Attending university, whether public or private, is such a privilege for Palestinian refugees like us. In practice, higher education is mostly unattainable due to the exorbitant tuition fees and the strained conditions of the camp. To compound the issue, even if someone managed—through scholarship and other means—to overcome their dire circumstances, their refugee status would not allow them to find legal work outside the camp. But Ameena's family was exceptional. Her father had money and the right connections.

Accordingly, Abu Nidal used his influence to help Yasser earn a driver's license and gave him a promotion. Yasser was to drive Ameena to work and campus and back. Naturally, infuriatingly, following the cruel course of nature consistent with God's arcane plan, Yasser envisioned himself in love with my Ameena. He cavorted and stomped the ground like a rooster, beaming with strength and pride. His version of love came with no diminished appetite, no sleepless nights, no depressed sighs nor frustrated outbursts. Every morning, he dashed to his duties with a cheerful attitude and returned home chipper, a spring in his step. Indeed, Yasser was happy, he lacked the haunting look in his dark eyes, anguish in his voice, and hiccups in his laughter that truly indicated passion. No, he did not love her, not wholeheartedly. I, alone, bore the full weight of misery that true devotion hurled at an enraptured soul.

"Don't be a fool, son," my mother told Yasser when he voiced his intention. "Abu Nidal will never give his only daughter to you."

I watched Yasser from my corner, not looking for signs of indignation and frustration—that was expected—rather searching for clues as to whether or not Ameena reciprocated his feelings. Beyond the occasional hellos and good afternoons, I hadn't seen much interaction between them. She kept to her weekly schedule, always visiting on Fridays while he was at the mosque with a book or two in her bag for me. And she never talked about him to my mother and sisters. She didn't fish for information about his interests like Maryam did with the pharmacist's wife about her son, Farook, which led me to believe Ameena simply viewed Yasser as a driver, nothing more. So, from where did Yasser get the notion that she could accept him as a husband? Was his sole fuel a naive, optimistic presumption?

"What's wrong with me, *yumma*?" Yasser asked. "If *ma'almi* didn't like me, he wouldn't have taken me into his inner circle. He trusts me."

I grunted to draw Yasser's attention, but he kept his eyes on Mother. What did the fool have to do to win a spot in Abu Nidal's circle? I had gathered intelligence from the plumber about the baker's secret activities inside and outside the camp. I didn't need to resort to manipulative tactics to draw the information out. As soon as I stepped into his stinking shack, *El Sabbak* shared a generous portion of fried goatfish he'd acquired during his latest adventure at the harbor and blabbered with immense pride how Abu Nidal consulted with *him*—no one else—over plumbing systems on large ships. The possibility their activities had anything to do with bakery business was remote. Things didn't add up. Abu Nidal's power had mushroomed over the past couple of years, and everyone at the center of the camp worked on gaining his favor—everyone except the pharmacist, who, as far as I knew, never set foot in the bakery after the day of the fight orchestrated by Ameena. And now my smitten brother wanted to be Abu Nidal's son-in-law?

My mother reached to pat Yasser's cheek. "Nothing is wrong with you, *habeebi*. But how can you support a wife with us depending on you? Where will you two live?"

"Don't worry. Ameena is a good girl. She will conform to our circumstances."

"Hmmmff," I scoffed as loud as I could. Ameena *conform?* What a blind, arrogant ass!

Yasser's mobile phone dinged, and he took off. As soon as he left, Maryam, who had been listening from the kitchen, burst out, "That's not fair." She carried a crate of fresh *Mlukhia* sprigs, sat next to Mother on the floor, and they both plucked dark green leaves from long stems.

"Wwha . . . aatt firrrrr?" I asked.

"I'm a year older than Ameena and here I am, nothing to do." Maryam dumped a handful of leaves into a huge plastic bowl. "Going to university like her is impossible. Tutoring the neighbor's children is not exactly a dream job."

"It'll pay for your brother's winter coat."

"And . . ." Maryam snapped a long sprig in half, "I have no husband."

"Your turn will come," Mother said in a hushed tone.

"No, it won't, *yumma*. No one will take me for a wife." She pointed at me. "Because of him. Women say that. To my face."

"Be patient. Every rotten grain finds its blind measurer."

I threw my arms up in the air. How could a mother be so cruel to her daughter? Maryam was not the weevil in our family's wheat sack, I was the source of rot. Maryam and the rest of my siblings were innocent victims by association.

Mother smiled at me, a warm and loving gaze in her eyes. I couldn't smile back. To soothe my feelings, she squashed Maryam's. Was she attempting to lower her daughter's expectations so she would accept the first *measurer* who knocked on our door? Damned if I would let that happen. Maryam had set her eyes on Farook, a university student who would take over his father's business one day. Why shouldn't my sister have the man she pined for?

I am crippled, but not helpless. I pay attention, and I learn. There were means to force someone's hand, and I had been holding on to one for years. It was time to draw the sword of knowledge from its sheath and use it on the respected *dactor.*

CHAPTER SEVEN

During the many visits I had managed to the plumber's shack over time, I learned that the pharmacist, our supposedly neutral *dactor*, smuggled in medical supplies from the northern part of the camp, and not through Abu Nidal's connections at the harbor. Bootlegging was common practice here, considered an established occupation, even. Rations provided by United Nations relief agencies were not the best of quality and could not meet the demands of the camp's growing population. Without the smuggling, we wouldn't have many of the things that make life bearable in a refugee camp that had endured seventy long years. But of course, everything came at a high price.

Among the various goods Abu Nidal smuggled into the camp were sacks of flour for his bakery. The plumber had eagerly talked about Abu Nidal's irritation with the pharmacist. I knew the source of his illicit merchandise eluded Abu Nidal, who wanted to impose his secret channels to establish a monopoly and solidify his hold on the central area of the camp.

It took a full pack of Camels as payment for Wael to carry me and my walker to the *dactor*'s shop—I refused to call it a pharmacy like everyone else. Wael was sixteen and already a committed smoker, but he wasn't tempted. He could afford to buy cigarettes and was too nosy, demanding to know why I needed to see the *dactor*. I grunted nonsense, making sure he couldn't understand a thing if he tried, which he didn't. He walked out mumbling. I sent my left shoe after him. It whizzed past Nabil as he came in.

Nabil was fourteen at the time and could handle the weight of my nineteen-year-old body, but I hated seeing him hooked on tobacco. I wanted—hoped—to postpone his initiation as long as possible. I refrained from offering the cigarettes and simply relied on his kind nature to fulfill my request.

Whenever I showed up on the streets, boys followed me and mimicked the way I walked and talked. It got on Nabil's nerves but not mine. By then, those boys and I had a tacit agreement. I provided entertainment, and they spied on anyone I pointed out, like a puppeteer animating figurines. They brought me news of what went on behind the closed doors of their homes, things other people, men in particular, couldn't know about unless women or shrewd children chose to inform them. I built an arsenal of secrets. It began as a fortunate accident. One day I clapped at a stranger with yellow snake-leather shoes wondering down our alley to applauded his courage for the ill-advised footwear. One of the boys who always followed me, named Ghazi, laughed and clapped, too. I pointed at the stranger, questioning if the boy could understand my gesture as a request to inquire about the man, who stopped frequently to wipe his eye-catching shoes. Ghazi skipped away and returned within the hour to detail the man's family tree, including his mother's maiden name and history, which was frankly more than I needed to know. My intelligence practice developed on its own from that day onward.

With me on his back, and my walker under his arms, Nabil headed to the *dactor*'s shop. I heard a familiar whistle behind me—a signal from my spy, Ghazi. I had flagged the pharmacist to him days earlier by clapping three times in the man's face. Ghazi clapped back twice to show an understanding of his assignment. The boy personified the full meaning of his name. It means "conqueror," and though small for an eight-year-old, he exerted dominance over other boys, some years older. With a father who used his fists more than his brain, Ghazi had found ways to endure a cruel childhood. His father was blind to Ghazi's unique leadership qualities. I never met the man but knew his story. After spawning seven children—Ghazi one of the youngest in the brood—the day laborer fell off the roof of an illicit addition to a cluster of rooms and broke his back. Paralyzed from the waist down, he stayed home and forced his kids to work.

Ghazi never complained, never ratted his father out, never showed scars, but everyone with an earshot of their home knew malice resided there. I vowed to myself after his extensive relay about the snake-shoes man if I ever saw a single bruise on my chieftain, I would drag his father onto the street and give him the flogging he deserved. His paralysis provided zero immunity from my wrath, but I never saw visible evidence of any beating, and my body's inability to inflict physical pain onto others prevented me from carrying out my pledge.

I squeezed Nabil's shoulders for him to stop and lower me down.

"I can carry you all the way to the pharmacy," Nabil said, panting.

"Nnoooo." I squeezed his shoulders twice to thank him—a system I had established since I was a child.

Nabil steadied me behind the walker and slipped away.

I maneuvered a path to the dim, stinking passageway behind the barbershop. Ghazi followed me, along with two annoying cats. The felines pounced around my feet while Ghazi shared the intelligence he had collected about my target.

Ghazi discovered that at the beginning of every month, the pharmacist visited his aunt, who lived on the perimeter of Abu Nidal's circle of influence. This woman's three daughters—each had her own family—resided in different alleys adjacent to the mother's. On that specific day, the trio bought crates of lettuce from the same vendor once the market opened in the morning, and again in the afternoon. When lettuce was not in season, all three daughters bought crates of the same vegetable, be it cucumbers, bunches of parsley, or tomatoes, but they continued to purchase two identical crates of produce from a particular booth on the same day.

To close every transaction, the vendor's delivery boys, who reported to Ghazi, followed each daughter's footsteps to their mother's home and dropped off their crates in exchange for a stingy tip. The boys hated it when these women showed up at their boss's stand. It took much longer than it should have to reach their destinations, sometimes close to an hour, with heavy loads on their backs and no compensation to speak of. But the boss was always eager to accommodate these particular clients.

I motioned for Ghazi to pick up a stick. "Mmm . . . aaapp." I moved my hand in circles by his feet. "Hooomm . . . sss."

"Let's say you are the aunt." He made a circle in the sand around my walker and me. "She's as scary looking as you are."

I growled to give the boy his expected fun.

Ghazi chuckled, skipped back a few feet and engraved Xs in three different spots. "Here's where each daughter lives. Nice places. Cement roofs and big windows." The cats followed the tip of the stick, erasing some of his map. He made a small circle to his right. "And this is the market." He drew intersecting lines to connect the dots.

I could detect four paths to walk to the aunt's place from the market. I pointed at each and touched my watch.

"Ten minutes, tops, for the longest way." Ghazi squiggled a mess of winding lines. "But the women backtracked often. Took too many turns, see?"

I nodded. The daughters walked unnecessary, long routes. These odd events happened to align with the pharmacist's visit to his aunt, a dutiful nephew's stopover that went well into the evening.

Now, what would the aunt do with so much of the same vegetable in one day? Unless she prepared a salad party for the entire block every month, which to Ghazi's knowledge never took place, she must have been bringing in contraband supplies for her nephew hidden in those crates. He must have been conducting his surreptitious business activities during those visits.

I set out to find out who the vendor was and flipped my hand back and forth in Ghazi's face. "Nnnaaa . . . mmme?"

"Who? The aunt?"

I stuck my hand in the empty pockets of my trousers, took it out, and mimicked paying money. "Bbo . . . sss."

"*A'am* Ahmad."

I rolled my eyes. So many called Uncle Ahmad in the camp.

Ghazi scratched his temple. "Women call him Abu Jamila. He doesn't have sons."

I knew who he was. Mother talked about him with one of her visitors, the mother of the epileptic boy. A camp northerner, Abu Jamila had the backing of a league as powerful as Abu Nidal's group, yet more dangerous. One nugget of information a couple of men once blurted in my presence was that in addition to medicines and pharmaceutical supplies, the Hawks of Freedom league smuggled weapons and ammunition into the camp. Small wonder the pharmacist didn't want to cross swords with Abu Nidal. A power struggle between the factions could quickly spiral out of control and end in violent clashes, with the allegedly nonpartisan *dactor* caught smack in the middle of a crossfire.

One of the cats, a shabby creature with bald spots on its back, leapt up and hooked her claws to the bottom of the cloth sack dangling from my walker. I shook her off and mumbled to shoo her away. What came out of my mouth sounded like a hoot of an owl. The cats scrambled in different directions. Ghazi laughed.

I flicked my hand in the air to dismiss him. In a poor aping of my walk, he hobbled away with an exaggerated limp that sent his left side too close to the dirt. Cupping his hands around his mouth, he shrieked, "Woooo, woooo, woooo . . ."

Armed with information, I pushed my walker to the vegetable cart parked next to the barber's shop. It was late afternoon and the donkey dragging the cart looked grateful for the break. I tried to pay for what I wanted, but the old man tending to his donkey insisted I didn't need to, claiming that what was left of his load had begun to rot under the sun, and that I would be doing the docile animal a favor. I don't accept charity if I can help it, but I was short on time and didn't want to argue with the good man. I dropped everything into my sack and continued my mission.

I went into the *dactor*'s shop and plopped into a chair. He ignored me. I expected that. I opened my sack, pulled out a small head of lettuce and started munching, one wilted leaf after another. I waited until all the patrons left and motioned for him to close the doors. He threw a skeptical look my way and ignored me again, burying his large head behind a stack of white and blue boxes. I kept chomping and when I finished the last leaf of lettuce, I pulled out long cucumbers and ate them. They were surprisingly fresh and crunched nicely with each bite.

The pharmacist finally lifted his head and peered at me. I could see my reflection in the glass pane of the medicine cabinet facing me. I smiled; green shards stuck between my jagged teeth.

"Can I help you with anything?" he asked, his tone edgy and cautious.

I pointed at the doors again. He rose from his rolling chair with difficulty and did what I had asked him to do half an hour earlier. He closed his shop and lumbered back to me. "What do you need?"

I shook my head, which made my entire body jerk from side to side. "Waaa…nt," I said as clearly as I could.

He plopped down and rolled his chair closer. "Fine, what do you *want*?"

"Amm . . . eeenaaa," I said, thumping my chest and rubbing my index fingers together. "Frrri . . . nnd."

"Yes, I know Ameena is your friend."

I shook my head again. "Spe . . . speci . . . aaal."

The pharmacist laid his hand on my knee, steadying me before my spastic twitches threw me off the chair. "Okay, okay. Your special friend."

I felt sorry for the man for what I was about to do, for he seemed genuinely attentive. Nevertheless, I continued on, "Faa . . . the . . . rrrr."

"Her father? Abu Nidal?"

I nodded. It would have taken us an hour of back and forth if I had led with Abu Nidal's name, for I could never enunciate it to the point where it was clear to any audience other than my mother.

The pharmacist averted his eyes to papers on his desk. "What about him?"

"Prrro . . . ppro . . . ttt . . ." Struggling to get the word out, I smacked my thigh in frustration then slapped my cheek.

"Take it easy," he held my wrists. "What's the matter?" His tone shifted to one laced with concern. "Are you in trouble with Abu Nidal? Is that it?"

I spasmed in denial, my entire body shaking along with my head. "Himm prrro . . . tte . . . cccttt meee," I managed to sound out.

"Oh, Abu Nidal protects you." The pharmacist threw his head back. "Well of course he does. For his daughter's sake. Everyone knows that." He let go of my wrists and patted my knee. "No one in the entire camp is foolish enough to bother you, Waseem. Doesn't your brother work for Abu Nidal?"

"Yesssssss."

"Well, if Yasser is having issues with his boss, I can't help you. No one can. But like you said, Abu Nidal only listens to his daughter. So talk to her—"

"Fff," I cut off the rambling man, grabbed his arm and tried again. "Fffaaa . . . rrrooo . . . kkk."

"My son? Farook is not in trouble with Abu Nidal," the pharmacist said through a chuckle. I could tell he forced the mirth, for his plump face lost color.

I sucked in several deep breaths in an attempt to control my muscles and sat straighter in the chair. "Www . . . ill beee."

The pharmacist's eyes widened. He clamped his hand on my knee, only this time, his grip had more force. It hurt. "Why do you say that?"

I flipped my sack and dumped the remainder of its contents at his feet. Several cucumbers, smushed tomatoes, and another wilted head of lettuce scattered on the floor.

The pharmacist scooted back and lifted his confused eyes to me.

"Abbu Jammeellaa," I said. The name left my lips so beautifully, clear and just right—I had practiced saying it on my way here—and it hit the mark.

The pharmacist's cheeks turned red, his features seemed to gather themselves closer to his nose, morphing confusion into anger, then panic. "What do you know?"

I tapped the glass pane of the medicine cabinet and swept my arm, drawing a circle in the air. "Evvv . . . rry . . . thin . . . ggg!"

It was his turn to shake his head. "Abu Nidal will not believe you. Even if he could understand you."

Jutting my pointy chin in his face, I said, "Ammm . . . eeenaaa."

As if the mention of her name were a lightning flash hitting him square in the eye, he squinted; the wheels in his head working hard to make connections and projections, no doubt. I gave him time, ticking seconds as I counted the scattered vegetables.

Releasing a heavy sigh, he nodded. "I see, I see."

I didn't need to say more. He understood. He realized the bind I could put him in.

"What do you want, Waseem? Why are you telling me all this?"

I grabbed his left hand and rubbed his wedding band. "Mmarr . . . yyamm!"

"What?"

"Mmy ssiss . . . tterrr."

"You have a sister?"

I nodded and repeated, "Mmarr . . . yyamm."

"Maryam. What of her?"

I tried to twist the band around his chubby finger but couldn't establish a good hold on the slippery ring.

"Oh! You want me to help you marry off your sister. Sure. I can do that." He pulled his hand out of mine and turned. His thick shoulders shook, which I assumed was due to a relieved silent laugh, as I couldn't see his face. "I'll pay for a wedding. And whatever else she needs. Rent? furniture? No problem," he rambled on as he left his chair and went behind his little desk. "Who's the fortunate young man?"

"Fffaaa . . . rrrooo . . . kkk!" I bellowed.

I left the man cursing a storm, though resigned to how he must proceed. I accomplished what I had set out to do that day but paid the price at night. All the vegetables I had stuffed my face with exerted their cleansing power over my digestive system, which drove my brothers to sleep on the roof. Mother and sisters had to suffer the night cleaning after me. Their disgusted *oofs* and *ews* didn't bother me. I secured for Maryam the husband she wanted and finally seized my place as the head of the family, whether they knew it or not.

CHAPTER EIGHT

Ameena was there on the day Farook and his father were to officially ask for Maryam's hand. Once the good news hit the streets, Ameena came over before everyone arrived, shrieking her congratulations in obvious, genuine delight. Laughing and ringing a loud *zaghrouta*, she dashed through the door to hug and kiss Maryam. Though she had moved up in the world, so to speak, and left my sisters behind, she never changed toward them, never wavered in her devotion to the girls she grew up with, and never failed to light up my entire universe whenever she graced us with her celestial presence.

Farook's mother and three uncles accompanied him and his father to our humble abode after Thursday's midday prayers. The men—all taller than any of my brothers—sat on cushions, their shoulders touching. Facing them, Yasser and Wael flanked me while Nabil remained standing behind us. Mother took one of the plastic chairs she had borrowed from the neighbors and offered the other to Farook's mother, a thin woman half the size of my mother. They sat by the open door. Ameena watched from the kitchen with my sisters, holding the dividing curtain open.

"*Bismillah Al Rahman Al Raheem*," the eldest man in Farook's entourage started and everyone went silent at once. "Following the teachings of the Holy Qur'an and the traditions of our prophet Mohammad, peace be upon him, we gather here today in the noble mission of requesting your honorable daughter's hand in marriage to our righteous son, Farook." He handed me a wooden box twice the size of my hand.

Baffled, I fumbled to open it. Yasser came to my rescue. Nestled in a bed of green velvet, a copy of the Qur'an lay flat. Yasser lifted the holy book, kissed and passed it to his forehead, then returned it to its nest. He passed the box around until it reached Farook's mother, who hugged it with folded arms over her pathetic flat chest.

"Forming a bond between our two families is a sacred affair," the uncle continued with his evidently well-rehearsed speech. As his calm voice orated tenets of marriage in the background, I fixed my gaze on the women by the door, struck by the glaring contrast between their expressions.

Pride and joy shone in each and every pore of my mother's face, her eyes glistening, pregnant with unreleased tears. She kept her open palms face up in her lap. Her fingers twitched every now and then and—though smiling—her lips moved nonstop. Throughout the ongoing formality that filled the room with a somber air, my mother sat praying.

The groom's mother stared not at Maryam, not at my mother, and sure enough not at her son or husband. She stared at me with sunken eyes. Her lower jaw jutted forward, nostrils flared wide open, and eyebrows—thicker than any woman's I'd seen—pulled into a straight line. If she possessed the same strength of olfactory senses as mine, I could have attributed her sour look to the collective odor of men's socks as they had removed their shoes at the door. But I knew the reason behind that disgusted, bloated-intestines expression. I'd seen it stamped on the faces of those women who used to visit my mother, the ones who decided my sisters would never marry because of me, the look that epitomized loathsomeness.

Maryam's future mother-in-law hated me, detested my existence and possible infiltration into her son's blood line. She sat before me, pulsing with animosity for the way God mashed me together in the womb, the same God my mother was praying to right beside her. Clutching what everyone in this room believed to be *the* Word of God housed in that wooden box, this abhorrent mother passed judgment on the ultimate judge.

I shook my head at the irony. Let her subsist in hatefulness on top of fear then—of me, if not of the god she worshiped. I raised my upper lip to expose sharp fangs and snarled at the hypocritical woman. She flinched and cut her gaze to her solemn husband.

On the morning of the wedding a month later, Ameena was again beside my mother and sisters, all busy bees fluttering about in bridal preparations. They ushered a teary Maryam to a hairdresser, which was a first, as my sisters could never afford the luxury. Ameena insisted it was her gift to her dear friend on a very special day.

No one knew of my cunning measures to secure Maryam's marriage. It was in the pharmacist's best interest to keep it that way, and I, of course, never disclosed my involvement to anyone. What mattered was that my sister was happy, and Farook seemed eager and willing. Although Maryam was not of the same caliber of beauty as Ameena, she had my mother's attributes: a healthy, curvaceous frame to complement her round face, long dark hair, and hazel eyes that reflected an intellect far greater than her grade-school education. And Maryam loved Farook. I don't know what more the man could ask for.

My brothers scattered in different directions to help the men in Farook's family set up a big tent on the clearing at the end of our alley for the wedding reception. There was limited space where big celebrations could be held in the camp. Families who lived in structures that had decent rooftops usually held their parties there, but I was told the roof of our dwelling consisted of zinc-plated metal sheets held together with patches of cement. It may have been enough for a man to lie down on during a hot night here and there, but it was nowhere spacious nor sturdy enough for a group.

Farook wanted to book one of the restaurants, but since the wedding was somewhat rushed at my request—as I didn't want my blackmail to lose momentum—he couldn't find an available date within our time frame. His building was the same structure as ours, so I consented to having a tent in the street. The groom's father consulted with me on every logistical step, especially at the time of writing their book—I worked the details of this official religious agreement as if I knew what a marriage contract and a wedding entailed. To protect my sister from the possible wrath of Farook's mother, I stipulated as part of Maryam's dowry that she and Farook should have their own place, not move in with his parents. Yasser told me such demands rarely occurred in our overcrowded camp, but I insisted until Farook complied. His father dismissed his wife's loud objections by siding with his son. It showed how eager the pharmacist was to curry my favor, a position that was new to me. I embraced it, even abused it, in my persistence to hurry up the wedding, and people took notice, especially my mother.

I caught her eyeing me several times; lips shaped midway between a smile and a thoughtful appraisal, as if she couldn't determine whether my elevated position with the in-laws was a blessing or a curse. My brothers also noticed, starting with Yasser. He took it in stride and didn't voice objections. That wasn't unusual, Yasser had hardly spoken in full sentences since the day Ameena turned him down. I never learned how she did it, but if I wanted to guess, I would say it was straightforward, clear-cut, leaving no room for misunderstanding. She continued with her visits to us as if my brother's marriage proposal was never extended. Ameena's perceived carelessness could explain Yasser's dramatic deflation and social withdrawal.

Home alone, I waited for one of my brothers to come for me when the ceremonies started. I sat on my cushions, dressed in a white shirt and my best trousers—the black pair that had a knee patch on only one leg. Mother had sewn padded patches on all my trousers, as my knees rubbing together when I walked stripped the fabric. I hadn't worn this special pair long enough to fray the cloth of both legs. Mother had also attached short chains to the zippers of all my trousers, which helped me dress and use the toilet unaided. I double-checked the clever accessory to make sure it was securely tucked in. The shirt was a hand-me-down from Yasser. I wanted to wear a suit, but none of my brothers owned one. I pulled out my father's necktie from a bundle Mother had kept in a special pillowcase since he passed away.

I don't know why Father owned a necktie. I don't recall ever seeing him wear one. He used to drape a checkered black and white *kufiyah* over his shoulders sometimes, but it wasn't in the bundle. On the anniversary of his death, year after year, Mother would spread out the contents of the pillowcase on her lap and run trembling fingers over each and every article of clothing: a blue shirt, a white undershirt, a maroon-checkered white kerchief, and the gray necktie. Taking her time refolding the pieces, she would silently stare into the space separating us. On a few occasions, she would open her mouth to say something about him, and then force her quivering lips closed without a word. She never reminisced about good times with my father, shared their adventures of courtship, or anything of the sort. I imagined that before my arrival into the world, there were pleasant times between them worth recounting, but I learned to keep my mouth shut while these annual episodes passed, leaving us engulfed in strained silence.

It seems to me that my mother's entire life hung on those moments of unspoken stories she failed to convey. Pleasant memories no longer reached her tongue, perhaps because our austere, day-to-day struggle banished them from her focused mind.

To pass the time, I attempted to properly tie my father's necktie around my neck, a useless exercise for I didn't know how to manipulate the ends of the tie with my hands jerking in different directions. But I kept at it and surveyed the bustle in the alley from my window. I couldn't see the tent from my angle. Music filled the air. A male singer started to serenade the crowd with love songs too loud and a bit out of tune. Perhaps I shouldn't have insisted that the pharmacist hire a live band, I thought to myself. I had heard having one was the trend, an added luxury for those who can afford to, and I wanted Maryam to have more things to boast about to the women who had deemed her un-marriageable. Yet again, I was probably the only one whose hearing detected the poor acoustics.

Three men walked by, single file, each balancing a big round tray of *ba'lawa* atop his head. They disappeared around the corner of the alley.

A teenager ran after them with a jar in his hand, yelling, "You've forgotten the syrup!"

Heading my way, Wael bolted up the alley, bumped into the teen and almost caused him to drop his jar. He let out a string of profanities. I closed the window and faced the door. It was time to join the festivities. I thought about abandoning the necktie, but I wanted our father represented at Maryam's wedding. So, I double knotted the ribbon under my collar as I would a length of rope and thought nothing of it. I figured no one would give me a second look, anyway.

"*Yalla*, let's go." Wael panted as soon as he walked in.

I raised my arms. "Rrr . . . dddy."

"No, you're not," Ameena said from the doorway behind Wael, standing with her hands on her hips.

I smoothed the top of my hair with stiff fingers and stared at her magnificence. Dark curly locks passed her shoulders to rest just above her elbows and contrasted with her cream-colored traditional Palestinian *tobe*. Red cross-stitches embroidered the entire chest area, long sleeves, and front of the dress, running down the sides in thick strips all the way to the floor. A belt striped with red and gold fabric cinched her tiny waist. She wore no makeup, save for a thick black line of kohl around her eyes. Her spotless, tanned face sparkled with a veil of perspiration.

She came running? to me?

"Everyone's waiting," Wael said.

"Five minutes will not kill anyone," she snapped.

"Mother won't let us proceed without him. She said Maryam should have her big brother by her side."

"Yes, I know." Ameena approached. It seemed to me as if she moved in slow motion. I smelled grass and lemon and then something sweet when she reached to undo my knotted tie. Red henna tattoos covered the back of her hands and the tips of her fingers. The dangling sleeves of her *tobe* brushed the top of my thighs. I slammed my palms down to halt my muscles' spasmodic jump.

"Let me show you how to do this." She winked, a spread of a single palm between our faces. "We can't have the bride's big brother show up as if he had just survived a suicide attempt."

Somewhere in the background, Wael laughed as I tried to follow her instructions, all the while wondering if I would succeed in choking myself to death and have Ameena as the angel in charge of my soul.

CHAPTER NINE

As the years passed, I established a routine in which Wael carried me down to the little bookshop at the corner on his way to work almost every morning. I struck a special friendship with the owner, *Ustath* Ihsan. I dubbed him "Professor," though he possessed no formal degrees, because frequenting his shop was the closest I came to attending university—Ameena's childhood offerings were of course my grade school education. And I loved his name—Ihsan means "kindness"—which was so indicative of his personality. Perhaps he knew of Ameena's book theft and turned a blind eye for goodwill. Yet again, maybe she was too clever to be discovered.

Ustath Ihsan treated me well and loved to discuss with me the books that I read. I mostly listened to his analysis and critique, and only offering my own by sounding out simple words he could interpret and ending with either a thumbs up or down, or a shake of an open palm when I wasn't sure of my opinion. If only I was able to control a pencil or pen to paper, I would have written essays to impress the professor. At least I could keep a book propped up and managed to flip pages. I should have been thankful for that. But I was not—am not still. I want to be able to write and walk and run and fight and sing and say everything that was on my mind. I want to dance, too. I don't want to overcome my limitations. I reject having them in the first place. The more books I read the more this rejection burned inside of me.

Learning about the outside world made me thirst for more. *Ustath* Ihsan did his best to buy or borrow a variety of books from his contacts outside the camp. I read the tremendous trove written by the blind Egyptian intellectual, Taha Hussein, and became inspired by his journey from a rural village school in Upper Egypt to the renowned lecture halls of the Sorbonne. Anointed as The Dean of Arabic Literature, Hussein was nominated for the Nobel Prize fourteen times.

Extremely stirred by his life story, I nearly memorized his autobiography, *Al-Ayyam,* line by line. Taha Hussein's intellect was not impaired by his childhood blindness, caused by the mistake of an unskilled practitioner, he excelled in spite of it, and demonstrated brilliance on a grand scale. He embraced the darkness and lit up an entire world with his words. He explained this himself in *Al-Ayyam,* written as a story about an unnamed boy: *And that is likely because notwithstanding his ignorance as to whether it was light or dark, he just remembers on leaving the house, meeting with soft, gentle, delicate light as though darkness covered some of its edges.*

I was not as courageous as he was. I could not grow up in a world of deprivation and emerge a tolerant man. The more I read, the more I became unfulfilled, unhappy, and unsatisfied. Gone were my days of resignation, of accepting my condition, or whatever you would call my wretched station in life. Anger hooked its mighty claws in my chest and poisoned my blood. I curled onto my cushions with a promising book every night and woke up enraged at the nonexistent possibilities in my world. I had no choice but to read more and intensify my fury. What else did I have as a means of escape?

And so, I kept on reading through *Ustath* Ihsan's stock. He brought me many of Shakespeare's plays translated into Arabic. Though I syllogized love with Romeo, schemed revenge with Hamlet, and conjured up magic with Prospero, I couldn't quite see why Shakespeare was the god of English literature. Even his first name was mangled. I kept sounding it in my head as *Waleem*—after the way it was typed in Arabic without the diacritical marks—and since I couldn't clearly articulate the name and *Ustath* Ihsan only used Shakespeare, the professor didn't know of my mistake and never corrected me. Only after I heard it pronounced in an English documentary on television, did I find out that it is enunciated as "William."

Ustath Ihsan explained that Shakespeare's genius lay in his ability to use, and sometimes invent language to convey his characters' emotions, much like Van Gogh and Monet used specific brush strokes and color pallets to evoke sentiments and create distinctive moods on canvas. I'd seen reproductions of these artists' paintings in books and magazines and read about their techniques, but that didn't help me appreciate Shakespeare's writing style. It might have been different if I were able to view those paintings in person to understand what all the fuss was about, but that was something only for dreamers in my world, and I identify as a realist.

Yet, one cold evening, when just Mother and I were at home, a notion jumped into my mind as I noticed how she gazed at her broken tile on the wall. While I failed to share her devotion to the flawed object, I detected a subtle shift in her countenance. Adoration roamed in her eyes long enough to induce a slight smile before, too quickly, those hazel windows to her soul closed and succumbed to tears of longing. As I had for years focused on the cracks caused by my mischievousness, an appreciation for the designer's artistry had escaped my attention until *Ustath* Ihsan's explanation of Shakespeare's brilliance finally dawned on me and I made the connection. Upon gazing at that damned thing, my mother replayed her imaginary happy childhood stories in *Yaffa*, where the tile held a prominent place in her family's house. I tilted my head slowly from side to side and stopped focusing on the glued crack splitting one of the triangles at the top left corner of the tile. I narrowed my eyes as if shining a beam and conjured up jovial bath times under Nabil's caring hands, hearing his carefree singing and poetry in my head. Several seconds ticked before the tile's colorful design became more prominent than its imperfections. Once the pleasant memories sharpened my vision, I saw the artist's tessellation through my mother's expressive eyes. I began to share her temperament and realized the great sentimental value of her memento. With a gentle squeeze of her hand, I tried to show my understanding and delayed regret.

Now enlightened, I came to accept that much of Shakespeare's creative intellect is lost in translation. I decided that evening to try to learn English and sought my professor's help. The old man didn't know the language but provided me with the necessary books and audiotapes. If I knew how to work a computer, I would have tried to use the desktop collecting dust on a top shelf at the bookstore, but he said it didn't work, and I had no way of knowing otherwise. So, I relied on an ancient tape recorder for my studies.

I discovered God's purpose in gifting me fine-tuned hearing: it facilitated audio learning. I learned the basics of the language in the summer, enough to be able to read and appreciate some children's books. Dr. Seuss's play with words and whimsical characters amused me, but more complex English literature in its original language remained beyond my full grasp. Eventually, hundreds of books and many years later, I caught up with the rest of the world in its adoration of Shakespeare's literary gifts. How fitting it was for me to truly understand the words in his play, *Twelfth Night*: *Alas, I took great pains to study it, and 'tis poetical.*

On a special afternoon, Ameena showed up with a copy of the *National Geographic* magazine to celebrate my success. She had been following my progress and providing incentives with various reading materials, including published reports and statistics from her work. Having learned English and French, she believed she was progressing in her job at the UNHCR office because of her knack for languages and communication skills. I tried to tell her that she excelled because she was good at everything. Whatever I conveyed in my attempt made her smile, though doubt lingered in her beautiful eyes. I resorted to our special *Abooh* code, which drew out her unreserved, confident chuckle.

That night, I flipped through her magazine and landed on an article about zebras. I studied a number of amazing photographs. I immediately related to those striking animals. They had such distinct markings and, like me, a lone zebra did not blend with its surroundings—the stripes combination a giant bullseye for predators to target. Other than being a satisfying meal for lions and leopards, could those beasts have ornamental value? A variance from the shades of brown and green in nature? If there was beauty in their special prints, where was the charm in mine?

Perhaps the fox in me was camouflaged in the guise of a zebra. I stood out. Rather than imbue awe and admiration, I confused onlookers; my misshapen limbs acted like those black and white stripes. Though no predators chased after me—not inside the refugee camp. If I ever managed to escape these confines, and snarling jackals pursued, I imagined Ameena would be with me at each step and tumble.

If there were truly a merciful God, he would not allow her to witness my capture.

CHAPTER TEN

What I remember the most of that fall afternoon is the smell, dank and pungent, as if I washed my face with the same saltwater that soaked my feet. Weighed down by a damp wool jacket, I left *Ustath* Ihsan's company with a head full of Rumi's mystic poetry and sloshed through murky pools under thundering gray skies to go home. One of my spies spotted me struggling up the alley and ran to tell Nabil at the body shop. My sweet, gentle brother came to my rescue. Ignoring the muck I transferred onto his oil-smudged overalls, he quickly dropped me off and returned to work.

Mother greeted me with a big smile. "Mention the cat, and it comes pouncing." She closed the door, helped rid me of my heavy jacket and muddy boots, and wiped the wheels of my walker. "We were just talking about you."

Behind my mother's bent frame, sitting on cushions with crossed ankles, Ameena clawed the air with both hands and mouthed a silent meow.

I forced a smile to hide my embarrassment. This cat was more like a sheep caught in the rain. I stank of wet wool, and the room was small, and whatever Mother had stewing in the kitchen didn't smell close to being edible yet, and the cold humid air was too stagnant without open windows, and . . . and Ameena was there, resplendent in black slacks and a beige blouse. Nude, sheer socks revealed toes with red nail polish.

Edging onward, the front wheels of my walker caught on the rim of the rug and sent me flying, landing face down at Ameena's feet. She jumped to help and tried to insert her hands under my arms.

I rolled away and laughed to cover my humiliation. Pulling up on all fours, I crawled to my corner.

Adding to my embarrassment, she followed, waited until I settled, and dropped a stack of papers in my lap. "Read through these, Waseem. It's an opportunity of a lifetime. I have it all sorted out. Started the paperwork already. If all goes well, they'll take care of everything." A new spark danced in her eyes. She spoke fast, ticking her fingers. "Travel documents, permits, visas, fees, accommodations, expenses and . . . and everything. Oh, Waseem, imagine the possibilities. Just imagine." She squeezed my arm and whispered, "This could be our ticket out of here. I have to go now, but I explained everything to *khalto*." She rose and turned to kiss my mother. "Like we agreed. I'll bring him tomorrow at nine."

Bring who? What was she talking about? I glanced at the papers stamped with the baby blue UN refugee agency logo. Was she traveling on some work-related assignment? Good for her. Where to?

"Can't you stay?" Mother asked. "Maryam should be here any minute. And Fayzeh just went to get yogurt. I'm making *mjadd-ara*. I know it's not much, but you are welcome to eat with us."

"Oh *khalto*, I looove *mjaddara*." Ameena exaggerated her tone, catching on to my mother's unease, no doubt. The simple lentils and rice dish was a staple meal for the poor throughout the camp as a rich source of protein cheaper than meat.

"I have to head home," Ameena said. "I promised Mama to model a dress she's been working on and help her with the hemming."

"She's still taking clients?"

"No, not anymore. But she likes to sew and indulge her friends every now and then. This dress is for an engagement party. You know *khalto* Aida?"

Mother tilted her head, pretending to concentrate. She didn't know the woman, I could tell. Ameena's mother moved in higher social circles. "No, I don't think I know Aida."

"The dress is for her eldest daughter." Ameena put on a sleek black raincoat and slipped her feet into tall boots. "Is Maryam still craving chalk? It has to do with her calcium levels. I'm sure Farook knows to check." She grabbed an umbrella propped up in the corner behind the door. "I asked my Mama's friend in *Saida*, the obstetrician? She said it could explain her strange craving."

"Maryam wants sour things now. Pickles, lemons." Mother opened the door. "The midwife insists it's a sign of a boy. I told her we don't care. Boy, girl, it doesn't matter, as long as the baby is whole and healthy."

I caught Ameena's eye. She didn't look away, or wince, or mumble something agreeable. She freed hair strands trapped under the collar of her coat. "I thought Maryam plans to deliver at the hospital."

"*Inshallah.* Farook wants to take her to Qudsi hospital, but that's very difficult to reach. If only Al-Aseel hospital was still operational. Do you think it'll open its doors again?"

"Funding for UNRWA is dwindling fast. I'm afraid it won't happen in the near future, if at all."

"One more week to the due date, maybe ten days. A first delivery is almost always late. The midwife is an old friend. I asked her to be ready just in case."

"Yes, that's a good idea." Ameena hugged my mother, threw me a wink, and left.

I read through her documents. In collaboration with a non-profit, a Dutch orthopedic specialist had arrived at our UNRWA clinic to examine cases and arrange for eligible patients to travel to the Netherlands for treatment. I lifted quizzical eyes to my mother. Before she could respond, Maryam arrived and commanded her full attention. Fanning her red face, my sister lowered her pregnant body onto a cushion with theatrical difficulty. Mother handed her a glass of water.

I waved a stack of papers in the air.

"Isn't it great?" Mother sat next to me. "They already showed him your medical file. You know, the one they prepared before they gave us the walker. It's very old, you were what, six? Seven? That's why the doc—"

"Nnooo," I blurted to slow her down. I was eight. I remember that day in the clinic very well. The doctors had prodded and probed, stared at my test results, and then scratched their heads. At the end of a very long, painful day, they had sent us home without naming a diagnosis.

"Don't worry." Mother patted my hand. "You don't have to go to the clinic. Ameena will bring him here to examine you tomorrow."

"Nnooo," I repeated.

"Who is coming tomorrow?" Maryam asked.

"A special doctor from *Holanda*. Ameena talked to him about your brother. He thinks he might be able to make him," Mother opened her eyes wide, "walk on his own."

Maryam arched an eyebrow. "Really? Without the walker?"

I raised both eyebrows. Yeah, really? Was this Dutchman a magician?

"I know. It sounds too good to be true. Ameena said the operation, well maybe more than one, will be in *Holanda*. If this God-sent doctor finds that your brother is a good candidate, of course. That's why he's examining him tomorrow. Where is *Holanda*, anyway?"

"It's in Europe, *yumma*," Maryam said.

Mother's face dropped. "That's very far away."

"Another continent."

"Oh, I don't care if it's in the North Pole as long as they help my son."

"Nnooo!" I bellowed, fed up with the two of them talking as if I were invisible. But they continued to ignore me.

"And who will pay for all of that?" Maryam rolled her swollen ankles. "If he qualifies."

"The doctor's organization. Long, complicated name." Mother pointed at my lap. "It's in those papers. Ameena is working on it. Such a wonderful girl, she jumped on this the minute she heard of this doctor's visit. I gave her all the papers we have to move forward. We need to take Waseem to get special photos for the application and—"

"Aaahhh!" I screamed, agitated and angry. Spasms started in my legs causing them to twitch. How come no one asked me if I wanted this or not? How could Ameena go behind my back? And why? Why would she give this sliver of hope to my mother? I rocked my hips, twisting my legs to kick pillows and shake the papers off my lap to scatter them away from me.

"What's the matter?" Maryam asked.

"He's getting too excited," Mother said. "Take it easy, Waseem."

Maryam rubbed her belly. "I need you here, *yumma*."

"Oh, of course. I'm not going anywhere. You know we can't leave the camp, let alone travel out of Lebanon." Mother twisted her lips from side to side. "Even if, with Abu Nidal's help maybe, I or Yasser manage to get a Lebanese Ess . . . Essae Pasay—"

"Laissez-Passer," Maryam corrected.

"One of those. Still, we can't afford to go. Ameena said the organization does not cover a family member. They do it only for the patients they approve."

"So, he'll be all alone?"

"Ameena promised the people at the organization will look after him. They take refugees from all over the world, and they have been doing this for many years. If this works, they will bring him back walking." Mother flipped up her open palms and sent her prayer toward the ceiling, "*Yaa Rabb*!"

"Aahhh! Aahhh!" I yelled, my tongue stiff as a rod of steel. I thrashed in my corner, fury and angry spasms taking my body hostage. What if Mother's heavenly messenger failed to perform his miracle? What would happen to her if they take away her hope? How could she go on? How could I? I jerked every which way, no longer able to control anything. My head slammed against the wall.

"*Habeebi*," Mother attempted to hold my arms, but I lashed out and shouted at her, my throat shrieking sounds like an injured mule. I was in pain. Ameena hurt me. She introduced hope and, in my world, hope was as dangerous as a handgun. One successful shot, and I would cease to exist in my present state. A missed one, and I would become like my mother, drifting through life, praying for miracles.

"Oh, help me." Mother struggled to wrap her arms around me, but I was far-gone. A Sufi dancer in a trance, I twirled faster and faster away from reality. No longer confined to my cushioned corner, I ran, skipped down the stairs, jumped over potholes and cement chunks. What if I could? I arrived at the seashore and dove in, chased waves and kicked my feet—my normal looking, perfectly aligned, scar-free feet. What if Ameena's dream doctor could make it all happen? What if? What if?

"I can't do anything!" Maryam screamed. "Sit on him, *yumma*."

Mother did just that. She climbed on top of me, trapped my arms with her knees and pinned me down. Framing my face with both hands, she started reciting verses of the Qur'an, as if my despicable condition was a demon she could exorcise. Her tears wet my face; mine collected in my earlobes.

"Please stop, Waseem. Can't you see how much you're hurting her?" Maryam's voice came from somewhere distant, panicking, accusing.

Gradually, with the full weight of my mother's enormous love pressing onto my chest and abdomen, my muscles began to release their tension, my outburst passed. She wiped my face with her palm, bent over to kiss my forehead and eased off.

Ashamed and completely spent, I turned to face the wall and buried my face in a pillow to muffle my sobs. To appease Mother, to stop her pain, I would have to go along with Ameena's plan. I would allow Ameena to pull the trigger.

Perhaps it was time for Mother's God to have a change of heart about me.

I remained in my position for a while, Mother clanged pots in the kitchen, Maryam watched television, some Turkish drama series dubbed in Arabic, and related its events to my mother. Fayzeh came home and talked of chaos on the streets from heavy rains. The Market turned into a mushy mess as vendors scrambled to protect their merchandise. Some classes at the UNRWA secondary school flooded and teachers turned dry areas into shelters for those whose homes were worse off.

Maryam decided to sleep over since Farook didn't want to risk having her go to their place. He phoned from the pharmacy to tell her that their alley flooded. Primitive sewage canals couldn't keep up with nature's onslaught. Since our home was on a hilly incline, we hardly had problems when it rained, aside from a few roof leaks here and there—nothing a couple of strategically placed buckets couldn't handle. The incessant hammering on metal sheets of the roof drove me crazy, though. As if an electric drill screwed nails into my bones.

The fierce storm continued throughout the night. Nabil and Wael stayed at the body shop to do whatever they could to keep water away from valuable equipment. Yasser called to say he was helping his mentor at the harbor and for Mother not to worry.

I kept my back turned to everyone and bit the corner of my pillow to alleviate a savage headache. Sometime during the night, Maryam moaned in pain. Mother told her to hang in there and breathe slowly, then instructed Fayzeh to boil water. Mother knew what was coming; I could hear it in her calm voice. Maryam's voice was panicky and frantic, her moaning escalated to screams too painful to hear. I curled my body to make it as small as possible and had no choice but to listen to the sloshing noises. Agonizing shrieks interrupted heavy panting and grunting. I kept quiet until I heard a baby's cries and flipped over to see. Big mistake.

Blood covered my mother's hands and arms all the way to the elbows, her face was sweaty, her damp hair shot in all directions. Fayzeh was on her knees, wiping Maryam's face and neck with a wet cloth. Mother was working on a crying baby between Maryam's raised knees tenting a bed sheet that covered Maryam from the waist down. Mother lifted a boy, head bloody and shiny, body covered by whitish patches of a butter-like layer. She placed him on Maryam's chest right under her chin. The bluish umbilical cord dangled from Maryam's side while Mother snipped and tucked. Baby stopped crying. Maryam started laughing. I gagged and threw up in my mouth.

So, yes that was the birth incident I had witnessed, the graceless deliverance of a poor, oblivious soul to my world.

CHAPTER ELEVEN

The arrival of my nephew called for a change of plans. Mother called Ameena to tell her the good news and asked her not to bring the doctor to our home. Yasser would take me to the clinic instead. I didn't object. With all the commotion and constant noise, I needed relief.

Once we arrived at the clinic, Ameena dismissed Yasser, clasped my arm, and guided me through groups of people to an examination room, the same room where I had been prodded as a child. Time, however, had chipped and smudged the baby blue paint on the walls and cast it in a disgusting hue of moldy green. The white linoleum floor had acquired a yellowish tint. I avoided rips in the cover of the padded examination table as I let go of my walker and, with the help of Ameena, climbed onto it. She flurried around with enthusiastic professionalism. Wearing a lemon-yellow shirt over a brown skirt that reached her tall black boots, she bustled left and right, talking to nurses and checking papers.

"I'm not supposed to be here, you know," she said with a sheepish smile. "I don't work in the clinic, but I told Doctor Van der Sloot I should be here to help with communications since *khalto* couldn't come. I promised her I wouldn't leave you alone." Ameena tilted her head, spilling her neat braid over one shoulder. "And I don't believe Yasser has the patience."

I sighed in agreement and refrained from pointing out that Yasser hadn't offered to stay. Banishing childhood memories of this room from my mind, I promised myself not to disappoint Ameena before her Dutch doctor, resigned to give her what she worked hard to secure, even though the likelihood of making it to the chosen list was dismal. I was twenty-one years old. It didn't take a genius to realize that my skeletal structure had settled in its deformed shape. Corrective surgeries would be complicated and costly, and no organization would be willing to fork up so much of its resources for a single patient—a crippled Palestinian refugee, of all people. The hope Ameena and my mother willingly clung to hadn't rubbed off on me. I was a highly effective repellent.

A number of people walked past the door, some seemed lost or looking for something, others hurried along crying children. Ameena talked to someone in the hallway and closed the door.

"So, you are an uncle now." She clasped her hands in obvious excitement. "All this planning, the hospital, the midwife, and what does Maryam end up doing? She gives birth at home. During a raging storm! What was it like?"

I stuck out my tongue and cleared my throat with a loud, "*Eeekhkh.*"

"I can't imagine," she chortled. "Isn't it strange? Life is exciting that way. Oh, I don't know. It's hard for me to think of Maryam responsible for a tiny human being. And *khalto*? A grandmother? She's too young . . ."

As Ameena cheerfully chatted, the noises outside faded, and my apprehension slipped away. I began to relax, swung my dangling feet to and fro, carefree in Ameena's nurturing presence.

We were alone in the small room, a first since . . . ever, and I had her full attention. I hung on to every word, move, blink, and breath. And, in her flurry, when she sat next to me to show me pictures of a hospital in The Hague, my heart picked up speed. A tenacious alien invaded my body, settled in my gut, and weighed me down, as if rapidly laying swelling seeds. Pleasing tingles started at the pit of my stomach and spread to my limbs. I couldn't shake the feeling. I wasn't myself, afraid to move a muscle. I remained silent, nodding or smiling every now and then so as not to spoil the experience with my abrasive voice. The precious moment shattered when a man came in pushing a wheelchair.

"This is Abdo." Ameena left my side and lifted something off the wheelchair. "He's going to help you change and take you to the X-ray machine." She placed a folded gown dotted with colorful balloons in my lap and headed to the door. "I'll see you back here afterwards, okay?"

I gave her a thumbs-up and allowed the middle-aged man with a beard streaked with silver threads to help me out of my clothes, except for my underwear.

"You must be very special," Abdo said in a thick voice that seemed to come out of his chest, not his throat. "All the patients Doctor Sloot has seen so far were children. It's easier to correct young bones, you see. Miss Ameena insisted he examine you, too. He agreed, of course. You know what they say about her around here?"

I shook my head, eyeing the loose knot at my waist Abdo made with the ties of the faded gown.

"He has not yet been born, who can say no to Miss Ameena." Abdo chuckled. "You are lucky to have her in your corner."

I shrugged. Sometimes, luck could be mistaken for a curse. In my case, that might be true. I was helpless, locked in a brutal battle between unmitigated, cruel reality and futile, grand aspirations. I couldn't dare to entertain a sliver of hope. How could my broken body handle so many conflicting emotions? I wanted to stay close to Ameena yet move away from her at the same time. Perhaps if this Dutch doctor succeeded, I would finally be able to do just that, run as far as I could from the fair, bewitching Ameena.

On our way to and from the X-ray room, Abdo shared his vast knowledge about each person we came across. There was the young, pretty nurse whom everyone dubbed "Feather" because she had the lightest touch giving injections, the janitor, referred to as the "Savior," who was sure to have a chocolate bar or a handful of pistachios in his pockets for whoever missed a lunch break, the clerk at the registration desk, nicknamed "Popcorn" as she could be heard popping her chewing gum from the end of the hallway, and then there was the "King" radiologist, who knew everyone depended on his work and behaved as though a crown floated atop his head.

Abdo told me who was married and the names and ages of their children, who had been there the longest, who were the newcomers, and so on. He talked about people I would probably never see again—some I would make sure to avoid—and all the while I wondered why he was telling me. He could have filled the time talking about sports or whatever dominated the news, yet he chose to speak of strangers, to give me glimpses into their lives as if I had the need to know. And yet, his chatter made me forget I was alone and put my mind at ease.

I liked Abdo. He helped manipulate my body into various and somewhat uncomfortable positions required for X-rays without making me feel awkward. Once back in the wheelchair, I poked his chest, flicked my wrist and asked, "Naammme?"

"I told you. Abdo, my friend."

He didn't understand that I wanted to know his work nickname. It didn't matter. I decided to call him "Mayor," as the good man seemed to know everyone in his domain.

Back in the old musty room, Abdo draped a flimsy sheet over my lap and left me to wait for Ameena. I spent thirty minutes alone, eyeing my bare feet, expecting my ugly toes to turn blue from the cold. Good thing Mother had remembered to clip my nails this morning.

A very tall man in a white coat opened the door. "Hello there," he said in English and walked in, Ameena on his heels. He extended his hand. "I'm Yaap Van der Sloot. Very glad to meet you, Waseem."

In the papers Ameena had given me, the doctor's first name was spelled as Jaap. He couldn't have misspoken his own name, which led me to conclude that it must be how the Dutch sound the letter J. Although I would never call the doctor by his first name, I made a mental note to remember its correct pronunciation. "Waleem" Shakespeare jumped into my head, and I winced at my past ignorance. Never again.

I returned the handshake.

Doctor Van der Sloot creased a wide forehead when he raised both eyebrows. "Ameena told me you understand English?"

I nodded and waved at Ameena, who stood in the corner behind him. She winked back.

"Good. Good. I studied your X-rays. And now, I want to examine you." Wasting no time, the doctor straddled a round chair and rolled it toward me. I stared at his ash-colored hair pulled into a ponytail. It dangled like a dead snake between his shoulder blades. I had never met a man with a ponytail, nor one with features resembling Vincent Van Gogh. I had studied a rendering of one of the painter's self-portraits in a magazine.

This man had the same pinkish-gray face as Van Gogh's, small green eyes, and sad-looking untidy beard, though his was brown, not red.

"Tell us when you feel pain, okay?" He started at my toes, and then moved to my ankles and knees, inspecting, tugging and turning. Aware of Ameena silently observing, a groan escaped my throat.

"Am I hurting you?" the doctor asked. He turned to Ameena. "I need to know if he's in any kind of pain."

"Waseem?" She met my gaze and spoke in English, "do you want to tell Doctor Van der Sloot anything?"

Had I been hurting, Ameena would have obliterated my ache with the care she showed. She made the point to the doctor that she wasn't there to interpret from Arabic. She was there merely to convey my unclear speech. She had faith in my self-schooling, in me.

"Nno," I responded in English.

"Good. Good. Let's lay you down on your back." The doctor towered over me and gently eased me onto the table. I adjusted the sheet over my midsection, relieved that Ameena hadn't left her spot in the corner. He lifted my left leg, bent it at the knee, and paused. "I'm going to rotate your hip joint, now. It will hurt a little. When it becomes too much you must tell me."

I braced myself by clutching the sides of the table. "Okkayy."

Absorbing some tolerable discomfort, I looked for something to concentrate on. No posters or pictures hung on the depressing walls, so I locked my gaze on a dark smudge in the ceiling as he moved my leg around. Once he pushed it inward to cross it over my right leg, my lower back caught fire. I screamed in agony.

"Good. Good. That's what we were looking for," he said in a triumphant tone.

A vile curse shot out of my mouth in Arabic concerning the doctor's mother. Must he sound so pleased? I trusted innocent Ameena didn't understand the profanity even if she could detect my speech. The doctor probably thought I was just making unintelligible noises from the pain.

"Sorry, young man. I had to do it." Doctor Van der Sloot slowly lowered my leg, pulled me to a sitting position and pressed his thumb to where the flame ignited in my back. "That is where it hurts the most. This here. This is it!"

"Hmmmfff," I breathed and wiped beads of sweat off my forehead. I glanced at Ameena. The pained look on her face confused me. She couldn't be that upset by my vulgar outburst, even if she could imagine it. Perhaps it was my childish screech? She didn't work in the clinic, after all, and wasn't hardened by suffering patients. I arched my eyebrows. She blinked. Tears rushed down her cheeks. What was going on? Why was she distressed?

The doctor grabbed my walker. "Now, I want to see how you walk. Come." He helped me off the table. I hobbled to the other side of the room, wincing and moaning despite myself. I prayed Abdo did a good job on that single knot holding my gown together and turned to face Ameena. She brushed tears with the tips of her fingers and buried her face in a folder.

I edged closer. "Ammeeenna?"

She answered my question with a flash smile and squeezed my forearm, as if to tell me she was fine. The doctor came up behind me.

"We're done for now. Ameena, you were right. I'd love a chance to help this brave young man." He placed both hands on my shoulders. "If you're not too attached to your walker, I believe I can rid you of it. Two stages of operations, the first to correct hip joints, the second to align your knees and ankles. You'd have a limp, of course, but you'd be independent. What do you say?"

My gaze still on Ameena, I barely registered what he said. Tears swelled in her eyes. She scribbled something in the folder. She was trying to hold it together. Were these tears of joy? But why did she cry before the doctor made his decision?

"Will you allow me to help you?" he pressed. "Should we go for it?"

"Yesss gggooo," I mumbled.

He released my shoulders and addressed Ameena. "Let's get the ball rolling, then. I'll write up my report and leave it to you to work out details with staff."

"I will. Thank you, doctor," she said, her voice strained.

He opened the door. "Waseem, if everything goes well, I will see you in Holland."

After the doctor left the room, we faced each other in silence for several seconds.

"Waseem, it's happening," she whispered. "Aren't you excited?"

I nodded. It was a lie. Excitement hadn't hit me yet, I stood perfectly still, no spasms or shakes.

"I'm so happy for you, Waseem. I know it will be a long, painful road. But you can handle it. You're strong. I have to admit, I wasn't sure doctor Van der Sloot would be willing to take on an adult."

Her words were joyful, her voice steady, yet her beautiful eyes shielded a negative emotion I couldn't detect. Was it sadness? Disappointment? Did she think her doctor should have also examined my arms and hands? Fix my jaw and teeth while at it? Did she imagine my body could be, somehow, reshaped into normalcy? Ameena couldn't be that naïve.

Searching for a way to lift her spirits, I tugged on my earlobe. “Dddocc . . . trrr Vaannn Goo . . . gghh!”

She smacked my shoulder and burst out laughing. “I thought the same thing the instant I saw him. He *does* look like him, doesn’t he?”

I nodded, gazing intently into her eyes. Even with laughter, that hiccup of a look hadn’t disappeared. She *was* hiding something.

I pointed my finger at her. “Youu ssaa . . . ddd.”

“Oh no, no. I’m happy for you. Really I—”

“Ssaa . . . ddd,” I cut her off. “Wwhyyy?”

Abdo came into the room. “I will help you get dressed, my friend.”

“I’ll call Yasser to take you home.” Ameena brushed past me.

I grabbed her arm. “Sspppee . . . eakkk,” I commanded.

“Oh Waseem, the way doctor Van der Sloot made you scream,” she pressed her lips together and shook her head, “so much pain all the time, I had no idea that’s how you—”

“Vinnncenn . . . ttt,” I interjected and wiggled my eyebrows for dramatic effect, forcing her lips to break into a hesitant smile.

She hugged her folder. “I guess we’ll call him Vincent from now on.”

Abdo clutched my clothes from the hook behind the door. “Who are we naming Vincent?”

CHAPTER TWELVE

Things developed at a faster pace than everyone expected. By the time March arrived, I had all my papers ready. Even with full sponsorship from the non-profit, my travel documents wouldn't have been issued so fast, or at all, if it weren't for Abu Nidal's connections with certain entities in the Lebanese government. Yasser made a point to tell me that bit of information each time he went out on an errand for his mentor. He neglected to mention it was, in fact, Ameena who secured my treatment credentials and pulled strings at her work, and with her father, to grant me the temporary refugee passage papers, Laissez-Passer.

Once we knew the scheduled date of travel—the first Sunday of April—my mother went into a frenzy of preparations. She instructed Nabil to find a way for me to bathe myself, forcing me to rely on no one for personal hygiene. Sponging off using a bucket of water with stiff hands was frustrating, but I managed a decent routine. Mother and Fayzeh sewed new clothes, specifically trousers, making sure to attach sturdy extension chains to the zippers. Mother also insisted on buying new shoes for after my feet were fixed. That was the term she used. To come up with the money, she formed a club with five of our neighbors. Women would pay a specific amount at the beginning of each month, and a member would use the sum on a rotational schedule. Mother asked to be the first to collect the interest-free loan from their ad hoc community bank. She said our budget could handle a conservative, five-month commitment and even asked Maryam to chip in. I told her to leave my sister out of it, given the added expenses of feeding her growing family. Mother hushed me, indicating that Maryam breastfed her baby.

The more Mother got involved in the arrangements, the more her hopes soared. The only other time I had seen that spark of lively energy in her eyes was before Maryam's wedding. I didn't have the heart to dampen her mood. I was trapped, not just inside my body, but inside my mother's bright world of great expectations as well. I was stuck, tied on the tracks of a train speeding in my direction—well, maybe not so much as speeding—but coming at me at a pace I couldn't slow, nor stop. Things were happening fast. The fact that I didn't want them to made no difference.

The crying started about a week before my departure. I would catch Mother sniffing and dabbing at her eyes at different times of the day, but mostly at night. On the day of travel, I had to leave the house at three in the morning to arrive at the airport in time for the midday flight. Yasser indicated the one-hour drive from *Saida* to Beirut involved a level of unpredictability. None of us had ever set foot outside the camp, so we didn't know what he meant.

He refused to explain. I entertained my own suspicions. Working for Abu Nidal, Yasser had a special leave permit and drove a car. He must have smuggled goods for his boss at one point or another. Since he secured Abu Nidal's permission to take me to the airport, I figured he must have been mindful of police presence on the road to the airport and worried we might be delayed during a routine stop.

Sensing Yasser's edginess to start the journey, I quickly said my goodbyes to everyone. Mother wet my shirt with her tears, Fayzeh tied colorful ribbons to my walker, Maryam's baby whimpered when she hugged me, and Nabil carried me down.

"I wish I could go with you," he whispered as he helped me settle in the passenger seat. Yasser opened the trunk so Nabil could place my walker and battered suitcase, telling him to be careful not to scratch the car. While the girls gathered around Mother, reassuring her that everything would be fine, Wael thrust his head through the open window and tucked a handful of folded bills into the inside pocket of my coat. "Euros. Keep them hidden."

I attempted to pull out the money. "Nnoo."

"Yes," he insisted and clasped my hands in his. "I know they said they will pay for everything, but a man should always have money on him. It's not much. You never know what might happen."

It was my turn to tear up. I had always deemed Wael a tough character, distant and abrupt. His considerate gesture surprised me. It took me several seconds to realize his watch was missing. A pale, winged disc circled his tan wrist instead.

When we finally took off, I twisted in my seat to look back at Ameena's house. Not a single light on. I expected her to bid me farewell, or at least wave from her window. She had briefly visited the day before, promising and double reassuring my mother that I would be fine. When she neglected to say goodbye to me before she left, I assumed she saved a slew of good wishes for this morning.

"She's not there," Yasser quipped.

I swallowed my disappointment and slumped forwarded. That must have been how my brother felt when Ameena turned him down. Her disregard bore a hole in my chest. The farther we drove, the bigger the void grew until it engulfed my foolish heart.

A representative of the organization met us at the airport, a woman in her late fifties. I had seen her talk to Ameena in the clinic. Untidy, grayish, short hair gathered atop her small head and exposed extended earlobes. The boyish hairdo reminded me of an abandoned bird's nest. Her ankle-length, green leaf-print dress helped cement the image. Yasser examined the name badge dangling from her neck when she introduced herself as Emma Van Gastel. She spoke Arabic with a broken Lebanese accent, yet she was surprisingly comprehensible. She turned to a man behind her in his late twenties clutching a clipboard and gestured for him to show his badge. It identified him as Dirk Van Eedin.

Yasser and I shared a questioning look. Do all Dutch names have "Van" in them? I promised myself to find out what the word meant once I was settled and gained access to books, perhaps a library close to where I would be staying. Bird Lady Van Gastel glanced at her watch with a regularity beyond what I considered polite. Arriving five hours before the flight, we were very early. Why was she so worried about time?

After checking my papers, she led us to a group of five children and asked us to wait. Yasser deposited my shaggy brown suitcase on a big trolley with the group's luggage—identical black bags with a circular yellow logo. How come the organization didn't give me a bag? Yasser fell into a seat nearby, whipped out his phone, and typed with his thumbs at a fascinating speed. I discredited the notion he was researching the Dutch name matter, because every few seconds an annoying sound dinged from his phone.

I eyed the boys and girls, all seemingly under ten years old. I couldn't recognize any of them. Where did they come from? And why were there no family members waiting with them?

A boy in a wheelchair with his left leg extended on a rod approached.

"I'm Saeed. What's your name?"

"Wwaa . . . ssseeemmm," I responded with an exaggerated drawl, exposing my jagged teeth and sounding my name more as a growl to dissuade conversation. I wasn't in the mood for chitchat.

Saeed hurried backward and wheeled himself away. He lifted his hand to his forehead in a military salute. The others followed suit, including the girl with one arm. I knew what they were doing. They were anointing me their leader because I was an adult and clearly the most disadvantaged. Or because they were scared, sick children traveling on their own and needed an advocate from their ilk, someone big and mean like me, to be in their corner. I returned the salute. *There, feel safe and leave me alone.*

They chatted and joked. It seemed that they knew each other from somewhere; they probably came to the airport together, as they talked about a minibus that collected them. Well immersed in my miserable abandonment, I didn't care to know more.

"I made it," Ameena's voice came to me before I saw her. I almost lost my balance when I turned around. Running past families and groups of travelers with her father not far behind, she skidded to a stop before Bird Lady and waved at me.

I closed my open mouth. She came all the way to the airport to see me off? I waved back, then noticed the shiny hard-shell suitcase behind her.

Abu Nidal talked with the two women. I couldn't hear their conversation. Ameena handed the suitcase to Dirk, and he brought it to our trolley. She hugged her father and took off toward a ticket counter.

Yasser stood to attention when his boss signaled for him to go over. My brother clapped a hand on my shoulder.

"Take care of yourself. Ameena will let us know how you're doing."

I poked his forehead. "Yyouu knne . . . www?"

"*Ma'almi* stressed not to tell anyone. He wasn't sure her papers would be ready in time. She's not sponsored by the organization, so it was more than iffy." Yasser dipped his chin to his chest. "Once she sets her mind on something, no one can stop her. Not even her father." Yasser snapped up his head. "It may help you to remember that."

I waited for Ameena on the same seat Yasser vacated. He left with Abu Nidal after talking to a man wearing a black suit and dark glasses. The mysterious man nodded a lot and patted a bulge under his jacket.

I watched travelers lug suitcases, drag carts, and push strollers every which way. Children whined and cried. Porters frowned or smiled at whatever tips they received. An old man parked in a wheelchair looked lost and confused. Announcements about departing flights blared, sometimes indistinguishably. A woman in red high heels and a white dress dragged a cat-sized dog on a sparkling leash. Surrounded by commotion, for a moment, I forgot about my impending journey to the unknown.

The group of chosen children gathered around Dirk as he examined tags and scribbled on his clipboard. He then handed out sandwiches and juice boxes. I declined his offer when he approached me and remained aloof, suffering a mass of conflicting emotions and entertaining strange thoughts.

Ameena hadn't deserted me. She had been my champion, my only friend, teacher, and savior. It was evident she would also be my traveling companion. What other roles could she be planning to assume?

~

It took Ameena a long time to join us at the gate. The girl with one arm glued herself to Ameena's side. I caught Dirk stealing glances at my precious friend, appraising, admiring. She paid him no attention. I doubt she even registered his enthrallment. Bird Lady frantically went over rules and piled papers onto Ameena's lap, said she needed them filled and signed right away, before Ameena was to leave the country. When it was time for us to board, Ameena lifted up her head from her homework and signaled that she would come find me.

I landed an aisle seat several rows behind the group. Dirk tried to switch places with the man next to me, but the jackass refused to give up his seat, leaned his head against the window and closed his eyes. I knew what to do to chase him away. A couple of farts wouldn't be hard to release given the nervous mess I was in. I held it until boarding was complete, then fired my cannons. The sleeping beauty didn't even flinch.

Ameena boarded at the last possible moment and sat sandwiched between a man and a woman a few rows ahead of the group. After talking with a clean-shaven flight attendant, she swapped with a woman sitting next to the girl with one arm. Everyone in the group ended up on the same row, except for me. I didn't mind as my intestines kicked into overdrive and competed with the churning of engines under my feet as the plane sped on the runway. I gripped the armrests and looked out the window.

Lights flickered on the tips of the wing, a couple of flaps lifted off its metal surface. Loud rumbling assaulted my hearing. We started to ascend. Invisible hands pressed my head and torso onto the back of my seat. My ears hurt from inside my skull. I unlocked my jaw to relieve some pressure. White blobs whizzed by the windowpane. The plane pierced a layer of clouds to clear skies, then penetrated another cluster of clouds. An image of my mother's needle sewing my ripped pants popped into my mind's eye. I laughed and laughed, releasing the gases bubbling inside me until we leveled off.

To my horror, as soon as the pilot announced he was turning the seatbelt sign off, Ameena left her spot and came toward me.

As she steadily made her way past elbows and extended hands spreading newspapers, a couple of men turned their heads with leering gazes. I imagined myself rushing at those men and punching them in their smug faces. I considered yelling profanities from my seat, which would probably sound like howls. Causing a scene would embarrass Ameena, who seemed unaware of what went on behind her back. Alas, all I could do was watch, curse under my breath, and add my envisioned acts to the list of things I could do once Vincent performed his medical artistry on my body.

"Hey. I wish I could sit next to you," she announced to everyone on the plane, shooting disgusted looks at my neighbor. He didn't open his eyes.

I crinkled my nose and fanned my face, not one bit guilty for blaming the smelly vulgarity onto my seatmate. Ameena frowned at the man. "Some people are just too rude." She squatted in the aisle and lowered her voice. "I thought this would be exciting, but I'm beyond that. Barely holding it together for the sake of the children. It's terribly overwhelming, isn't it?"

I nodded. Her admission relieved some of my apprehension. I raised my hands to my lips and crossed my index fingers together.

"I know, I know. You're upset I didn't tell you. I couldn't, Waseem. It was a very long shot. To secure the needed documents and visa, I had to prove my services were essential and my expenses would be covered. I didn't want to use funds allocated to a child, you see." She spoke fast, almost bouncing on her heels. "It took some convincing to have Baba agree to pay for my trip. Doctor Van der Sloot . . . I mean Vincent, sponsored me personally on papers, told Baba he couldn't communicate with the children without me, that he needed me as an in-between person, you know? I only found out the visa was issued last night. And you know what? Emma is the organization's communications specialist. She speaks Arabic. The doctor lied to Baba." Ameena grabbed my arm with both hands. "It was you, Waseem. You're the one who persuaded Vincent to bring me along."

I scowled and shook my head. When did I do that?

"Those children? They're all orphans. The organization's charity cases. Humanitarian work and stuff. It wasn't difficult for Vincent to decide on them." Ameena moved one of her hands to my shoulder. "You, Waseem, your condition presented a medical challenge. Vincent wanted you so badly, but he couldn't get his organization to cover your treatment. They only sponsor children. So, he's paying from his own pocket. Convinced two other doctors to help and included you on a special, official list to grant you entry into the country." She tucked stray hair strands behind her ear. "I told him you wouldn't go without me. If he wanted to have you, he must take me too." Chuckling, she winked. "You didn't think I would leave you alone, did you?"

My stomach growled an answer, loud enough for everyone around us to hear. The angel that she was, she pretended she hadn't and rose to her feet.

"Look, Emma taught me things here." Ameena demonstrated how to work the entertainment system, showed me how to open and close the folding tray, where to find a reading light. She pointed at a button on the armrest, "When you want anything, anything at all, just press this. It will alert the flight attendants, and they will let us know." She leaned closer to whisper, "When you need to go the bathroom, Dirk will help you."

Returning to her seat, I counted five people tilting into the aisle in her wake. Her white, long-sleeved top was loose-fitting over her jeans and reached mid-thigh. Men would have ogled her even if she were covered head-to-toe. It was the way she moved—sure, steady steps with shoulders pulled back, arms straight down, and head slightly tilted to one side. Ameena didn't walk, she glided with an air of humble confidence that demanded attention. A cosmic star trapping everything within its magnetic field, people gravitated toward her, if not sensually attracted, then emotionally drawn, curiously captivated at the very least. Poor Vincent had no chance of refusing her requests. Nor mine as she had acquired my voice and merged it with hers. What would she do with it?

I turned to my comatose neighbor. Had he ingested medication that knocked him asleep? Perhaps this was his first time on an airplane, and he was as anxious and apprehensive as I was. If I had access to such pills, I would have swallowed a couple.

CHAPTER THIRTEEN

I decided to banish the word "comfortable" from my vocabulary. I hate it. Never mind the chronic pain, when one was scared, one could never be comfortable. And I was terrified. The airplane engines roared inside my body, around my heart, and between my jaws. With a woman praying out loud in the seat right in front of me and a man with gut-wrenching coughs somewhere behind, I couldn't concentrate long enough to read what happened to wild Heathcliff after he fled the farmhouse in *Wuthering Heights*.

Everyone I encountered on the journey kept enquiring if I was comfortable. Flight attendants generous with tiny pillows and flimsy blankets wouldn't leave me alone, repeatedly asked if I needed more. During the first four-hour flight to Paris, I refused to eat or drink anything to avoid a complicated visit to the toilet.

Even though they had their hands full tending to the children, Dirk and Bird Lady frequently checked on me. I finally relieved myself during the layover in Charles de Gaulle Airport. I pushed Dirk out of the toilet stall with my walker, after he offered twice to unzip my trousers, and pulled out my zipper chain extension to prove I wasn't helpless. Though I appreciated his attention and assistance, the man took it too far. The flight to Amsterdam lasted an hour and a half, and this time "Helping

Hands" Dirk sat next to me. Taking my cue from my previous neighbor, I hid under a blanket, clutched the chain to secure my zipper in place, and pretended to sleep the entire time.

On the bus from Schiphol Airport to The Hague, the bus driver gave me questioning looks after each bump and turn, sticking up his thumb questioningly to verify I was okay. He dropped off the children with Helping Hands at a special facility and drove away. Bird Lady explained that a Dutch family of Moroccan origins had volunteered to take me in. And since Ameena was a last-minute addition, the family also offered to host her as they have a daughter her age.

Ameena was the only person who didn't request a report on my level of comfort. I appreciated that. She understood asking was pointless and saw how strange, how distressing, everything was. Dedicating her attention on the children, she showed affinity by squeezing my arm or shoulder whenever she passed.

By the time we arrived at the door of the host family late at night, I was a walking, or rather dragging, zombie. Bird Lady introduced the head of the family as Mr. Rasheed Alaoui. Though the man's hair was all white and his tan face showed deep wrinkles around the eyes, he sounded younger than I expected. The problem was, I couldn't catch what he said to Ameena and me. He spoke an Arabic dialect with intonations of what I inferred to be a French-Spanish mix. Latifah, his nice, heavyset wife, chatted with Bird Lady in Dutch, which sounded very different. The same happened with the daughter, Samra, who as expected, took an instant liking to Ameena.

The petite young woman—with a name that literally described her as tanned—smiled a lot, showing an entire spread of perfectly aligned, bright teeth. Her frizzy black hair formed a circular frame around an adorable face. Though twenty years old, her big brown eyes, long lashes, smooth rosy cheeks, and a delicate frame made her resemble a pre-teen girl. Dressed in a sleeveless top and skinny jeans ripped at the knees, she spoke with a whining, high-pitched voice. I couldn't take my eyes off of her, wondering how this dainty person could produce such powerful noise.

After Bird Lady left, Ameena gave up her attempts to communicate in Arabic with the Alaoui family and switched to English. Exhausted, I couldn't stop laughing at the irony. It was obvious Vincent and Bird Lady had chosen this wonderful family to host us because of its Arab origins, yet we couldn't understand much of their North African accent. I stayed silent and stuck to either nodding or shaking my head whenever I had to answer questions. Had I opened my mouth, my chopped-up speech would have added more layers of confusion and miscommunication. I feared my abrasive voice would hurt delicate Samra's senses. To compound my discomfort, a fit of chuckles escaped my throat, making me sound more like a clucking rooster.

Clasping Ameena's hand, Samra dragged her suitcase to her room. Rasheed led me to the back of the house. Pale wood panels covered the entire floor—no rugs to sidestep or catch my walker on. We passed a room lined with bookshelves all around. I stumbled to a stop at its door. Talking quickly, as if I understood every word, Rasheed pointed at an enormous section full of Arabic and English books. I gathered that I was welcome to spend as much time as I wanted in his study. Convulsing and chuckling with delight, I couldn't believe my good fortune—a library within my reach.

We continued on to a spacious bedroom with an attached private bathroom. Rasheed talked and gestured with his hands to help me comprehend as he took off my shoes and unpacked my suitcase into a wardrobe. The good man didn't offer to escort me to the bathroom and left me alone to prepare for bed. My nervous chuckles died as soon as my head hit the pillow. I recall making a promise to myself to apologize for my rudeness in the morning.

Whatever barriers the language discrepancy erected, good food tore down. The Alaoui family won me over during breakfast. I was famished. Judging from Ameena's delightful exchange with the family, I knew I wasn't the only one who found the spread of hummus, olives, white cheese, and fried eggs perfectly satisfying. They even had welcoming, warm loaves of pita bread.

Samra, partially dressed in tight leggings and a strapless top that showed a rose tattoo on her left shoulder, attempted to serve me slices of orange-colored fish. Trying my mightiest to remain quiet, I smiled with my lips closed and shook my hand to reject her unfamiliar offering. She followed with a jar of small, headless, silvery-white fish.

"Raw herring?" she asked, as if she were presenting chocolate.

Repeating my polite rejection, I held my breath and watched her grasp a fish from its tail, dip it in chopped onions, slide it whole into her mouth, and swallow the huge bite.

Ameena broke my mesmerization by coughing behind a closed fist. Samra failed at enticing her to try a sample of the traditional Dutch food. Samra joked about our weak sense of adventure and promised to have us both eat a whole fish by the time we left The Netherlands. Eyeing the herring jar at the center of the table, I thought of the stuffed lamb intestines dish that my mother once made for Eid. If the situation were reversed, and Samra sat at our floor spread during such a meal, would she be able to hold back a gag as I just had?

I inwardly agreed to Samra's challenge. I would eat a whole herring before I left and share her tradition. I would do a lot more in this foreign place as well; so much to explore and experience.

Every now and then, Mr. and Mrs. Alaoui would slip into French when they conversed with Ameena. She would immediately translate their exchange for my benefit. I loved Ameena's French and enjoyed watching her full lips form the smooth front-rounded vowels. Though she stuttered a bit, she seemed at ease, as if she had known this family all her life. But as soon as the meal was over and everyone cleaned up, she excused us from the kitchen, saying she needed to go over some logistics, and signaled for me to follow her to my room.

"Oh, Waseem," she said as soon as she closed the door. "What have I done? This is too much. I mean, what a wonderful family, right? But I can't in good conscience stay here like a parasite." She clasped her hands under her chin and paced the room. "I mean, they planned to host *you* from the start, but not me. Vincent put them on the spot when he told them I was coming. Oh, Waseem. I didn't think this far. I'm an idiot. I should have brought gifts. Maybe I could pay rent. Baba gave me cash for incidentals, and I have some money saved from my paychecks. It might be enough. I barely convinced Baba to let me come and cover my ticket. I can't risk asking him for more. Besides, he thinks I'm under Vincent's sponsorship, but I do have a job, you know? I need to find out what my duties are." She finally stopped and opened her hands. "What do you think? Should I offer to pay rent? How much?"

I had never seen her unsure of herself. It disturbed me. I sat on the bed and reached for my jacket draped on the bedpost. I opened my mouth, but before I uttered a sound, Ameena rambled on.

"Would that offend them, you think? I mean, how fortunate are we to have such a nice, generous family take us in, right? We can't risk hurting their pride. And this house is perfect. Look," she turned a full circle, "your own room! And Samra's room is big and bright. I'm not used to sharing, but she's really sweet. I think we'll get along well." Ameena squatted before me. "You've been so quiet. Waseem, don't worry too much. Let them hear your voice, get used to your speech. After all, you and I?" She gave me a mischievous wink. "We need to get used to theirs." Sighing, she stretched to her feet. "Oh, Waseem. What should I do?"

I pulled the Euros from my jacket and offered them to her.

"What's this?" She took the folded bills. "Where did you get this?"

"Wwwaa . . . ell."

She dropped onto the bed next to me. "How nice. I didn't think Wael had it in him. See?" She slumped her shoulders. "Everyone thought this through, except me. I bullied Baba and Mama, even Vincent and his staff, to get us out of that camp, and didn't stop for one moment to plan the next step." She wiped her eyes. "So much for my plan to take us where we belong."

I cleared my throat to ask about the path she had envisioned for us to reach Palestine from Holland, but she stopped me with a heavy sigh.

"Waseem, what is wrong with me?"

I poked her arm. "Pperrr . . . ffccttt."

"Yeah, a perfect fool." She put the money in my hands. "Thank you for this. Keep it with you, though. I'll find out how much the Alaouis want for rent. If what I have isn't enough, I'll let you know." She briefly closed her eyes. "God, I hope I'm doing the right thing."

"Asskkk Vinnncenn . . . ttt."

"Yes, that's a good idea. I'll talk to him. See what he says. We're supposed to go to the hospital the day after tomorrow. Vincent is very straightforward. He'll just tell me if I'm expected to pay rent." She blew a long breath. "Thanks, Waseem."

Wanting nothing more than to make her feel better, I tried to nudge her shoulder with mine, but my body jerked sideways and almost knocked her off the bed. I clutched her arm and said, "Bbrrreaa . . . dd—"

"Pita bread?" She asked through a giggle, immediately knowing what I was trying to convey. "You saw how pleased they were when they served us the loafs? They're wonderful. Doing everything to make us feel welcome and comfortable." She rolled her eyes. "But that smoked salmon and raw herring? Why would anyone eat that? And for breakfast?"

I wanted to retort with a reminder of the bull's testicles that the butcher, Abu Ali, saved for special customers such as her father, but I couldn't bring myself to mention the aphrodisiac to spare her additional discomfort.

CHAPTER FOURTEEN

I remained in the hospital for four straight months after the first set of surgeries, went to the Aloui's for a six-week reprieve, and returned to undergo a second round of operations. Whenever able, I would roam the halls of the hospital with my walker, which Vincent repeatedly adjusted to accommodate the changes in my body. I would visit those sponsored children—my clan—who underwent treatment at the same hospital. I absolutely refused to use a wheelchair or replace my walking aid with a new, sleek-looking gray one. My glow-in-the-dark, creaking wheels demanded attention, much like a circus trumpet announced a clown's arrival. The children knew I was coming to check on them before I showed up at their bedsides and always greeted me with smiles, no matter the conditions they were in.

Their resilience amazed me. Homesick, scared, and in pain, they often cried in my arms. I tried to comfort them, but there were limits to what I could offer. Kissing both index fingers and tapping them to my forehead three times, I promised to visit as often as possible, even crawl over to their wing if I had to, which drew wider smiles on their innocent faces. Much as my walker remained the one constant in my changing life, I thought I could serve as the children's familiar anchor.

I assigned an animal to each child and provided pictures ripped from magazines and bits of information about characteristics to keep the children interested. I invented some traits, too. I would encourage them to chortle, gibber, grunt, roar, or clack according to their animal avatar, any way to entice them to express their misery without reservations. As a stipulation for my visits to continue, they promised not to use their animalistic sounds in my absence. The one exception was if anyone attempted an inappropriate touch. Then the young ones had my permission to bite, claw, kick, and screech until the entire hospital staff came running. Thankfully, nothing happened to warrant such drastic measures.

There was a kangaroo constantly seeking hugs with his short arms, a monkey digging into things with his club fist and one finger, a camel moving in slow motion because he couldn't bend his knees, and a tigress missing an arm who lashed out at everyone but me and Ameena. I designated Saeed, the clever boy with one leg shorter than the other, to be a dolphin. The list stretched to include an owl, a frog, a bear, and a couple of elephants for a pair of twins.

On the days I couldn't leave my bed, I took comfort in knowing they were not all alone. Ameena, Dirk, Bird Lady, and volunteers frequently looked in on them. Still, I would send notes through nurses, scribbles my stiff hands managed to draw of misshaped hearts and crooked balloons, include more pictures of designated animals, anything to let the little ones know I was thinking of them.

~

During the course of my entire eight-month stay, I received many precious gifts. The eventual diminishment of constant pain, the slight height gained as I no longer stooped over my walker, and the newfound dignity that accompanied an independent freedom to roam the hallways whenever I felt the urge. All these new experiences finally excused my existence.

The greatest material gift was an iPad. Rasheed brought it to the hospital one day after I had my first procedure. I mimed my thanks, but disappointment must have shown on my face because he usually carried a stack of books. With a calm fatherly smile, my benefactor explained that I had devoured most of what was in his home study and burned through his allocated quota for the public library. He claimed I would have access to more knowledge via the smart tablet. I knew what it was, had seen starry-eyed people glued to its glowing screen, and refrained from professing my dour opinion of a device I didn't know how to use.

There are very few things I could hold with my crooked hands, and the feel of a book bound within a cover was the one I cherished the most. Ameena understood. She continued to replenish my supplies—and soul—with the printed word.

For six long weeks, I lay flat on my back in a body cast from the waist down. A horizontal bar thirty centimeters long inserted in the plaster held my knees apart. A cloth flap covered my privates under a joke-of-a-bedsheet. Since I had to stay in that degrading position, I implored Rasheed to prevent Ameena from visiting. The man tried. His exasperation showed every time he trailed her into my room.

I should have known better. No one, or nothing, stopped Ameena from doing what she wanted to do. In the case of the Alaouis, she did whatever she liked, and if it went against their wishes, she claimed to misunderstand their Arabic accent. When they attempted to communicate using French or English, she pretended to miss the meaning of key words. It didn't happen often, but the tactic worked to her advantage whenever she wanted to avoid a sticky situation or make something happen. As much as it hurt me to deceive the generous family, I followed her lead, although it was far easier for me to plead ignorance.

Ameena came by every afternoon to inform me about her training on specific programs at the UNHCR offices. She left the room when nurses needed to tend to me—always male nurses after I hissed at a young blond woman who approached my bed with gloved hands—and returned to continue her reporting. Ecstatic, Ameena would talk fast, in a hurry to share possible opportunities that would help ease the plight of refugees. She established connections with professors and educators from all over the globe and extracted promises from them to visit our camp.

On weekends, while Rasheed and his wife kept me company, Ameena explored The Hague and Amsterdam with Samra. I vicariously experienced city life through my friend's breathless, detailed descriptions and came to fully understand why my mother had clung to her mother's depictions of their family home in Palestine and those distinct *Yaffa* oranges. Like me, she cherished a place only known through the description of another.

Ameena informed me of the multiple art museums that brimmed with works of renowned artists such as Vermeer, Rembrandt, and the true Vincent. She took pictures on her phone and showed me everything, including a couple she had snuck from inside the Van Gogh Museum of his masterpiece, *Sunflowers*. The photo was blurry and unflattering, but Ameena looked so proud of herself that I applauded her guile and hid the fact that I had seen better images in magazines. Besides, I had a whole field of sunflowers right before my eyes in Ameena, not just a select bunch in a vase. I did not tell her that, of course.

Some of her photos featured water canals, crisscrossed by streets teeming with houseboats and water taxis. The idea of a floating home appealed to me. Other pictures showed houses with pointed roofs fused together in long stretches along the banks of waterways. Several of these dwellings appeared to be leaning sideways as if they were close to sinking under the still water, yet smiling residents waved from windows and balconies adorned with colorful tulips.

Ameena described the difficulty of navigating a path strewn with pedestrians, skirting around bicycles, mopeds, cars, or metro trains, and chasing shuttle ferries. I demonstrated my walker maneuvering skills. She stopped for a moment, flashed a smile, and continued to add detailed depictions of strange places. Dark, hazy coffeeshops that had nothing to do with serving coffee, and red-framed windows displaying semi-naked women. When I raised my eyebrows at a photo of a vacant window, she shook her admonishing finger at me and quickly swiped to a photo of giant windmills.

How I wished I could join Ameena on those adventures.

The following week, I reluctantly allowed Rasheed to teach me how to use the iPad, and my wish came true in a way. I didn't expect the vast, novel world it ushered into my small hospital room. Like a street beggar attending a lavish banquet, I hopped from one website to another, sampling or stuffing my mind with information, images, endless articles, and excerpts from books. A bat emerging from a dark cave, I sucked on varied fruits of knowledge with the ravenous hunger of the flying mammal. Fixated, I ignored my pain, avoided sleep, I no longer cared which blond washed me. The rectangular metallic computer wasn't a machine, it was the most effective sedative, a potent stimulant, a shameless aphrodisiac, all of which I embraced.

Anchored to the bed by my body cast no more, I soared to the top of Mount Everest, dove deep into the Mariana Trench, and visited diverse patches in between; deserts, volcanoes, jungles, rain forests. I floated in zero-gravity on spacecrafts, explored the battered face of the moon, and landed on the dusty surface of Mars. I roamed the halls of the Rijksmuseum, Smithsonian Institution, Le Louvre, Acropolis, and the British Museum. At the tip of my stiff fingers, everything I summoned simply materialized on the screen. I rode camels around the Pyramids, swam among stingrays in the Caribbean, and migrated alongside zebras intermingled with wildebeests on the Serengeti. I even saw what those red-framed windows displayed. And then some.

I felt no shame, no remorse, only hunger for more.

Once I passed the stage of bewilderment and awe, I gorged on specifics. I learned that the "Van der" in Dutch names meant "of the," similar to the structure in some Arabic names. I started to view Vincent in a different light after realizing he was Jaap, of the Sloot area. Somehow, that nugget of knowledge changed my perspective, and I became more accepting of the Dutch doctor, seeing commonalities between us instead of divisions. And yet, the more I explored this digital world, the sadder I became—not that my mood was great to begin with, given all the doctor's visits and never-ending injections—but I grew more dejected, mournful for the wasted time, angry at my years of deprivation and darkness.

It is one thing to live in ignorance, another to learn and see what you were, indeed, ignorant of. I traveled on a magic carpet—my tapestry was Google Maps—and when I navigated through the streets of *Yaffa*, my mother's teary eyes traveled with me. I hated myself for not being on the internet before. I had never ventured into one of the internet cafés at the camp to use a computer, never learned how to—the expense a big deterrent, as well.

We talked, Mother and I, using different video chatting apps on Yasser's cell phone, beholden to whatever worked on the signal strength at the internet cafés he patronized. Once we passed her crying episodes, she talked, and I mostly listened. I nagged her to rake her memory for my grandmother's detailed descriptions about the location of their home in *Yaffa* so I could see it on my tablet. She pinpointed its location within walking distance to the shore, the Drama School, and the Cultural Theatre.

I couldn't find the whole neighborhood. A vast public park and a synagogue had replaced the entire area surrounding the theatre. But from her recalled account, I savored the view my grandmother must have enjoyed from the window: azure Mediterranean waters, white sandy beaches, and proud, centuries-old buildings of established communities. I begged Yasser to do a search and show her on his phone, but he didn't see the point, so I took screenshots, sent them to his phone, and watched her sad eyes flicker with excitement when I insisted that she see the images. The stubborn dimness returned with a savage vengeance when she realized her family's home which she heard so much about from her mother no longer stood, and that its neighborhood grove produced the exceptional *Yaffa* oranges no more.

At that moment, I made a promise to myself. No matter the outcome of my medical treatments, and no matter how much time it would take, I would go to *Yaffa*. The need to experience for myself this colossal, all-encompassing power that held my mother's tormented psyche hostage for those long years overwhelmed me. This oath kept me sane through the painful, complicated physical therapy sessions that followed each procedure. With Ameena's ardent persistence, the Allouis' heartfelt encouragement, and Vincent's unyielding insistence on seeing his project succeed, I made steady progress. My personal motivation, however, was the image in my head of sinking perfectly aligned feet in Palestinian soil.

Staying at the hospital for an extended period of time, fully dependent on nurses and caretakers, I was exposed on so many levels, constantly touched and prodded, my wounds repacked. I needed to cling to something private. I kept the solemn vow to myself, never mentioned it anyone, not even to Ameena.

By then, I was able to communicate through typed text. It was the easiest thing, as if my deformed hands were designed to accommodate the touch screen, not the other way around. I started with clear responses to Vincent's probing and gave simple instructions to my nurses. Limited by having to use the English language, I would type hurts, or I can't, or go away instead of baring my teeth and hissing at them whenever they failed to understand my vocal rejections of their demands. I gradually engaged in short conversations in Classical Arabic with Rasheed. The printed language is understood by anyone who speaks Arabic, which removes the cumbersome comprehension difficulties encountered with different dialects. Our initial exchanges were slow at first because I had to steady my spastic hands and search for letters on the keyboard. But once I memorized their locations, both on the Arabic and English keyboards, no one stared at me with an open mouth anymore.

Ameena didn't like my newfound communication tool, which hung from my neck to dangle across my chest. She lacked the patience to wait for me to type what I wanted to say. She would brush my hands away from the iPad and nudge me to speak. I couldn't understand why she had this irrational, impractical insistence to carry on like old times.

Her stubborn rigidness annoyed me. Why did she work so hard to bring me to this point of bodily improvement and then deny me what I needed the most? It didn't make sense. I defied her, repeatedly thrusted the glowing screen with my typed words in her face. She would respond by cutting her visit short. One day, she neglected to show up, then another.

Upon hearing her sure footsteps pierce the loneliness of a quiet Wednesday afternoon, I relented, turned off the tablet, and declared defeat.

I continued to talk to Ameena, and as always, she never missed my beat.

CHAPTER FIFTEEN

Relinquishing my dependable walker was gruesome. I didn't expect the physical pain, as if the orthopedic specialist was sawing off one of my legs without sedation. I screamed, spit, and tried to bite the doctor when she hauled away my walker. Her efforts to showcase a weird-looking cane with a four-pronged base fell on deaf ears. In the back of my mind, I knew I was being unreasonable, I had known this day would come. Yet I couldn't fathom losing my sturdy wheels, the one constant that anchored my history, my family, and my home to the very core of my existence.

Spasms raked my body and terrified the gentle specialist standing next to Ameena, who had just arrived. To the best of my knowledge, Ameena had never witnessed my undoing to this degree. I grappled for control, but it was too late. Roaring and convulsing, I fell off the bed and rolled along the floor.

The slender specialist approached, knelt to administer an injection. To everyone's horror, a strong jerk of my arm threw her against the wall.

"Waseem!" Ameena screeched, crouched behind me, and locked her arms tight across my chest. "Breathe," she commanded in my ear. "In . . . and . . . out." She gently squeezed my ribs. "*Yalla*, do it with me, in . . . and . . . out, in . . . and . . . out. In and out."

"*Emmmmm*," I growled, locked my jaws, and closed my eyes. Mortified by her intuitively mimicking my mother's calming technique, and humiliated by my outburst, I followed Ameena's rhythmic coercion until I gradually regained composure. My weary body sagged against her softness. Turning my head sideways, I nestled my face in the crook of her neck and sighed.

She rubbed my chest. "*Abooh*?"

I nodded, ashamed to say anything.

"*Abooh ya* Waseem?" she repeated.

I opened my eyes to see her smiling, her wet cheeks almost touching mine, eyes loaded not with fear or sadness, but warmth, concern, and familiar sincerity.

"*Aabbooh . . . oohh*," I mumbled and gave her the smile she had beckoned using our particular catchword.

"He's good now," she declared to the bewildered specialist and two nurses who weren't there before. Ameena released me to allow a nurse to check my blood pressure. The other wiped my face and neck with a wet towel and helped me settle in bed. Avoiding eye contact with Ameena, I caught her from the corner of my eye whispering to the doctor before they left.

The following evening, the same specialist entered my room, turned off the lights, and summoned Ameena. She walked in with the horrid cane, only its tentacled base glowed with a metallic, green color, an identical hue to the wheels of my walker. I had behaved like a spoiled child, and she, clever as always, presented a fitting solution to pacify a brat. I had no choice but to accept the damn thing. What else could I have done after the meltdown that reduced me to a mere *boy* in Ameena's eyes?

That night, I eyed the blasted cane standing with its spider-like base glowing by my bed, mocking me, taunting, goading, challenging me to grab it. I had allowed this offensive intruder to replace my walker but absolutely refused to try it while Ameena watched. After my tantrum, the least I could do to redeem myself was train my body to use it.

Showing off to Ameena was motive enough to nudge me out of bed. I turned on the light, landed my feet on the cold floor, and grabbed the cane's rubber handle with my right hand. Forcing my fingers to establish a firm grip, I clasped my left hand on top. I leaned slightly forward and gradually increased pressure onto the cane to lift my backside off the mattress, certain I would topple over any second. My entire body perspired, sweat dampened my palms to the point I had to let go, dried them on my nightgown, then tried again. Concentrating on the edge of the window shade ahead, half drawn above my eye level, I held my breath as my backside finally cleared the safety of the bed. I straightened. Ears buzzed, head pounded with my loud heartbeats. Lights outside the window tilted to the left. The room spun. I closed my eyes, blew a steadying breath and opened them. Streetlights, walls, and furniture pieces settled back into place, but something around me was still amiss. What was different? What changed?

Legs shaking, I looked up and down, left and right. Nothing in the room moved but me. The experience must have turned me into a mad man. My eyes landed on the window shade. It drew down to *below* my eye level. How could that be?

A shallow breath caught in my throat. That was it! For the first time in my life, I stood upright to my full height. My head cleared the shade's edge by a good hand's span. Delirious with excitement, I took one step forward, then another and another, intending to reach the window.

Running footsteps echoed behind me. My laughter and glorious crash must have awoken the entire wing.

~

One overcast morning, I finally experienced weightlessness, not as magnificent as I had imagined. Supported by three members of the physical therapy team, I lowered my body, feet first, into a huge swimming pool inside the hospital orthopedic center. Nervous, yet eager, my throat released all sorts of childish noises. Two sitting assistants sandwiched me on a submerged step. My muscles jumped, limbs flailed in all directions and splashed everyone. The men laughed. I howled.

Once the wave of excitement subsided the instructor's voice pierced through the fog swirling in my head. I relaxed and gradually let go. My re-shaped legs floated toward the surface right before my eyes. The scarred knees—partially covered by the long black shorts I had insisted on after they brought me some tiny joke-of-a-swimsuit—shimmered just below the surface. I babbled and giggled like a baby.

Encouraged, my assistants coaxed me off the step with exaggerated flattery, which they really didn't need to do as I was too willing to comply and gain the full sensation of this dream-come-true occurrence. Two men gripped my arms and the third supported my neck. They laid me flat on my back to face the vaulted glass ceiling. Their calm, gentle voices offered instructions on how to loosen up and permit my ears to get wet as they turned me in slow circles.

I never thought a lot of water could weigh so much. My chest and abdomen dunked under the surface, I struggled to breathe, as if my mother had suddenly jumped into the pool to press her heavy brand of love onto my body. Panic struck, intent on thrusting me toward the deep blue tiles. I gasped, jerked, and twitched with a certainty I would drown. The team held my thrashing body with firm grips, but they were no match for the might of a frightened, drowning man. I clawed at their shoulders and arms, striving to keep my nose above the water.

Chlorine burned my eyes and singed my lungs. The more I struggled, the worse my predicament grew. After what seemed like an eternity, I peed myself, and felt the warm stream slither between my tired legs. I was certain at least one of the men knew what I had done. I didn't care. I vowed if I survived, I would never endure this form of therapy again. When they finally lifted me to dry safety, I suffered an episode of spasms that left me in more pain than ever before.

On the cold floor by the edge of the pool, under a frenzy of probes, checks, and shouts, Tolstoy's words in *The Death of Ivan Ilyich* rang in my head: *Always the same. Now a spark of hope flashes up, then a sea of despair, and always pain; always pain, always despair, and always the same.*

Why did I ever dream of swimming? Why even bother to dream at all?

~

On a rainy afternoon, I escaped my short-tempered physical trainer earlier than scheduled. I had withstood the burly man's sadistic exercises for close to an hour and could no longer remain upright. Seeing the outline of my face on the speck-free linoleum floor more frequently than on the walls of mirrors in the spacious exercise hall, I decided the so-called therapy session was done and staggered away. I could hardly storm out of the hall with the clumsy cane but, using the walls for support, I hobbled to my room over the loud objections of the Incredible Hulk turning green before my eyes.

Clutching the side bars for balance, I stepped into the shower and lingered longer than necessary to steal precious moments before the onslaught of nurses. The experience of bathing under continuous running water was something I would never get used to. How many of our bath buckets at home could I fill in the span of one shower? Probably enough to wash my entire family. Do the week's laundry, too.

Toweling off, I admired my straighter legs. Long scars ran along the sides of each hip to mid-thigh, more marred, even, was the area around the knees and ankles, but by all that is holy, I stood upright. And I could walk without my knees rubbing together, using my legs according to their intended function. Approaching twenty-three years of age, I was born again, reincarnated into a better functioning body. My prominent limp would serve as a mere reminder of the profound transformation my lower extremities had endured. Soon I would have no need for the despicable cane but would certainly need some sort of support. I didn't want an old man's walking staff. Perhaps I could find a stout, straight stick like the one Sherlock carried. *A formidable weapon*, according to Watson.

I heard Ameena's voice in the room. "I know we're early. He should be done with PT soon," she said aloud.

It didn't take me long to figure out who her companion was. Samra's piercing voice came at me like an axe breaking through the closed bathroom door. "It's only a week. Five nights. Six days. That's all. I don't understand why you need his permission."

"No, nothing like that. I just . . . need him to hear it from me. It's . . . important, Samra."

I draped my towel over the toilet lid and sat down to listen, doing my best not to make a sound. I could have slipped into the clothes I had brought in and walked out, but the way Ameena sounded, unsure and conflicted, tempted me to eavesdrop onto possible confessions. Whose permission? And to do what?

"You feel responsible, I get it. But this is a chance of a lifetime, girlfriend. You shouldn't let him stop you."

"He won't."

"Let's just say he asks you not to. What then?"

"I'm telling you, he wouldn't do that."

"So why not submit the application? Why the delay? You should've informed him the day they told you about it. These things take time, and time is a luxury you don't have."

"The papers are ready. Tomorrow morning. I promise. As soon as I tell him. Now go home, Samra."

"I'm not leaving. Not before I make sure—"

"I appreciate your concern, but this is a private matter between me and Waseem. Now, I promise to tell him, okay? I'll see you at home."

"Fine. Fine. But don't be late."

Sounds of ruffling clothes followed, as if they hugged. Then, a door closed. I didn't know what to do. If I started to dress, I would make noises loud enough for her to hear and realize I was eavesdropping. The best thing to do was to remain motionless until she gave up and went looking for me. Then I could rush out. When she returned, I would tell her I was checking on Saeed, the last remaining boy of the sponsored children. That seemed like a reasonable fib.

I waited, naked and cold on the toilet seat until I heard her footsteps fade away. Forgoing underwear, I easily pulled up the elastic waist pants of a training suit, hastily donned a T-shirt, dashed out, and barely made it to the window by the time Ameena came back.

"There you are," she said out of breath. "I was looking for you."

Holding on to the windowsill, I lifted my cane to the side and sounded a throaty train of clicks.

"Oh, I should've guessed you were with Saeed. How is our brilliant Dolphin?"

I flipped my open palm back and forth.

"Poor boy, his body is too weak to handle the frames they embedded in his leg." Ameena swiped hair from her eyes. "I'll visit him later." She pointed at the chair in the corner. "Sit. I have something to tell you."

Ever direct and unapologetic, my friend decided to tell me what was on her mind without frivolous introductions or a chance to catch my breath. I wouldn't have wanted it any other way. Bracing for grim news, I accepted her offer and slid onto the vinyl recliner. A squeaky sound vibrated under me. We pretended not to hear it.

Ameena stood before me, clasped both hands under her chin. "I was asked to attend a conference about refugees as part of an international team." She took a step forward. "I'm to talk about the situation in our camps. Offer inside information on realities of refugee life." She arched her eyebrows, her eyes questioning, expecting.

I gave a thumbs-up and added another.

"Can you believe it?" Kneeling, she laid her hands on my knees. "They asked me, Waseem. *Me.* A Palestinian refugee from nowhere, a nobody. I'm to speak to officials and dignitaries."

Her absentminded touch lit up things in my body, ushered powerful sensations as if she had plugged my rear end into a wall socket. I struggled to turn off a powerful response. What was I to do with myself at that moment? To distract her from shameful possibilities infesting my mind and tingling my skin, I pointed at my iPad on the nightstand.

"No." She shook her head. "I know what you want to say. You're proud of me. You think I deserve this. Worked so hard." Tears swelled in her eyes. "I know, Waseem. I know all that."

She should be happy, not about to cry. Searching her drawn face for reasons that caused her restlessness helped me simmer down. I touched her nose with the tip of my finger. “Wwhaa . . . ttt’sss wwrronn . . . gg?”

“The conference? It’s in Berlin. I’m going to Germany for a week!”

“Aha,” I muttered. So that was what bothered her? She expected me to be upset that she would abandon me for seven days. She thought this little of my recently acquired independence? I pulled back my hand and repeatedly clapped, showing enthusiasm. I was no suckling infant, damn it.

“Oh, Waseem, I just knew you would be happy for me.” She rose to stand. “And, you know what else? They are going to give me the blue book, not just a special document like the one they used for us to come here, but an actual UN passport. Valid for a year. Do you know what that means?”

I swallowed. Those were tears of joy dancing in her eyes. It was inevitable; she would move to a better future and leave me behind. Though fully expected, the notion still stung. Masking my panic, I clapped harder.

“Once I’ve earned vacation days, I can travel anywhere.” Spreading her arms to her sides, she whirled around. “Any . . . where! I’m free, Waseem. I’m finally free.”

“Fffreee!” I pumped my fists overhead to surpass her excitement.

“Waseem, I can go to Palestine!” She stopped, dropped to her knees again and whispered, “How about you go with me?”

Dumbfounded, I bit my lower lip.

Incredible Hulk walked in, mumbling something about a necessary massage.

"I'll work on the papers after I return from Berlin." Ameena winked and left me to the mercy of the Hulk's giant hands.

Once again, hope wiggled its way into my life and played havoc with my nerves. Travel to Palestine? Ameena had not pitched the suggestion haphazardly. She knew the high mountains we must climb to deliver me to the Occupied Land. A crippled Palestinian refugee with—unlike her—no credible value, there was no way I would qualify for that UN passport to cross borders.

She knew that, yet dangled the possibility, the fulfillment of my dream, before my desirous spirit as if it were the most natural consequence of her acquiring the coveted travel book. Did she see me as her extension? Where she went, much like an appendage, a strand of hair or a lost lamb, I must follow.

CHAPTER SIXTEEN

I was in the Netherlands for nearly a year. My medical adventure reached its conclusion as Vincent accomplished his impressive transformation of my body. The Netherlands sojourn approached its end. Doctors discharged me from the hospital ten days after Ameena returned from Berlin, and I was booked to travel to Lebanon three weeks later.

Rasheed took me to a special store to pick out a cane. I found what I had been envisioning as soon as we walked in. A deep lustrous black stick, costing most of the Euros I had. Rasheed offered to buy it as a parting gift, but I absolutely refused. I needed to give Wael the respect he deserved for selling his watch for my benefit and show my brother what I gained by his selfless act.

Ever since her Germany trip, Ameena had been running in place, as if suspended above the ground. I couldn't shake the image of her moving like the British hovercraft I read about crossing from Hampshire to the Isle of Wight. I watched videos of how the vessel operated. Ameena, though level and steady, churning energy hummed underneath. She would burst into the Alaoui's house, talk fast, flash official documents, then dash away as if behind schedule.

She dressed differently. Subtle changes in the way she styled her hair, often shaken free of its ponytail and pulled back from the sides, enhanced her vivacious vibe. She livened up professional pencil skirts and plain shirts with colorful scarves and belts. Sometimes, she abandoned her old outfits all together in favor of black leggings, short dresses, and clunky ankle boots. She didn't reach Samra's level of fashionable taste, or, in my opinion, her friend's distinct lack thereof, but Ameena was clearly influenced by the European fashion around her. I couldn't say the new style made her appear more mature. For the sake of precision, I would concede it demonstrated a blossoming sophistication and reflected her maturity. Something I was sure I should not take notice of, nor find pleasure in.

Refusing to accept my imminent departure, she kept pushing for more time, more tests, possible procedures, imploring other doctors to examine my shoulders, arms and hands, even appealing to speech therapists, anything to keep me in the country. When none of her efforts were met with a favorable outcome, she enlisted Rasheed to help me write letters to immigration officials and non-profits. These letters were endeavors to showcase my hitherto obscured intelligence and potential—though, for the life of me, I couldn't think of any specific possibilities. Yet, I pled my case: If I am returned to the refugee camp, I would resume a wretched existence, with no prospects for a brighter future, and my physical advancements would amount to nothing. A squandering of precious time and resources.

Feigning elation to keep her happy, I met with UNHCR and UNRWA representatives and endured humiliating displays of pictures and videos taken before and after my procedures to demonstrate how inordinately medical intervention had improved my health and quality of life. My cherished retired walker became a prop in a show which I knew would result in nothing substantial, not because of Ameena's lack of effort, or a shortage of good-willed people, but because such was the life I had been allotted. This ingenious performance made a cameo appearance onto my tattered stage once, and that was the end of my good fortune.

I do not believe in miracles, nor do I share my mother's faith in angelic saviors. I credited my transformation to Vincent's medical intrigue and Ameena's clever, stubborn nature. Perhaps a heavenly hand had aligned the stars to allow the events of the past year to happen, but such a feat could have also been coincidental, couldn't it? I didn't know the answer. And I really didn't care.

What difference would it make whether I believed or not? The end result remained the same. Even if my body were a perfect picture of health, as any of my brothers', I would always be a suffering Palestinian refugee, preemptively disadvantaged, overlooked, and cast aside by an indifferent world.

I see my entire existence as unnecessary, a frivolous attempt at life, and I am unable to envision how a soul born into the same circumstances could flourish during three lifetimes trapped in a refugee camp. I think of my healthy, chubby, screaming nephew and the dire hardships he would have to face growing up surrounded by our collective misery.

To continuously have faith festers hope, and I had banished such pestering activity from my mind long ago. My beloved literary scholar, Taha Husain, would be ashamed of my eternal pessimism. Indeed, after exposure to what normal life ought to be, my idolization shifted to another blind writer, the Abbasid era philosopher and poet, Abu 'Ala' al-Ma'arri. The eleventh century deist, visionary, childless freethinker summarized my attitude in a single verse he instructed to be inscribed on his epitaph: *This is what my father inflicted upon me, which I myself never inflicted upon anyone.*

And yet, and yet, and yet again . . . there was Ameena. A spark crackling to illuminate my darkened world. How could I reconcile her glaring, luminous presence with my sensible, practical conviction?

I did not dismiss her promise to someday whisk us away to Palestine. Despite nagging certitude that even Ameena with her Herculean abilities would fail to procure this prize, I chose to ignore the facts that govern our painfully predictable world and continued to believe she would succeed. Perhaps my blind trust, surrendered with utmost will, was the source of her strength. I liked to think that it was. Nurturing faith in someone harnessed power. My mother presented a sterling example. She plowed through a dreary existence because my brothers never doubted her ability to overcome her husband's loss and never gave her a break. To my knowledge, none of them witnessed the hiccups in her chest when she silently caressed my father's belongings. Year after year, she just kept going, rising. And when the time came to send her disadvantaged son to a land far away, she silenced her fears and chose to believe in a foreign doctor's skill. Her courage imbued my admiration as an individual beyond that of a loving son's. Couldn't my steadfast adoration of Ameena provide her with such nurturing sustenance? I began to consider my presence, finally, to be providing a service. The words of the Irish poet and playwright Oscar Wilde echoed in my mind: *Women are meant to be loved.*

All forms of love, freely granted by a parent, husband, lover, child, sibling, student, colleague, friend—or whatever combination of the sacred elixir was out there—presented as less honorable if the core of the woman's spirit wasn't cherished. And I respected, revered, even canonized Ameena's essence.

Wilde, in his romantic wisdom, did not condition his statement with *deserving* women, and the love to be arduous. He understood that love was vast and should have no stipulations. Though, for the life of me, I couldn't fathom any man's romantic bond to my sister, Fayzeh. I, myself, was destined to *blood-love* despite tremendous dislike of her petulant character. However, a man, a stranger, forming a passionate connection with Fayzeh escaped my imagination. But Ameena? Ameena was meant to be truly, undeniably, entirely loved in every aspect and form by no one other than me.

So, as long as I drew a breath, I would concentrate on the one thing I craved above all else; to remain the central focus of my savior's unwavering attention.

Alas, I could not escape al-Ma'arri's pessimism infesting my soul. I was condemned to be a wretched realist anticipating the eventual denial of even benign, platonic desires. And if Ameena, aided by some supernatural occurrence, proved me wrong, and my corrected feet ever trod upon the ancient streets of *Yaffa*, my heart would most likely fragment into a million pieces until there was no more love to bestow onto Ameena nor anyone else.

Alone in my room with my revelations in the quietness of night, the golden voice of the Lebanese national treasure, singer and musical icon, *Fairuz* serenaded in my head: *A Lilly sword, I am. Break me on the soil of my homeland.*

~

A breakthrough, that was how Ameena described it. One cold gloomy afternoon, she barged into my room full of vitality and immediately brightened each corner as if the heavy curtains parted to reveal a sunny day outside. Something was different with her hair, and she had on a red dress, no leggings or those thick, nude stockings she regularly wore. Her smooth, tan legs shimmered below the fiery dress skirt. What on earth was going on?

Balancing on black, high heels, she snatched the book I had in my hands and checked the title, *Unnecessary Necessity*.

"Al-Ma'arri again? Enough with this pessimism." She tossed the collection of poems by the skeptic philosopher onto the pillows. "You are not like this double prisoner. You are not blind and definitely not alone. You should embrace what Mahmoud Darwish wrote: *We have on this Earth what makes life worth living*."

I pretended to examine the book as it had fallen open-faced to hide my grin. Such an eloquent response to calamity from Palestine's most eminent poet suited Ameena's personality so well. She never gave up on anything. True to Darwish's impassioned description of the unfaltering resistance of our people in his poem *State of Siege*, Ameena does what political prisoners do *with country on the verge of dawn*. She nurses hope.

Up to this stage in my life, I had been besieged by a restricted body, captive in a land where the mere thought of a new dawn plowed and tilled one's heart to no avail. Ameena had been sowing seeds of hope in mine all this while. Would she ever reap a bountiful harvest?

"Get up. *Yalla*." She extended her hand. "We have a breakthrough."

I arched my eyebrows in question.

"Doctor Younis. Here to see you." She looked around for my slippers, found them in the closet, and brought them over. "I met him in Berlin, but he's here now. Lives in Sweden. His father is Palestinian, originally and . . . and he's interested in you."

Inserting my feet into the slippers, I could have sworn her flushed cheeks emanated heat. She had met the Swedish-Palestinian doctor in Berlin, and he traveled here to The Hague because he was interested in me? I found that hard to believe. Before I accepted her extended hand, I pointed at her hair.

"Wwhaa . . . ttt happe . . . nnedd?" I asked.

"Highlights. A hint of red. Like Henna." She smoothed locks in place. "I went to the salon with Samra this morning." She checked her reflection in the mirror above the dresser and faced me. "It's not too much, is it?"

I shook my head. It was a tad over the top.

"You like it?"

I nodded. I didn't like it one bit.

Seeing through my lies, she slumped her shoulders. "Oh, I shouldn't have listened to that girl." She gathered her hair with one fist, snapped a tie from her wrist, and worked on tying a ponytail.

"Nnoo," I grabbed my cane and limped over to stop her, hating to upset her. "**Different, but nice**," I typed on the iPad dangling on my chest, smiled and pushed her ahead of me out of the room before I changed my mind.

Younis had his back to us, conversing with Rasheed and his wife, Latifah. As he heard us coming, he rose from his chair and turned around. In his mid-thirties, he stood a full head taller than Rasheed, which meant he literally looked down at me as he shook my hand. Even though he was dressed in neat cream slacks and a brown corduroy jacket over a white turtleneck, he projected a rugged look that contradicted his refined professorial attire. With tan skin, gray eyes, thick eyebrows, and jet-black hair, he could have easily been one of the men my brother Yasser hung out with in the camp. In my mind's eye, I dressed Younis in a shirt unbuttoned down to his mid-chest and stuck a lit cigarette between his fingers to bind the image. And then there was the way he looked at Ameena with his clouded eyes, the way he smiled and greeted her—too friendly, too warm. Yeah, this fellow was *not* interested in me. I disliked him immediately.

"*Marhaba*," he greeted in Arabic, as if sensing my displeasure and thought that speaking in my mother's tongue would appease me. Fat chance.

Rasheed offered me the seat facing the doctor, which obliged Ameena to sit next to Doctor Turtleneck on the two-seater sofa. I didn't like that orchestrated chicanery, either.

"I heard so much about you from our friend here," the Swede said in a soft voice that clashed with his rough features. He waved his hand toward Ameena. "Good things. All good things. I just had to come and meet you. It's a pleasure, young man. May I call you Waseem?"

I plastered on a Cheshire cat's smile and nodded. Go on, plow past the bullshit.

"I don't know what this lovely lady told you about me," he said.

"Nothing," Ameena quipped. "I didn't think you would actually come here."

"I promised, didn't I?" Turtleneck pivoted closer to draw her in. "Once you know me better, you'll find I don't make promises I don't intend to keep."

Double negative, was that what passed for a doctor these days? And when would she know him better? Why would she want to? Did he just bat his eyelashes at her? My ebony cane twitched in my hand. The *formidable weapon* could come into use very soon. I contemplated employing it to wipe that self-righteous smirk off this sleazeball's face.

Samra entered the room. After introducing herself, she squeezed next to Ameena on the two-seater, forcing her to slide even closer to him. He returned his attention to me.

"As a rehabilitation specialist in Stockholm, I work with a number of organizations that help disadvantaged people. Perhaps you've heard of Doctors Without Borders?"

"Who hasn't?" Rasheed asked.

"I also work with local entities that help refugees." Turtleneck kept his gaze on me, disregarding Rasheed. Smart move. This guy knew where I stood with Ameena, or was it the other way around? It didn't matter as long as he realized the importance of our bond.

"I'd like to accompany you back to Lebanon," he continued. "Help you along the way and offer my services at the camp."

"Waseem is fairly independent now," Rasheed said, a hint of hurt in his voice, as if taking offense to the condescending offer from the doctor on my behalf.

I drew an arch in the air with my cane to stress Rasheed's point. I could hold my own. I didn't ask for, nor need, any assistance, especially from this rude stranger who was shooting moon eyes at my Ameena.

"You said there was a way to include Waseem in a resettlement program in Sweden?" Ameena asked in a firm tone. I knew that tone. She wasn't asking a question. She was demanding the delivery of a promise. Why would I want to go to Sweden?

Turtleneck shifted his gaze to her. "The program requires time and some finesse. It's always best to start the process of resettlement from the place of origin."

I typed fast and lifted the tablet for everyone to see. "Palestine."

"No, no. Your place of residency is Lebanon. So, we must start the process at the refugee camp." He turned to Ameena again. "I looked into the UNHCR resettlement program you mentioned. Found a number of success cases for secondary language teachers in Sweden. I think I can tap the same nonprofit that worked within the program. It's a long shot, worth pursuing, but we have to be patient. These cases take time, we have to prove Waseem would be an asset to society."

"*Ehmmmm*," I cleared my throat to snap the knave's attention back to me. Our? We? When did this guy become part of our team?

"Based on what merit?" I typed.

"Waseem, you have so much to offer," Ameena answered. "Just look at what you've done with the sponsored children. How you guided them and made them feel safe, spent time with each one whenever you could. You were the parent they needed during terrible times." She reached over to lay her hand on my knee.

I tightened my fist on my cane to suppress any muscle jumps.

"Saeed told me how you used to show the wounds on your legs as they were healing to give hope and help little ones manage pain," she continued. "You've done so much. Every one of those children returned home in a better state. Physically because of the treatment they received, and emotionally . . ." she squeezed my knee, " . . . because of you."

It cost me tremendous effort not to trap her warm hand between my knees.

"You could earn an online degree in counseling children with special needs," Samra suggested. "One of my good friends is doing it. Baba, you know Anna? She's about to graduate and already has two or three jobs lined up. There's a big demand."

"Right, right. I can try to set it up with the university," Rasheed said. "I have no doubt Waseem will pass qualifying exams and be admitted."

I darted my eyes between the four of them. How long have they been scheming this? Me, earn a university degree? With no proper schooling whatsoever? What world did they live in? Not mine, for sure.

Expenses? I asked, despite my skepticism.

"We'll apply for scholarships, tap several non-profits dedicated to supporting Palestinians' education needs," Rasheed said. "I have this covered."

Ameena withdrew her hand, sat back, and crossed her legs. "Well, then. We have a plan. Younis will go to Lebanon, meet with UNHCR and UNRWA representatives to start the process. I'll stay here and finish projects they have me working on. Most likely until June."

"And when I return, you'll come to Stockholm," the overconfident Swede said. "See the house. Meet the family."

"Yes, yes," Ameena hurried to say, as if as an afterthought. She placed her elbows on her thighs and clasped her hands. "Waseem, once you receive residency in Europe, you can travel." She winked. "Anywhere your heart desires."

Finally, I understood her roundabout plan. Get me settled in Sweden, acquire official status as a resident, then travel to Palestine. If everyone's efforts were successful, how long would that take? Years, no doubt. Would the mesmeric, men-magnet Ameena still be by my side, lighting up my world? Or would she soon lose interest and move on to accept worship by the likes of the healthy fool sitting beside her?

"Since I've met your best friend, Ameena, I uh . . ." Turtleneck ran blatantly fawning eyes over her from head to toe and adjusted the lapels of his jacket, " . . . as we discussed, look forward to meeting your father."

Latifah, who had been quietly studying him, squared her arms over her bosom and asked, "And her mother?"

"Of course." He ran a finger under his turtleneck and lifted his chin. "Can't wait. Parents. I meant to say parents. Do I have your permission, Ameena?"

Locking her eyes on mine, and with a demure smile I hadn't seen before, she nodded through a deep blush. "I don't mind."

My lungs stopped working. All of my many, many wounds burst open. My Ameena called a man she barely knew by his first name, colored her hair, wore an enticing red dress. She would go to Stockholm to check out the house, his house, not where I would stay, meet his family, not my host family.

There was my answer. I would have this man, this parasite, push me down a new path which my beloved Ameena blazed, and at the same time, snuff out the candle that had been the light of my life since I could remember. She had summoned Younis and brought him to heel so he could dutifully answer her commands.

For my sake, she would allow this worm to wedge and wriggle between us.

CHAPTER SEVENTEEN

As my departure approached, I tried to catch up on all the things I promised myself to do. One exceptionally sunny morning, I bit into a whole pickled herring and managed to force the piece down.

"Woohoo," Samra jumped with excitement, her bright pink pajamas revealing a studded bellybutton ring. "One more bite. Finish it!"

"Nnnoo," I declared, standing firm.

Dangling a herring before Ameena's face, she goaded, "Your turn. Come on. Waseem is not more courageous than you."

"Uh-uh." Ameena retreated toward the door. "I'm no angel."

I hid my smile behind a tall glass of milk. The salty, slimy clump elevated me to the station of an angel in Ameena's eyes—worth the gag and near vomit.

I left Samra chasing Ameena around the house with the fish to start a routine for the remaining days. Rasheed had gifted me a generous amount of money for Eid-al-Fitr to celebrate the conclusion of the month of Ramadan. Although I was not his child but a full-grown man on my own, I had appreciated his sentiment for treating me as a son and accepted his kind gesture with some resistance at first then relented. I let it slide that I had not fasted that Ramadan—nor any ever in my life—but the man kept up with traditions, and I liked that.

I established a consistent schedule for the days leading up to my departure. I would stuff a few bills of Rasheed's gift into my pocket and leave the house after breakfast. I would walk the wet, cobblestoned streets of The Hague, enjoy numerous exhibits, and tour most of the city's museums, thirty-five on my count. An ill-fated visit to the Prison Gate Museum rattled me, as I came across a particular torture instrument on display eerily resembled a contraption used on my legs after one of my procedures. Stupid enough to have wasted limited funds on that ticket, I stumbled out after losing precious time and having taken in numerous testimonies to the cruelty of Man, something I already knew and didn't need to see.

To eliminate my disgust, Ameena and Samra accompanied me to the Peace Palace the next day. I was disappointed that we were not allowed entry past the small exhibit hall, where videos and displays recounted the history of the building. Standing outside the iron gates, I stared at the stone structure open-mouthed, as if examining the architecture of an alien species. Manicured gardens surrounded the driveway leading up to the Neo-Renaissance mansion adorned with two bell towers.

"It looks sooo peaceful," Samra said.

I couldn't stop laughing. What an idiotic thing to say about a place that housed the International Court of Justice, which was supposed to enforce accountability and bring world leaders together for the single purpose of establishing peace. In today's world, the establishment had fallen far too short of its mission.

I read in a gilded frame at the exhibit hall the famed prediction by the financial engineer of the project, Andrew Carnegie, at the Palace's opening ceremony in 1913: *The end of war is as certain to come, and come soon, as day follows night.*

What an audacious declaration. A year later, the entire world erupted in war, closely followed by another one. The third war was predicted to begin any day. And now, more than seventy-six years since my people were subjected to a brutal military occupation, maliciously persecuted, massacred, and violently ejected from their homeland, the dawn of justice had yet to crack on the Palestinian nightmare.

The three of us continued to the city of Delft. I read about its renowned, hand-painted blue and white pottery, an obvious source of pride for the Dutch. Admiration poured out of Samra's eyes as we examined Delftware plates, bowls, and endless rows of tiles. My mother had a similar look whenever she glanced at her artfully colored tile, only her gaze was always marred by longing, the sadness prominent even before I broke her single tangible Palestinian inheritance.

Samra urged Ameena to buy a souvenir, but Ameena refused. I had set aside money to buy gifts for my family, so I lifted a square tile depicting a boy and a girl holding a basket between them.

"Mmyy ggi . . . fftt," I said, placing the tile in Ameena's hand.

"It's not the same." She returned my offering to its shelf and walked out of the store. For the rest of the day, Ameena remained in an unapproachable mood. Samra was at a loss.

I knew exactly what my friend meant. She thought I wanted to buy the tile for my mother. She had mistaken my intention, but she was right that it wouldn't be the same.

Alone the next day, I continued to check off items from my wish list. I balanced on one of the ferries, clinging to the side railing among cyclists and motor-bikers, savoring cold mist on my skin. I rode a smooth metro train to Scheveningen and sank my feet into the sand of the North Sea shoreline. The new experience baffled me. Though it was sunny, everything was harsh and cold. The strong wind slapped my cheeks and coarse sand scratched my soles. When I approached the shore, icy waters attacked my ankles, and I hurried back to the safety of the sidewalk. Loud families and hyper teens crowded the area. I found a spot on a rocky promenade and stood still for a moment.

Boundless waters stretched before and all around me. The vast, mystic sea calmed my nerves. I closed my eyes and listened to the rhythmic song of the waves. Their esoteric poetry lulled me to quietude. I waited until the sinking sun wiped every speck of blue from the sky, taking it all in. For the first time in my life, I pulsed in harmony with my surroundings. As darkness engulfed me, a notion sparked to light in my head.

I believe I touched the depth of my mother's wishful, sentimental longing for her family's home in *Yaffa*: a single, imagined, careless afternoon by the Mediterranean shore that continues to bring peace to her agonized soul.

On another excursion, this time to Amsterdam, I pushed past droves of hurried people. A powerful stench slapped me in the face as I crossed a street just outside the central train station. The familiar odor transplanted me for a moment to the cat alley behind our barber shop. Stopped dead in my tracks, I looked around for the source and found a man, partially concealed by a short, metal wall, peeing right in the middle of the busy sidewalk. A yellow stream hit a drain by his feet. Another man stood waiting on the other side of that circular wall while people bustled all around. He went in as soon as the first man left and relieved himself.

I couldn't stop staring. This public restroom was not in an obscure corner or alley, behind a tree, or inside a proper closed stall, but stood exposed in the midst of the busiest spot outside the huge station building. I guessed I hadn't ventured that far from the camp, after all.

I continued on to the Van Gogh Museum. I looked the artist in the eye in one of his many self-portraits. I related to his uncategorized madness, his trapped genius within a disappointing body. How hard had he fought to break out of his cell to grant us the pleasure of his exceptional talent? Lost amidst Van Gogh's bright sunflowers, gnarled olive trees, and swirling corn fields, I sensed him standing next to me, pointing, whispering, explaining each divine brushstroke and color palette. Beauty seeped under my skin like paint on canvas, and I crawled into the paintings to become part of the scenery.

For the first time in my life, I felt normal.

~

I asked for a window seat on the two flights home so I could experience the view, an opportunity I had missed the first time I flew on an airplane. An older gentleman sat next to me and hid behind a Dutch newspaper. Other than a quick hello, he ignored me. Savoring the solitude, I gazed out the window. Clear afternoon skies allowed me to track a network of canals snaking through verdant lands—a magnificent sight I would never forget. As the plane tilted sideways, nausea kicked in, but I refused to close my eyes, not wanting to miss anything. Taking deep breaths, I overcame the dizziness and followed the murky Rhine on its way to the delta.

While bidding farewell to the Alaoui family, I had dissolved into a bowl of emotional soup. Everyone cried amidst the flurry of hugs, kisses, and promises to stay in touch. I had arrived at the family's doorstep with so many unknowns and parted ways a different person. I wrestled with sadness for leaving them. Yet, as I watched the no-longer-foreign land beneath me fade away, a euphoric realization tempered my dejected mood. During my journey, I traveled farther than I had imagined. My body didn't just transform and change. *I* grew into someone else, an experienced person with a broader mind and a nurtured soul.

Sometimes, the unknown was not that scary.

Leaving Ameena behind, however, was torture. She gave me a reserved hug at the door, a move I never thought even daring Ameena would venture had we stayed trapped in the camp. Our embrace was graceless, awkward, and somewhat comical. Her arms wrapped my neck for a breath, long enough for me to detect a trace of lavender in her hair. She patted my back and pulled away as I raised my stiff hands to brush her shoulders. Our arms bumped. I lost my balance and clamped firm fingers onto her forearms, pulling her sideways and down with me.

My gracious angel laughed as she sat sprawled on the hardwood floor, legs entangled with mine. Luckily, she chose to wear a pair of jeans that day, not a dress or a skirt, which would have caused me to dissolve like a bloated snail covered with salt. Once we scrambled to our feet again, Ameena presented me with a parting gift: two books for the long journey.

"Something different this time," she said with the familiar mischief dancing in her eyes. "To broaden your outlook."

Clutching her present, I stumbled to the car. To my horror, I cried—bawled, drooled, and sniveled—all the way to the airport.

We rose above the clouds. Whiteness covered everything before my eyes. I turned to Ameena's gifts, which I had stuffed into my backpack. One book was written by an Egyptian feminist writer, physician, and psychiatrist, Nawal El Saadawi.

I knew of the activist's cultural, revolutionary literature but I had not read any of her work. She was imprisoned for what was deemed controversial and dangerous social views by the president of Egypt, Anwar Sadat. Denied pen and paper, she used a stubby eyebrow pencil and a roll of tattered toilet paper to record her thoughts until she was released a month after the president's assassination. That summed up my familiarity of this writer, described as "Egypt's Most Radical Woman."

I admired El Saadawi's tenacity and could relate to the fever that drove her to extreme measures to express herself in words. But I didn't know what her views actually entailed, and had no idea if Ameena shared any of them. I promised myself I would dive into the book with a clear head once I had the time to devote the required energy. Ameena, I thought, might want to discuss its topics in letters or even calls while we were separated. I couldn't let my denseness stand in the way of a much-craved conversation. Never ever was ignorance a bliss.

The second book was Mark Twain's *The Adventures of Huckleberry Finn*. The Great American Novel held me captive on the plane with its scathing satire of the racist attitudes held by people residing along the Mississippi River. Even though the events were set before the Civil War in the United States, the injustices Jim faced on his travels echoed what my people faced every day as they languished forgotten in refugee camps. I struggled with the Southern vernacular in Huck's coarse language and settled for the general gist once I correlated it to the jargon I used to hear on our miserable alleys. Poor boys bear the same fierce inclinations everywhere in the world. A few boys in my makeshift spy network could equally inspire epic novels. My chieftain, Ghazi, came to mind. At times, having a father around was not an asset.

We landed in Paris after dark. Flickering lights dominated the vast view from my window. Rasheed had tried to convince me to arrange for a wheelchair at Charles de Gaulle airport, but I had refused. With a six-hour layover, I had ample time to walk to the gate to catch the next flight. When I finally slid into my seat on the plane, I was a sweaty, stinky, exhausted mess. I looked out the window and only saw darkness. I closed the shade and took a long nap, then passed the time alternating between reading and tracking the flight path on the monitor embedded in the back of the seat before me. After we crossed Greece, the pilot announced that he had to slightly change course, veering south to avoid a storm in the Eastern Mediterranean.

As we neared our destination, I set aside my book and lifted the shades. We had broken through clouds and were heading straight toward the Crescent Levant. I flattened my nose against the cold pane. We were flying over Palestine, its olive coastline arc prominent against the lustrous, blue Mediterranean. Strong thumps slammed my ribs. Loud, erratic beats drowned all noise as if a giant's heart sprang to life in my chest, dominating, tugging each and every nerve toward the window.

Too quickly, the plane shifted toward Lebanon. I pulled away and threw my back into the seat, hyperventilating, and sweating.

Eden lay down below, and there I was up above; like Adam, exiled. The moment of truth approached. Shortly I would reach home and see my family again. Or rather, they would see me—the new me.

CHAPTER EIGHTEEN

I acquired celebrity status at the camp. People gawked at me whenever I set foot outside, examining my legs admiringly and raising their eyes to the skies and praising God. Most commented on how lucky I was to have had such a transformation. A couple of women tried to converse with me, as if they expected that my vocal abilities had improved too. They shook their heads in sorrow when they saw me write on the tablet and walked away without reading my responses. Several men invited me into their homes to mingle with their families, which had the opposite effect of being hospitable. I felt more like a freak than before my operations, just a sideshow entertainer to call on, pity, and help others feel better about themselves at the same time. But I obliged and accepted, connecting with folks I never knew, learning more secrets than I could count.

I knew who was behind on paying rent and who was indebted to whom. I deduced which families secured extra income, often from activities linked to Abu Nidal's unconventional sources, by the quality of furniture and appliances inside the newly accessed homes. Some veiled mothers and daughters kept their hijabs in my presence, which had not always been the case before my medical transformation. Their restraint led me to believe that they finally viewed me as a man, a healthy man with threatening desires. In the dichotomy of combined repulsion and satisfaction that dictated my actions around these women, I avoided looking in their direction, lest one got the idea that I harbored interest in any female other than Ameena.

The biggest surprise was my mother's attitude toward me. It never changed. As if I returned in the same condition I had left in. Except for a couple of prayers and a tight hug she performed upon my arrival, she settled down next to me as she always did, and gave instructions to my siblings. She scolded Fayzeh for refusing to prepare a salt bath for my feet. One stern look from Mother's permanently sad eyes sent my sister rushing to the bathroom. It made me uncomfortable. I didn't need the bath, not at that moment, and couldn't understand the reason behind my mother's insistence to carry on like old times.

After admiring my modest gifts and chic cane, she told Wael to shift the stack of shoes outside our door from the right corner to the left in place of where she used to park my walker. Nabil helped Maryam in the kitchen, and they spread the usual celebratory meal of roasted chicken on the newspaper-covered floor. As I watched my nephew play with the tag of the tactile toy I brought him and wriggle in his father's arms, I suspected Mother spared Farook and Yasser from further chores since they were the ones who had picked me up from the airport.

The men updated me on the political cross-currents in the camp while I was away. They praised Abu Nidal's efforts to maintain a stable hold on our area, keeping the streets somewhat peaceful compared to the northern and southern sectors.

"How forceful?" I typed.

"Necessarily forceful," Yasser quipped. "*Ma'almi* has his ways."

"All in the shadows. No one knows details," Farook said. "We only see results. And your brother is a locked vault."

"Survival." Yasser pinched the bridge of his nose. "You know I can't open my mouth about my responsibilities. How do you think all of us here, our family, can live in—"

Mother cut him off to talk about more important matters, as she put it, and delved into details about our neighbors, trivial things I didn't care to know. I gave her my full attention, tabling the matter until I convened with my spy network. The boys would know the juicy details that Yasser and Farook assumed were hidden.

"You know Salma downstairs?" Mother asked and didn't wait for an answer. "She married an engineer who works in Nigeria. They moved there." Mother kissed the tips of her gathered fingers. "A great match. And the Shabrawas at the end of the street? They suddenly up and left. No one knows where they went. The entire family. You know who moved in their place? An old man with a very, very young wife." Mother shook her head. "Shameful. Such a pretty girl married to a man her grandfather's age. Oh, and Um Faheem next door kicked out Faheem. Loud fight in the middle of the day. Really sad. She threw out his clothes from the window, told me he stole her gold lira necklace. The single piece of jewelry she owns. He stole it to buy," Mother grabbed my arm and leaned in to whisper, "*hashish*. Poor woman. I can't imagine . . ."

Mother went on and on. I wonder if I weren't there, would any of my siblings give her the chance to talk non-stop like she was? I didn't think so. She burst with a flood of news, as if she had harvested it for my arrival. My mother, I realized, was lonely. I followed with polite silence, arching my eyebrows or nodding every now and then. Until she told me about the passing of her friend's son, the epileptic.

"Let us enjoy this moment, *yumma*!" Yasser chided her for dampening the mood.

"He needs to know," Mother responded with a shrug, pulled the fattest drumstick, and placed it on my plate.

I finally understood why she stuck to the way things were, as if to say that me returning alive was more than enough for her. All my operations and procedures—the answers to her prayers—were extra blessings, mere additional improvements to my life, sprinkles of spice to a well-flavored chicken. Did she not see them as corrections of vital shortcomings in my pitiful creation? Despite all that she had gone through, my mother remained optimistic.

CHAPTER NINETEEN

Nothing worked. Every association, program, and avenue that Doctor Turtleneck tapped failed to deliver. The delusional man showed surprise when he came over to our home to share updates, one predictable rejection after another. I kept telling him this was a waste of time, but he persisted. He had taken a leave of absence from his Stockholm practice to dedicate time for his two-pronged mission: volunteer at various refugee camps and secure my resettlement. His supposedly one-month stay in Lebanon stretched to two, then three.

Even though I detested his mere existence, I had to admire his perseverance. It reminded me of what Hemingway wrote in *The Old Man and the Sea*: *A man can be destroyed but not defeated.*

I imagined several scenarios of how Ameena would eventually vanquish the Swede once she extracted what she wanted from him, a flickering idea I kept alive despite my entrenched pessimism. Perhaps she would pen a curt letter, send a concise text or a dry email. She wouldn't place a phone call, wouldn't give him that much attention. Maybe she would use whatever tactic she had deployed to deflate Yasser.

Younis continued to dress like a foreigner and made zero effort to conceal his intentions to secure Ameena. Ameena's mother was the main megaphone of his proposal in our sector.

Everywhere I went, and I traveled to every ugly nook and cranny with my improved mobility, I heard people talk of the Swedish Doctor who reconnected with his father's Palestinian roots to ask for Ameena's hand. In my arrogance, I even wondered if she had requested my resettlement papers as her dowry.

I heard an endless string of different but always fawning titles for Turtleneck. Somehow, he became the most famous surgeon in Sweden, a world-renowned doctor, a peace award-winning activist, not to mention a UN goodwill ambassador. The fact that he did not have any of these qualifications mattered little to those who bestowed such luminous honors. To his credit, he attempted to correct these flattering misnomers, but people continued to use them. It didn't take long for him to abandon this quest to dispel them.

I didn't. Every chance I had, I would type in bold letters that the man was a regular doctor, one of many, and his services at refugee camps not a charitable act, but a duty pressing on the shoulders of any Palestinian with an ounce of privilege. I consider myself one, now. I was privileged, saw the world outside and savored a fleeting taste of normalcy. In spite of my short excursion, the fact remained I had experienced the life of regular folks, the unoppressed, nondeprived people inhabiting a bountiful land. I had witnessed a peaceful existence full of possibilities. I had slept on a bed in a room to myself in a thriving city with clean streets, sewage systems, art museums, and massive public libraries—a mythic setting none of my siblings could ever dream of sharing. With all my limitations, I had functioned and flourished in a respectable world.

Yes, I was privileged. I acquired the responsibility to put these experiences to good use and serve my community. I just needed to figure out how. I would start by reconnecting with my new clan. The sponsored children lived in the southern part of the camp, which explained why I hadn't seen them before that day in the airport.

I paced up and down our alley one Wednesday morning waiting for my chieftain, Ghazi, to assign him a mission to discover the children's whereabouts. Since my return to the camp, he'd fallen in the habit of checking in with me around eight while running errands for market vendors. His duties had elevated from mere deliveries to collecting payments and handling money. I wasn't the only one who saw promise in the smart, resourceful boy. I broadcasted my assessment of him to various merchants whenever I could. Ghazi expressed loyalty by continuing to answer my commands. He walked around with a pencil tucked behind his ear and a small notebook in his pocket.

On this day though, I kept on pacing. Ghazi was late. The hour approached nine when he showed up with a raw cut covered with congealed blood across his narrow cheek and slim neck.

I pointed at his injury.

He shrugged. "I fell."

I stared at his guarded eyes for a moment. Childhood; such a power to restrain adults.

There had to be another payoff for the improved mobility I had gained from all my operations. I could finally fulfill my promise to beat this boy's evil father. The weapon to deliver heavy blows twitched in my hand, the mighty Sherlock cane. Should I allow the boy to witness to his father's punishment? Why not? What sense of justice would prevail if he didn't? I could use Yasser to plant the fear of God, mainly the fear of Abu Nidal, in the father's black heart, but that would require some coercing and would deprive *me* of the satisfaction.

"Commme." I headed down the alley.

Ghazi followed. "Where?"

"Hommme."

"We're going the wrong way. Your place is behind us."

"Nnottt mmi . . . nnne." I thumbed his shoulder.

"My home?" The boy's voice cracked on a high note.

I nodded.

He skipped ahead and raised both hands. "Wait. Why?"

I stopped to type on my tablet, "Talk with your father."

Ghazi froze with his hands up. "You don't know my father."

"He knows me!" I dropped the tablet onto my chest and continued on my way.

Ghazi tugged on my arm. "He. Does. Not."

I shook his weak grip off and picked up the pace. Everyone in our sector knew me. I was a celebrity, after all. The man did not live in a remote cave. Even if his son had never mentioned who I was, he would have heard about me from his wife, especially after my return. Women loved to talk about my miraculous medical intervention.

"What do you want to say to him?"

I pointed at his facial wound, daring him to lie again.

He didn't, though he said nothing to confirm my suspicions either. I knew the general area where he lived but couldn't determine which particular structure it was. We arrived at the mouth of a dark narrow passage that smelled of garbage. The odor came from the piles of waste dotting the base of the graffiti-filled walls. Babies cried and wailed behind several broken windows.

I waited for Ghazi to show me the way to his place, but he stood still and quiet. I looked around and was about to signal to a little girl, who glared at me from a window, when Ghazi took my hand and shuffled to stand before a dented metal door painted an ugly charcoal. His family's makeshift residence was just that, a room squeezed between two outside walls to close off the narrow space in between. The boy's mother must be a slim lady, otherwise she would have to walk around sideways in this tight place.

"My father never leaves and won't come to the door. No one else is home now."

Did the boy think I planned to share a pot of coffee with his abusive father? I padded my chest to steady the swinging tablet. Had the man ever learned to read? No matter. What I wanted to communicate required no words. I raised my cane to the door.

"He's crippled." Ghazi's whisper stopped my hand midair before the first knock.

I gestured to scan my entire body then fumbled to type, "Me too."

"He's not like you." Ghazi shook his head, a pained look in his big, brown eyes I hadn't seen before, haunting, pleading. "Not as nice as you," he mumbled.

I staggered back a step. Nice?! *Nice*?! Ghazi thought I was nice?! All the meanness I'd been cultivating my entire life had escaped this bruised soul? How bad was his father for him to find me—*me!*—nice? Ghazi was a child but he was not stupid or naive. I'd read somewhere that children possessed a sixth sense strong enough to penetrate any shield. But this boy had a faulty intuition. He had created a grotesque, false image of me—a vulnerable, feeble one that failed to fit.

I stood before him dumbfounded. Innocence struggled to find a home in his little gaunt body before his father savagely beat it out of him. Yet, he endeavored to protect him from me. Fatherhood; such a fierce force to challenge.

"Look. I will be big and strong soon to handle him on my own." Ghazi shifted his bony shoulders back and beat his chest. "I'm the one who has to do it." He struck out his hand. "Agreed?"

I had no choice but to shake his hand, to let him retain this sense of control, have something to look forward to. I could always pay his father a visit behind his back.

A couple of boys came our way. They lifted their hands to their foreheads in a stiff salute. I waited for Ghazi to return the gesture before I did the same. He was their leader. I wanted to emphasize his rank before his comrades, should they detect his emotional turmoil. Perhaps they all knew—even shared—his misery.

Moving away from the black door, I wrote the name of the dolphin in my sponsored children's clan and his age on my tablet followed by a question mark.

Ghazi scratched his head. "Saeed. I don't know this boy."

"Southern sector. Operation on his leg. Home?"

"You want me to find out where he lives?"

"Yesss."

"Got it!" Ghazi backed away several steps then ran off. He left without ensuring I wouldn't tear down his damned door. Trust; what a detestable chain.

~

During the days Turtleneck spent at our camp, he resided in Abu Nidal's. I hated seeing the weasel creep in and out of Ameena's home from my window. I sought her reaction to her parent's hospitality—an undignified act of eagerness according to my mother—during our regular video chats.

I wrapped my palm around my neck. "Turrr . . . turr . . ." I refused to utter his name before her, as if doing so would give more space to his presence.

Ameena scowled. "Someone choked?"

I let go of my neck and pulled up the collar of my shirt. "Tlll . . . nneckkk."

"Turtleneck? Is that what said? What do you mean?"

I shook my head. "Wwhooo."

"Fine. *Who* are you talking about?"

I touched both ears then tapped my chest with gathered fingers, miming a doctor listening to my heart with a stethoscope. It was silly to go on like this, but I couldn't bring myself to blatantly say his name.

Ameena tilted her head to the side. "Are you talking about Younis?"

I nodded.

"You named him Turtleneck." Her face lit up with a wide smile. "Fitting, really. He does seem to favor them over shirts most of the time. He's doing a great job at the camp. Baba has told me all about his work. Younis turned out to be really sincere in his quest to help Palestinian refugees. I'm impressed." She wagged her index finger at me. "You, of all people, should be too."

"He slllee . . . ppss innn," I said and pointed at her close-up face, "rrooommm?!"

"So what?" she chuckled. "I'm not in it!"

"Nnottt okkayy."

"Oh, don't be silly, Waseem. It's the only decent bed available. I forgot to tell you. Samra has a nose ring, now."

Ameena seemed unconcerned. She brushed the matter aside and, whenever I mentioned Younis from then on, she would switch the conversation to a number of mundane topics. I half-expected her to bring up *Yaffa* oranges.

I couldn't tell if she was genuinely disinterested or masking a true affinity for the man himself and not just his volunteer work. If I were in the room with her, I would be able to tell if she was faking indifference from her body language. Instead, I choked on the fruit-flavored smoke at a crowded nargileh lounge where the internet connection was best, limited by what I could detect in her tone and see of her face through my tablet. At first, I typed my concerns, but she ignored my texts and beckoned me to speak into the microphone.

We had no privacy, no real connection. Such a lack of emotional clarity was one major flaw I found when using virtual chat channels. The continental distance didn't weaken our special bond, subpar technology accomplished the task. I hated the irony of it. These communication tools provided me with a necessary link, but they robbed me of its essential value.

Nonetheless, I hung on to our video calls like a desperate man dangling from a high wire in a gusty wind. Because of the time difference we could only speak at night, and the nargileh lounge was the only place in our area that stayed open late at night. Fees were also cheaper after midnight but since the place was always packed, the network frequently crashed or dropped sentences, creating a choppy conversation that compounded our already strained exchange.

As expected, my friend and savior asked if I had read her parting gifts. I discussed Twain's novel through typed text and stretched my analysis over many calls—stalling to give myself time for El Saadawi's book. I didn't know why I kept postponing it, as if I had a vague premonition that I would discover something disagreeable about its influence on my friend.

Finally, I read *Two Women in One* and hated it, or rather, hated what the author described. The novel recounted the social and psychological pressures to conform to expectations, expressed through the life of one woman, Bahia. A main character smothered by the presumptions imposed by her family and Egypt's male-dominated society of the nineteen eighties.

Bahia, at first a frustratingly passive conformist, is alienated from the desires of her own body and made to feel as an "other" to her true self; a vital, living force of creativity and sexuality. In my view, she takes far too long to reject her preordained path through life until she eventually shakes off her social restrains and learns to live in harmony with her desires. She adopts a life style that clashes with her judgmental society.

Ameena had underlined a particular passage in red ink: *She knew why human beings hid their real desires: because they are strong enough to be destructive; and since people do not want to be destroyed, they opt for a passive life with no real desires.*

I read and reread it many times and pondered its significance. Each time I read it troubled me to a greater degree.

Ameena never adopted this attitude. Since childhood, she was never a conformist, nor passive, nor defeatist, and most definitely never destructive. Just by taking me on as a friend, she had torched conventions and spit in the face of her female-dominated circle. And as far as I knew, her family, especially her father, never stood in the way of her education, employment, or anything she desired, including rejecting my brother's marriage proposal.

Her bold persona was absent in El Saadawi's novel. If Ameena was born and raised in the book's era, she would not have struggled to break free from shackles of oppression, or floundered about as a powerless woman. She would have embraced Bahia's long delayed rebellion as soon as she could form words. Nobody, no caste or suffocating social order could impose their limitations on my Ameena.

Learning of El Saadawi's life and impressive literary work, I realized her words must exert inspirational powers over girls and women everywhere, including the females of today, and my sisters should be included. Social revolutions crossed many borders yet sadly lagged behind many more. But not for Ameena. Other than the political prison we lived in, no social barriers stood in her way as far as I could tell.

Why did that passage appeal to her enough to highlight? Did she really connect with it? I don't know where she bought the novel, but I know it was a new copy—had the distinctive crisp feel of an unused book—so, she must have been the one who underlined that sentence. Had she thought my sisters or some of her friends were in similar situations? Or did she mean it as an indirect message to me, a tool in this male-dominated culture shed? If that were true, then I should take solace in the fact that, at least, she saw me as a man—whether disconnected from the female sphere or not didn't matter. How could *I* understand, criticize, or judge any woman's woes?

I decided to educate myself on the oriental feminism movement and study more of its writers' work. After all, when everything was said and done, I was a product of my society and, in the end, I was no more than a man. Nothing was stopping me from becoming an *informed* man of the female perspective other than a closed mind.

I fixated on this passage to the point of neurosis. Could Ameena's ulterior intentions in bringing that passage to my attention involve indirectly prepping me for some abhorrent event to come, perhaps?

I vowed that if she didn't bring it up in our discussions, I would never ask her, nor embarrass her in any way, and resigned to linger in the shadow of ambiguity.

"Finished Two Women in One," I typed on one of our later calls, ready to launch a well-thought-out analysis.

"I knew it would irk you," she stated with a wink. "I'm thinking of going on a diet before I come home. Mama would not be happy with all the weight I've gained."

Her response and annoying topic switch robbed me of the opportunity to show any hint of gallantry. Ameena understood me well, so well, beyond what I could ever imagine. I didn't feel the need to reveal my haunting thoughts on the matter and left it to her to elaborate. She never did. To this day, I don't know if she possessed an "other" within her.

CHAPTER TWENTY

I counted the days until Ameena's June return and tried to stay busy. I ventured into the southern sector of the camp to find Saeed, who was ecstatic to greet me. The Dolphin led me through a maze of narrow, squalid alleys before I was able to connect with the rest of the herd. Their area suffered terrible living conditions, much worse than my region, and it didn't have a bookstore like the oasis of knowledge *Ustath* Ihsan maintained.

The children's sole access to reading material was recycled UNRWA schoolbooks, cheap magazines, and a ramshackle nook with a meager group of illustrated primers. I made plans to engage the young minds in book discussions on a weekly schedule. I had found my calling, driven by one of the greatest Arabic bards, Ahmad Shawqi. The Prince of Poets once said: *The revolution of souls severs ropes, and the revolution of minds removes mountains.*

Austere economic conditions and onerous political mountains blocked the path to a decent life and prosperity for refugees like us. I aspired to lead an expedition to trek across one of the craggiest summits of literature and introduce the children to the nationalist lyrics of the Syrian poet, Sulaiman al-Issa, magical stories of the Egyptian writer, Kamel Kilani, and the heroic adventures penned by the Palestinian author, Rawda Alfarkh al-Hudhud.

Exposure to such Arabic literature whisked my clan to a world where heroes were their kin and next-door neighbors, kindred souls of a proud tradition renowned for perseverance and fortitude. *Ustath* Ihsan suggested translated classics, the Harry Potter series and other internationally acclaimed books, but those narratives were too far removed from our harsh realities.

My cadre already inhabited an unforgiving world. They struggled to maintain an existence in a bleak void, a severely skewed realm of physical and intellectual deprivation the world's sovereign citizens could not imagine, relate to, nor try to understand. To embrace a future these children needed to learn that they possessed special powers, inherited from our culture, history, language, and religion. With my small weekly allowance from Yasser, I persuaded *Ustath* Ihsan to secure the valuable literature from his usual channels, and depended on Yasser's connections to provide resources for other booksellers from outside the camp, legitimate or not, I didn't care. I had a mission to inspire that blasted through any barriers.

I asked Nabil to paint a wooden vegetable crate red and fasten the fluorescent wheels of my retired walker to its bottom corners. This became my mobile library. If I am not a sentimental fool, I am a practical one. Part of my faithful mobility aid remained by my side and soon proved invaluable. With its wheels repurposed, Mother hung the frame in the kitchen to function as an extra drying rack.

Very little went to waste in our camp. Rusty sieves and old tires held soil for herbs. Discolored sheets draped entryways and windows, serving as mismatched canopies. Mother salvaged a pair of socks bleached white to drain old yogurt and make *labneh*. I think the thick stockings were once my father's. About the only things that didn't find a lasting presence were us, the camp dwellers.

In my attempt to induct all of the members of the herd into my reading club, I ran into some opposition from the father of the Tigress. The cobbler refused to let me see his daughter, and only relented after Saeed showcased the stack of books I lugged along in my improvised, portable library.

The education-enthused widower permitted the Tigress to join my book circle on the condition that we held the discussions at his humble abode in the presence of her older sister, Jannat—a stipulation readily agreed to. With no toddlers underfoot in the home, the once sponsored children and I lounged in a room full of comfortable cushions. Though a tad damp and void of natural light, the private space was ours for a couple of hours each Friday.

Announcing my arrival, the wheels of my library creaked on the narrow paths in the still of communal prayer time. Children in the battered neighborhood followed as I trudged to our meeting place. My clan gathered before the door, swelled in number with the addition of siblings, neighbors, and more than a few trailing curious boys and girls.

Jannat walked in small, measured steps. She checked her hijab at the base of her chin often and smiled with kind, dark eyes. She flashed a special side grin with lowered eyelids whenever she glanced at her little sister. Like a prism, she fractured affection into wide waves. A fresh rainbow formed before my eyes to connect opposite corners of the dank room. I swear I could see its arched, layered colors blanket the tiny shoulders of the Tigress. Jannat's glimpse was so unique, so laden with love, yet so unmotherly, that I couldn't stop thinking of my own sisters whenever she entered the room.

Maryam's gaze always reflected sisterly adulation heavy with a sad, resigned acceptance akin to that of her revered namesake's depictions in most paintings. I reveled in Maryam's sentiment and reciprocated her uncloaked compassion. But never, ever in my life had I detected in Fayzeh anything resembling Jannat's tender, fleeting look. A sour disposition dominated my youngest sister's each and every glance, while Jannat's significant look cast a measure of peaceful stillness. Was it because of the way I looked at Fayzeh? Did my sister not discern any special fondness in my crossed eyes? Was I the source of my strained relationship with the sister I could not understand, let alone win over?

Jannat assumed the role of a trusted helper. She corralled excited kids and kept them in check—not that they acted beyond reason. My sponsored clan members taught newcomers the feral vocal greetings I had assigned to each of them at the hospital in Holland, adding other animals with more sound effects. This restored ritual turned the quiet room into a tiny zoo. Youngsters joked and played together before they settled down for a reading session, and I loved their exuberance. Refugee Children should have as many opportunities to laugh as humanly possible. How else would they endure the profound ugliness marring their lives?

During these sessions I took to observing Jannat, whom I estimated to be in her mid-twenties, because I knew she had left school after the ninth grade to care for her sister. She hid an elegant figure under a gray buttoned suit-like garment that reached her ankles over a pair of dark trousers. She wore thick black socks without exception, so I never saw her bare feet and had no idea if she painted her toenails. Ameena and Samra always did, as well as Fayzeh.

Jannat dressed in this same outfit each week and changed colors only with her hijab, favoring pastel shades of blue which barely contrasted her olive skin. If I were her fashion advisor, I would have suggested bright pink to highlight her interesting features. Her delicate, round face had only a little space between her thin eyebrows arching over big, banana-shaped eyes. She had a slim nose and thin lips reminiscent of a crescent after the birth of a new moon.

As an avid collector of secrets, I had always hated ambiguity. In search of a clearer image of Jannat, I studied her on our second meeting when she was helping the Tigress adjust her artificial arm, curious to know if she shared the same auburn color of her sister's smooth hair. When she suddenly lifted her head to look my way, I fixed my gaze on the single lightbulb above and pretended to examine it. With my crossed eyes, she couldn't possibly determine I was looking straight at her. The moment passed with little awkwardness, but my mental picture of the woman remained incomplete.

Jannat is the plural of "heaven" in Arabic—as if a single Eden wasn't enough for the greedy, human spirit—and when she spoke, her voice murmured with a soft hum as she sounded her m's. I imagined a little cherub blowing a tiny flute behind my ears.

"Waseemmmm," the flutist played at the end of our third session, "could I interest you in lending me some poetry *deewans*?"

Poetry? Yes, poetry interested me. And the chime of my name in Jannat's voice tickled my ears. Very peculiar and surprisingly pleasing.

"Your Favorite poet?" I prompted, eager to hear more of her voice.

"Antarah ibn Shaddad."

I hid my surprise behind a fake cough. A classic choice, linguistically complicated. The pre-Islamic Arab knight, renowned for his courage in battles and platonic love for Ablah, composed poems rich in war portraiture and idealistic romance. I didn't need to guess which side of Antarah's poetry beckoned to this woman. Jannat could surely be another young mortal tormented by romantic notions. I wondered what sort of dashing man galloped through her dreams. I labeled my flight of fancy about this woman as nothing more than mere curiosity and found solace in that.

"I'll bring what I can find," I promised as I helped usher children out the door.

An ever-present pang stabbed my chest. I would probably need to delve into discussions with Jannat about her literary interests—an endeavor I must confess I found exciting due to the intellectual desert Ameena's absence had created. But would Jannat come to understand and appreciate my quirks? Would I be able to fully express my thoughts, to be as honest with her as I was with Ameena? Would she grasp what I conceal between the lines of text responses as Ameena would before I finished typing? I very much doubted I would reach that level of kinship with this woman. And why would I want to? Ameena alone provided nourishment beyond compare. A mere angel could never ascend to the plateau of a goddess.

How I longed for Ameena's gravitational power to pull me into orbit again and transport me to a world free of hardship. If only Earth spun faster, and the days flew by until she returned to nourish my impoverished soul. Curse you, Jannat, I thought, for sending me home with Antarah's legendary words ringing in my mind: *I wish fate would bring my loved ones closer, akin to it drawing in my misfortunes.*

CHAPTER TWENTY-ONE

Yasser frowned upon me for crossing into the southern part of camp, which was controlled by a despised rival of his boss. He framed my community service as an opportunity to cast me in the role of a spy. He peppered me with questions about streets, alleys, and locations of certain shops which comprised the layout of the area beyond his influence. Undeterred, I accepted the spy charade and provided harmless information to continue my pedagogical mission.

Restless, unsatisfied, and annoyed at playing the informant, my patience with everyone faded, but most especially with my sister, Fayzeh. During my Netherlands sojourn, she had found unofficial employment with an affluent Lebanese family in Beirut, mentoring three children—a task I found strange as she lacked teaching credentials and proper references. She dragged herself home on weekends exhausted and sluggish while Mother handled all the housework to allow Fayzeh time to recuperate and unwind.

Fayzeh was no teacher, not even an aspiring nanny. My sister was, in reality, a hard-working maid. Because she was not legally allowed to work outside the camp, she possessed no rights, no official recourse if the family mistreated her or neglected to pay her honest wages.

Yet I was helpless to prevent Fayzeh from leaving to work. I understood her eagerness to escape camp life, even for a fleeting week at a time. I soothed my troubled mind with the idea that her job would provide a window to view what the outside world offered and might prompt her to seek a different path.

Nonetheless, I endeavored to place literary works by feminist authors in plain view. I scattered books, magazines, and snippets of articles by the Algerian novelist and filmmaker Assia Djebar, the Syrian journalist Ghada al-Samman, the Iranian professor Azar Nafisi, the Kuwaiti writer Laila al-Othman, and the Palestinian poet May Ziadeh among many others. I set out for her anything I could put my hands on. I even included El Saadawi's irksome novel, chancing an encounter that might light some rebellious fire under Fayzeh's feet.

To procure the needed publications, I reached out to *Ustath* Ihsan as usual, enduring quizzical stares and repeated head scratches when I offered no explanation for the peculiar list.

To my utter disappointment, Fayzeh would shove any reading material aside to make room for a make-up kit, the hair dryer, or to stretch out and admire a new article of clothing. She never even glanced at my extensive spread and seemed more than satisfied with her position—a quitter's attitude at odds with the Arabic meaning of her name, "winner."

It wasn't hard to secure a copy of Antarah's famous *Mu'allaqat*, reported to have been one of seven odes written in gold liquid and suspended from the Kaaba before Islam prevailed in Mecca. *Ustath* Ihsan kept a recent edition in mint condition on his shelves of cherished works and was happy to lend it.

Swallowing my frustration with my sister, I added a collection from another romantic bard for Jannat to enjoy. Considered the first modern poet by some Arab scholars,

Bashar ibn Burd thrived in the early Abbasid-period and opened the door for poetic experimentation. Although he was blind from birth and his face was scarred by a smallpox infection, the Zoroastrianism-admirer confessed his love and fascination with women through vivid imagery. Common people and not just the intellectual elite understood, accepted, and admired his poetry. This cornucopia of admirers testified to his timeless genius. If Jannat admired Antarah's complex platonic expressions, she would find contrast in ibn Burd's delicate and provocative flirtatious verses.

With both books tucked under my arm Friday, I hustled behind animated children toward our private library area. Passing a smudge-free window on the way, a face with a wide smile startled me. I stumbled to a stop to focus.

Elongated head and pointed ears. It was me! I looked different, though. I couldn't place the alteration, but I had certainly acquired a novel appearance, one that reflected satisfaction and perhaps even delight.

This was new. An additional disguise? Did zebras develop more stripes with age? Or could it be my real visage peeking out from under an old, tattered mask? Perhaps it was the excited look of anticipation. How would Jannat react to my books? Would she appreciate the selection? Which specific poems would appeal to her the most? I looked forward to uncovering the answers to these questions. Pure intellectual interest generated by an inquisitive mind hard at work.

For the sake of complete honesty, I could attribute my elation to the thrill of hearing her lyrical voice again. From a book under my arm, a specific line of Bashar ibn Burd's singed my skin: *O my people, my ear for some neighborhood longs, and the ear, sometimes, falls in love before the eye does.*

I switched my cane to the other hand to shift the books. Hold on, hold on, dear misguided, besotted poet. I was definitely *not* in love with Jannat, not even close to being infatuated. Admiring her kind character was all the emotion I could muster and honestly acknowledge. I simply found her unique voice pleasing and only wanted to enjoy another brief titillation. There must be a sonnet, or a stanza written about such discord somewhere. At that brief, revealing moment, staring at a stranger in the window, nothing came to mind.

As soon as I handed Jannat my literary offerings she sat down to peruse ibn Burd's Diwan, forgetting to help settle the kids down. The way books captured her full attention gave me an extra thrill. I howled and gestured to force the children to fall into line. Jannat snapped her head up. She had the startled look of someone jolted from a transcendental experience.

I really appreciated her focus, and in spite of my shepherd's angst, I found her contrite smile quite appealing. She set aside the thick volume and went to work, fluffing cushions, directing everyone to take their places.

Ego puffed my chest and stretched my crooked body to its full height. This endeavor to educate children had produced a most unexpected development, for I never intended to target adults outside my family circle. My efforts had opened windows to a wider range of knowledge to Jannat. I made a difference in her life. I mattered to this woman, a stranger who had only known me as a full-grown man. I was the benefactor this time around—a totally satisfying and fresh experience.

I summoned visions of benevolent Ameena in my head. Tell me, beautiful, intelligent, generous, all-knowing Ameena: What was I to do with this interesting woman sitting before me?

CHAPTER TWENTY-TWO

Madame, as Fayzeh would refer to the lady of the house where she worked, took my sister under her wing and granted her extraordinary benefits. Fayzeh accompanied the blond woman everywhere. She visited high-end shops in Beirut, dined at upscale Raouché cafes, attended the cinema, and enjoyed theatrical plays from patrons' balconies. For the first time in my sister's life, she owned jewelry—a gold necklace with a splendid pearl pendant *Madame* had gifted on her birthday—and now used one of those high-tech phones which she allowed no one to touch.

Much to her credit, Fayzeh spent a generous portion of her wages on our family. She bought a washing machine, reupholstered our mattresses and cushions, purchased a six-drawer dresser and a slightly used rug to replace the frayed one, and brought home her benefactor's hand-me-down clothing. Mother let out the seams on the pieces that were too tight and sold the ones that were impossible to alter for a tidy sum.

Evidence of Fayzeh's hard work showed in her dry hands and elbows. She would rub her skin with olive oil in the evening while relating her adventures. Excitement and sometimes wonder enlivened her tone, especially when she talked about *Monsieur*. The head of the house was a highly successful businessman and owner of multiple furniture stores. Whenever Fayzeh spoke of him, the gleam in her eyes delivered a punch to my stomach. My naïve sister was infatuated with him, her employer's husband—no wonder she didn't seek a different job. She *liked* to be in that house. She took extra measures to look nice before she left for work, dressed in her finest clothes, made her hair, painted her nails, and smeared her face with makeup.

That same sickening thought must have clouded my mother's mind. She would often stop Fayzeh at the door, wipe her lipstick away with a wad of tissues, and question the need for her stylish appearance.

"*Madame* wants me to look nice and presentable for her guests," my sister would groan. "Sophisticated society women. One is the wife of a minister. Another is the wife of a famous plastic surgeon. I'm the only one *Madame* trusts to serve their meetings. Don't you see how lucky I am, *yumma*?"

And with that, my mother would sigh, nod, and wish her well. I couldn't understand her reaction. Clearly her suspicions remained as they fled out of her chest with each heavy exhale. Why did she not pursue the matter further? I cornered her one morning after everyone left for work.

"Fffay . . . zzeh jobbb nnott gooo . . . dd," I said.

"It's not like she can be a teacher or a doctor, son. This is all she can do." Mother squeezed pinkish lotion from a white tube and massaged it over her cracked heels. "Maybe she will meet someone who can scoop her out of here. A person plans, and God manages."

I gave up on speaking and typed, "She is in love."

"Fayzeh says nice things about the cook's assistant, Khaled. He's Palestinian, from the camp here. Did you know that?" Not bothering to wait for my answer, Mother continued to speak and rub more lotion over her calves. "His family lives close to

Maryam's in-laws. The *dactor*'s aunt, I remember her saying. Khaled moved to Beirut a year ago. Now being a *Tabbakh* is not a profession I see a young man seeking a future in, but these are different times. I can't imagine why a woman would need a man *and* an assistant to cook in her kitchen. *Madame* must be very busy. A very important woman. Ah, this cream is fantastic. Not too oily and doesn't have a smell. I must ask Um Faheem where she bought—"

I attacked the keys on my tablet screen. "Monsieur!"

Mother slapped my fingers with her slick hand. "Stop."

"The way she speaks of him? More is going on."

"Fayzeh would never do anything wrong. I know how I raised my daughter. So, be quiet and don't dare mention this again." Mother went into the kitchen and said over her shoulder, "I'll squeeze some juice for you. Those oranges Yasser brought yesterday are full of seeds. If only we could taste the ones from *Yaffa*."

"Aaahhh!" I yelled, and tossed my tablet on the cushions in animated frustration. She ignored me the rest of the day. I set my mind to enquire about Khaled's family on my next visit to Jannat—and my students—on the other side of the camp. Before stepping on any toes, I needed to know if there were connections to the heavily weaponized militia controlling the area. As far as I knew, ever since my threats to the *dactor*, he became Maryam's father-in-law and changed pharmaceutical suppliers. He no longer used the Hawks of Freedom channel and had switched to Abu Nidal's. Did the abandoned league find a new outlet for smuggled medicines, and God knows what else, in Khaled's family?

Yasser and Wael didn't care one way or another about our sister's emotional attachment to her employer's husband. It was obvious they welcomed her financial contributions to the household, which eased part of their considerable burden. Attentive Nabil showed concern by escorting Fayzeh to work as often as his free time permitted. Passing through the guarded entrance of the camp was uncomfortable at best, suspicious sentries continually probing with pointed questions. Nabil's calming presence next to our sister eased the process. His mellow nature also helped him establish connections with staff members at *Madame*'s fancy house, and he managed to strike a guarded friendship with Khaled.

One evening, Yasser was tasked to run errands for Abu Nidal. Acting more secretive than usual, he barely uttered a complete sentence when he walked in to eat in a rush. After eating, he rummaged through his drawers and left in a huff with a bundle under his arm.

Mother and Fayzeh, preparing to visit Maryam, failed to notice anything amiss. They asked Wael to accompany them. It was obvious they were laying the grounds for another union. I heard Mother talk about one of Maryam's neighbors in very good terms and noticed Wael's eyes light up every time she mentioned the girl's name, Wardah.

Wardah is the Arabic word for "rose." Wael showed sudden interest in Beirut shops that sold fragrant flowers. Either he didn't find any roses that evening or deemed them to be too expensive because he came home holding a bundle of white carnations. Nabil chuckled and teased him about it.

As everyone was heading out the door, I caught Fayzeh slip a bottle of perfume from her bag and quickly stuff it under clothes in her designated dresser drawer. If it were a gift from *Madame*, she would have proudly showed it to Mother and let her enjoy its fragrance. But Fayzeh took measures to linger and hide the bottle. Nabil and I connected eyes and didn't say anything until the room emptied.

"We should do something," Nabil said, gazing out the window. "I know that perfume didn't come from Khaled, even though he is really taken by her."

I snapped my head up. What? Khaled, a man, admired Fayzeh in spite of her abrasive manner? I wouldn't need to learn more about this fool. Having romantic feelings toward my sister presented enough damning testimony about his character.

"You've been to his sector of the camp." Nabil's gaze shifted to me. "Did you learn anything?"

Ghazi had related nothing substantial about Khaled and his family of nobodies. I shook my head.

"The driver has heard rumors." Nabil crossed his arms over his chest. "Probably started by the old housekeeper. It won't take long for gossip to reach *Madame*, if not already."

I lifted my tablet to fill his eyes. "Explain?"

"Izzat . . . her *Monsieur*? He frequents an apartment in the suburbs of *Jdeideh*. Know where that is?"

"Nnno." What do I know of Beirut's suburbs? Other than reaching the airport, I've never been to the city.

"It's about a fifteen-minute drive northwest of Beirut," Nabil said. "Two days ago, I heard the driver say he was on his way there and he'd be careful as usual." Nabil knelt before me. "This time I followed him. I watched him take food and supplies to a corner apartment. I poked around. The neighbors say a middle-aged man frequents the place but keeps to himself. They know him as Abdullah Abdullah and think he's an airline pilot as he appears once a week." Nabil flopped down on his behind. "What a fake name. From the description, I think it's Izzat."

"Did anyone see Fayzeh?"

"They said maids also show up on a regular basis. No one pays attention to them, but God help us, several mentioned a well-dressed brunette." Nabil ran fingers through his hair. "I don't know. Maybe Fayzeh goes there to clean the place? Maybe she's embarrassed to tell us about this extra job?"

I went to Fayzeh's drawer and poked around her clothes.

"What are you doing?" Nabil seized my elbow.

I shrugged his hand off and exposed the perfume bottle, making a big mess of fondled clothing with my jerky hands. I showed the Calvin Klein aftershave to Nabil.

He narrowed his eyes. "What is she doing with men's cologne?" Then he slapped my shoulder. "Wait, whose birthday is coming up? Yasser. At the end of the week. Oh, thank God! It's a gift for our brother." He tucked the bottle back to where it was, too quick to dismiss our suspicions. He did his best to rearrange the drawer contents. "Look, is that how it was? I don't want her to know we . . . you did this."

Though I wanted to share his relief, something sinister kept nagging at me. The way Fayzeh conducted herself, exhibiting a confidence I hadn't seen before. I tried to contribute the change to her exposure to refined society, but I couldn't shake the feeling that there were other circumstances fueling her sure steps. To my knowledge, she never read a word in any of the inspiring literature I had laid around. Had Fayzeh's infatuation with Izzat developed into something more disastrous?

I continued to be vigilant. Yasser's birthday passed without her producing the gift. I waited a couple of days. Nothing. Nabil brushed the matter aside and suggested we wait for Wael's birthday in June.

Home alone on another sleepy afternoon, I raided her stash again. Next to the bottle, I found a man's watch and a pair of what looked like gold earrings, only they weren't. I snapped pictures of each item on my iPad and showed the one with the gold studs to *Ustath* Ihsan. He told me they were expensive cufflinks, men's formal wear jewelry. Once more, a gift for a man. I couldn't think of a situation where any of my brothers would ever wear something like that. So, it couldn't be another gift for any of them.

If she really liked Khaled, the hidden pieces could be for him. But where or when would an assistant cook ever don gold cufflinks?

Could Fayzeh have stolen these items? Why was it men's stuff? It would make much more sense for her to steal things from *Madame*, items she could use or easily sell to her friends. And what about this Khaled character? Could he be the instigator? Were they partners in crime?

Growing up, one of my resentments against my condition was that it robbed me the chance to protect my younger siblings from the ravages of a cruel world. Never in my wildest dreams had I contemplated the notion that I would have to protect others from my kin, my little sister of all people. I couldn't determine if I'd rather discover that she was a thief, than the other possibilities connected to that apartment.

CHAPTER TWENTY-THREE

I kept tight lips about my suspicions of Fayzeh's activities when talking to Ameena. Partly because I possessed no solid information to share, but mostly I believed that family matters should always remain within the inner circle. Moreover, Ameena was a part of *me*. Why would I inform myself of things I already knew?

Go ahead. Mock me. I don't care. I used the absurd, self-deceptive rationale to convince myself that I wasn't keeping secrets from Ameena. I salved my conscience and indulged my delusions with plans to orchestrate a phone call between her and my sister. The evident contrast between her exploits and the accomplishments of her childhood friend would spark my sister's jealousy and could nudge her to aspire for more out of life.

I wasn't sure if either of my sisters corresponded with Ameena after she left the camp. I never saw any letters nor heard them speak of chats. Had Ameena communicated with Maryam or Fayzeh, she would have mentioned it to me, wouldn't she?

Ameena asked about my book club activities with her usual enthusiasm. I told her about my growing cadre of readers and my literary mentorship of Jannat, and shared my excitement for my oldest pupil's fondness for poetry.

"Oh, Ibn Zaydun," Ameena immediately suggested. "Your student must read the work of the greatest neoclassical poet of

Al-Andalus. Most scholars endorse this claim." She held her hand up and winked. "I happen to agree."

I cringed. Another impassioned soul writing in sensual tones about love. Ibn Zaydun had a tremulous love affair with Wallada. The Iberian Peninsula poet expressed his adoration for the Princess of Cordoba, also a poet, with seductive passionate power and a grand poetic style. What sort of mentor was I to Jannat, exactly?

"And don't forget to add Wallada's work," Ameena continued, her voice laden with a serious tone. "It's only fair, so she can have the complete picture. Tell her how Wallada used to embroider her verses on the trim of her clothing. I'm certain your Jannat would find that intriguing."

I gave a thumbs-up. She wasn't *my* Jannat, she was my pupil. A Freudian slip, Ameena? Or was it intentional? I scratched my chin. This was the first time I ever expressed a favorable opinion of another woman to her. My body language must have exposed a gleeful reaction to the prospect of Jannat mitigating the intellectual void her absence had created. Ameena never failed to discern the reason behind each and every drool, grin, or growl I offered. She couldn't possibly be jealous of Jannat's presence. Or could she? Despite my extensive studies, I was still floundering deeper into darkness when it came to discerning how women think.

With exposure to the outside world, functioning in its realm longer than I had, Ameena must have changed. Even if I neglected to grant Turtleneck the weight he'd exerted on her emotional development, I needed to face the idea that my Ameena was bound to transform. She may have morphed into a woman, a sophisticated siren, I could no longer speculate upon her thoughts with a satisfying measure of accuracy.

"I have Wallada's *deewan* at home," Ameena said. "Please ask Mama for it, or have Yasser bring it."

I remembered that book. She had loaned it to me a long time ago, but I had thought the source was *Ustath* Ihsan as usual, not Ameena's private collection. I ought to refresh my memory and read it again before I present it to Jannat. I couldn't recall if Ameena had underlined a specific verse. Surely, I would have noticed if she had. And it was possible she had selected some passages after I returned the book.

A thrilling thought kept me awake that night: I could contrast Ameena's favorite lines of Wallada's with Jannat's. Luck could be on my side as I analyzed such sample exposure to the workings of both female minds, which was a mission well worth my efforts. It might also help me better understand my recalcitrant sister.

I found an opportunity to include Fayzeh on one of my calls to Ameena at the nargileh lounge during a late Thursday night. My mother, however, absolutely refused to allow Fayzeh to set foot in the place.

"You want your sister to be seen there after dark?" she admonished. "Very undignified."

"Many women go to smoke Thursday nights," I typed fast. "With their families."

"Women can do whatever they want. But not my daughter."

"Fayzeh *is* a woman!!"

"Exactly. She is a young woman, and she will never go there." With that upside-down explanation, mother marched into the kitchen to yank open the refrigerator. "Wish we had some oranges. Any would do right now, not necessarily from *Yaffa*."

I stared at my mother's back and bit my tongue. I should scatter some of that feminist literature about the room to educate *her* as well. My eyes met Fayzeh's as she sat quietly in a corner. She blew onto her fingertips to dry a fresh layer of nail polish. Fayzeh showed zero interest in attempting to argue, to defy our mother's unfair decree, or to even join a discussion concerning her best interests.

I snatched a tissue from the Kleenex box and waved it in mock surrender. Certain battles needed willing soldiers. My sister wanted nothing to do with this war.

~

On my next Friday reading session, I received a gift from Jannat. I dubbed it a gift because I didn't know what else to call it. As I was about to leave the room, she handed back Antarah's and ibn Burd's volumes.

"You don't have to return them so quickly," I typed.

"I read them cover to cover," she said with a scowl. "Ready for more, if you have any."

I nodded and presented books of the romantic duo, ibn Zaydun and Wallada. Why the sour expression? Had I offended her by suggesting she could have more time? Or did she not like these selections?

"Perhaps you could share your thoughts on the content next time?"

Jannat tapped ibn Burd's volume. "I wrote what I liked best on a piece of paper. I didn't dare scribble on the pages." She hurried to close the door but not fast enough for me to miss her cheeks turn a rosy shade of pink. Centuries onward, ibn Burd continues to touch women's hearts. His potent expressions caused Jannat to blush. Interesting. Very interesting.

I hastened home, eager to read her critique. She saved me the trouble of arranging a cumbersome back-and-forth discussion on my tablet. Smart pupil. This way, I could study her analysis and prepare a counter argument ahead of time. An exchange I was better suited for.

Walking as fast as I could, I passed Ameena's place and chuckled to myself. Oh, Ameena. I figured it out. Now I know what role I'm supposed to play with Jannat.

I dashed into my corner and fished for the report, fingers trembling, palms sweating, my entire body straining to stay steady. Leafing through numerous pages turned into a challenge more than usual. I found a sheet of paper folded perfectly in half and flipped it open with my tongue, drooling over the book at this point. My excitement burst as if my nephew's balloon had popped in my mouth, scorching my lungs, choking me. On the pale-yellow paper, Jannat had scribbled in pencil two lines separated by dots: *If I knew that love would kill me, I would have prepared, before I met you, my shrouds.* And then: *She kept offering, at night, lips for me to savor; a djinn wedded, in slumber, to a mortal.*

What? What? Were these selections directed at me? It shouldn't, couldn't be true. The spellbinding woman said she liked those verses above all others. Ah, but what expressive lines she chose to share! It was no wonder she had blushed so charmingly when she told me about her selections. But why must she be so brief, annoyingly concise, and so evasive? I could not help but notice that she chose inconsecutive verses from the very same poem of ibn Burd's I had recalled when I savored the charming textures of her melodious voice. What were the odds? Of the poet's extensive collection consisting of hundreds of poems and thousands of unforgettable expressions, she selected that specific one? And why did she choose two nonsequential verses? Did she add the second as an afterthought? Or did she intentionally include it to prick my soul and keep me reeling in confusion?

Oh, Ameena. I lay exposed, cut to the quick by another woman's hand. Jannat may yet prove to be a spellbinding student and most unexpected mind reader.

CHAPTER TWENTY-FOUR

Over the following days, I monitored Fayzeh's treasure while it dwindled. The watch was the first to go. She came home that week with a set of new pots for Mother—a whole set with matching, differently-sized pots and pans. Mother was beyond ecstatic. She abandoned the tube of body lotion she loved so much and examined the pots as if appraising heirloom jewelry.

"*Madame* bought them from a charity fundraiser," Fayzeh explained. "But the cook didn't like the feel of their plastic handles. She said I could have the set."

Calvin Klein departed next. Fayzeh toted home a pair of leather boots that week. "*Madame* doesn't wear them anymore. Isn't it great we have the same shoe size?" she exclaimed as she modeled the scuff-free new boots. On the day we prepared to make Wael's engagement to Wardah official, Fayzeh gave him a jewelry box.

"I've been saving for this a long time." She opened the box to reveal a gold bracelet and a matching necklace. "I hope Wardah likes it."

Ever short on words, Wael gave her a hug and mumbled his thanks. Nabil and I looked at each other over their heads. His lips broke into a satisfied smile. Though he didn't utter a word, his eyes seemed to shine and signal, "See? It's all good."

Mother wobbled her tongue into a *zaghrouta* loud enough to summon neighbors behind closed doors. While everyone mingled on the steps to accept congratulations, I slipped back inside to check Fayzeh's cache. The cufflinks were gone.

My family and I headed on our noble mission to join Wael with his intended. My limp became more prominent with each step as the weight of my sister's deception shackled my ankles. An image from the Prison Gate Museum popped into my head and slowed me further. I needed to find the right moment to face my sister and put an end to her thieving.

I took too long. A couple of mornings after Wael's modest engagement party, while everyone was out and I sat alone contemplating a strategy, Jannat's red cheeks formed before my mind's eye and prevented me from focusing on the problem at hand. She greeted me with her adorable blush every single time, and such a reaction to further poetic exposure became her permanent feature. I wasn't the only one who had attained a new look.

Jannat spoke very little to me, poured her energy and full attention onto the children. Before each session started, she chatted about the weather, general politics, recent events, and book themes, but always in brief. I hated having to type questions on my tablet to nudge her into extensive conversations after a couple of failed attempts. But during the few, brief moments of silence, when our zoo occupants were ensconced each in their sphere, completely absorbed by what they read, I would catch her studying me. She would blush, adjust her scarf, then flip a page of the book nestled in her hands.

Jannat's perceived interest and canorous voice ushered tingling sensations all over my body and sent heat to the tips of my ears. My pointed earlobes itched in her presence.

The experience of being the target of a probable admirer's glances was unfamiliar to me. I was accustomed to being the one who snuck furtive looks at Ameena when she wasn't aware. I had often traced the contours of her darling face with my mind's finger. Did Jannat do the same during her stolen glances? Was it possible she esteemed what her eyes registered? I found that hard to believe. And how would I reciprocate her subtle advances? I had not the slightest idea.

Flirting. I knew nothing whatsoever about such activity between adults. I could have been reading this situation totally wrong, of course. Jannat's focused gaze could simply have been a demonstration of her clever discovery of the many masks I wore and her intention of shredding them to pieces.

I ticked the days off until she completed her reading assignment. I told myself I must learn which of Wallada's words appealed to her the most. Instead of asking for an essay, I would succumb to vagueness and innuendos to prod her. I would condescend to play her game. Anything to distract me from thinking about Fayzeh's misconduct and Ameena's life—so very far removed from mine. Ameena had underlined nothing in Wallada's Diwan. Not a single word. I decided to ask for her preference the next time we talked.

Nabil stormed into the room and interrupted my trail of thoughts about the women in my life. He sported a swollen eye and busted lip.

"I put an end to the rumors," he huffed. "No one will dare talk about our sister again."

I tapped my cane to his shoulder and flipped my hand in his face.

"I taught the driver a lesson. He had the nerve to suggest I track her movements. He said *Madame* gives her free time

Thursday afternoons to manage personal things before she comes home for the weekend."

I nodded. Fayzeh arrived late on Thursdays. So, she had two to three hours to herself every week in the city. "Doo ittt," I said.

"What?" Nabil mumbled as he pressed a tissue to his bleeding lips.

I typed fast, "Follow her. We must know if she goes to that apartment. No smoke without fire."

Nabil shook his head. "I will not. I trust her. More importantly, I *respect* Mother."

Sure, he would. Nabil was a kind and sensitive soul, a poet. Romantic notions shaped his opinions of women. Our sisters were pure and innocent as Qays's Leila and Romeo's Juliette. Our mother had the leadership and saintly qualities of Sheba's Balqees and France's Jeanne d'Arc. And in his black-and-white vision, I was more like Othello's Iago, driven by self-destructive obsessions. What did he think of our brothers?

"I will tell Yasser."

Nabil stumbled back a step. "You can't."

"He will know what to do," I continued with my empty threat. Of course, I would not bring Yasser into this. There was no telling where his anger would lead. Even if my suspicions were wrong, he would not follow Fayzeh or anything of the sort. He would act. I know what he was capable of. Moreover, I know what his boss could do. "I can't follow her without drawing attention. Wael is too involved with his fiancée. Yasse—"

Nabil stayed my hand on the tablet dangling from my neck. "All right, all right. I'll do it. Just don't tell Yasser, okay? Not even Wael. You and I will handle this. There could be a very simple and innocent explanation, right?"

I briefly closed my eyes. I feared not.

"I'm not sure I can on Thursday," Nabil admitted, "I promised Wael I'd cover his shift at the shop Thursdays. It's the only day he can spend time with Wardah's family as her father commanded." He aimed for the wastebasket in the corner and threw the crumbled bloody tissue. He missed. "I can't just take off to follow Fayzeh."

"Close shop."

Nabil picked up the tissue ball and back stepped to the window. "Clients expect their vehicles ready on time. Can't afford to lose any." Balancing on his heels to focus, he made the shot. "And what would I tell Wael and the owner, huh?"

I wished my spy network extended outside the camp. This task would have been easy. *Ustath* Ihsan was the only person I knew who had connections in the city. I couldn't involve him in this delicate matter. If Ameena were here, I would rely on her.

"One! One Thursday afternoon is all we need. I will man the shop if it comes to it. Say you have a friend's funeral to attend in Beirut."

"Funeral?" Nabil arched an eyebrow. "Why so gloomy?"

"Aaaah!" I threw my hands up in the air instead of smacking the back of his head.

"Fine, fine. It's your idea. We'll clear up this misunderstanding soon."

~

Continuous heavy rains turned our alleys into muddy rivers. Nabil and I had agreed to meet inside the closed shop once he returned from his intelligence gathering mission. Listening to nature's assault on the roof, I leaned my cane against a stack of tires and waited on a torn, leather seat that had been removed from a totaled car. Nabil trudged in, his face as dark as the mud clinging to his boots. I waited for him to run a towel over his hair and arms.

"She went to the apartment," he said, flopping down on a tattered backseat. "Stayed for two hours. Then a man arrived. I took pictures of him." Nabil kicked a Pepsi can and clanged it against another. "Not Izzat."

"Hmmmm," I grunted and breathed slowly to control my anger. I gripped the sides of my seat in anticipation of a spastic episode. Spongy foam filled my palms.

"Here's the twist," Nabil raised his index finger. "*Madame* showed up five minutes after him. Only she wasn't blond." Nabil patted his head. "She wore a wig. Long brunette hair. Fayzeh left the minute *Madame* arrived." Nabil leaned over to stick his face close. "I told you our sister is innocent. She must have been cleaning the apartment."

"Madam having an affair with Abdullah Squared?"

Nabil stared at my typed line for a second then chuckled. "I would have named him Double Abdullah, but okay, we'll go with Squared. Anyway, who knows how these rich people live, huh? It's clear our sister goes to prep the place. She gets paid extra and that's how she can afford the things she brings home." He leaned back. "It's simple. Fayzeh doesn't tell us because she can't rat on *Madame*."

"What about the things she hid in her drawer?"

"That, I can't explain." Nabil flicked mud off his trousers. "Worst case scenario, she stole them from *Madame*'s lover. Best case, she found them in the apartment after the secret meetings and hid them until she gave them to *Madame*."

"I have to know. Have to talk to Fayzeh."

"Yeah? Well, I'm convinced." Nabil clapped his hands once. "Your suspicions are groundless."

I wished I could dismiss the issue as easily as he did. The fact that our sister could be a thief working for a woman with loose morals didn't bother this idealistic dreamer alarmed me.

Several heartbeats passed in silence. Nabil flipped out his phone to show me the photos he had taken of the mystery man. "I should find out who this Abdullah character really is." He raised questioning eyes. "Just in case we're wrong about *Madame*?"

"Yesss," I said and squeezed his shoulder twice. The ethical brother I knew and hoped for had returned to share my concerns. Nabil's momentary relief that Fayzeh wasn't the one having rendezvous in that apartment must have overpowered his sense of righteousness. His lapse in judgment passed fast.

"Don't talk to Fayzeh until I ask about him," he said.

We plodded home. After supper, everyone huddled around the propane heater in the middle of the room to watch an Egyptian film on television. I washed, dressed in pajamas, and snuggled under a thick blanket in my corner, intent on exposing the conspiracies in Dan Brown's novel, *Angels & Demons*.

A deafening boom sent us to the window. My brothers ran outside to the darkness, yells filled the alley. They came back with the news that an explosion had taken out the power station and phone towers covering the entire central area of the camp, including our sector.

News on the streets spread that lightning was the culprit. But there was no big storm, and the gathered clouds had cleared that night. I was sure something else was afoot. Yasser's reaction to the event, standing outside on high alert, told me it was most likely a deliberate act—someone engaged in sabotage to weaken Abu Nidal's iron grip on his turf.

Two days after the blast, a young man who worked in the store next to our body shop disappeared. Wael said his family looked everywhere for him. Another went missing the following day. By the end of the week, four men in our sector vanished without a trace.

Everyone behaved as though a bomb was about to drop from the skies, taking extra measures to stay in good standing with Abu Nidal and his men. Our neighbors singled out Yasser, as if he were an iron dome guarding the area. Men greeted my brother with extra cordiality, raising their joyful voices whenever they passed him on the stairs, some even slightly bowed their heads when they came across him in the alley. I saw and heard these exaggerated gestures from my window. Those actions reflected fear, not respect. The way they shuffled and skipped out of his path showed dread. People held their breaths in anticipation of Abu Nidal's next move.

Scrumptious dishes appeared at our doorstep most days; meat stews with green beans or peas, lamb kababs over rice, chicken and potato casseroles, and other dishes my family could not readily afford in such abundance.

Mother refused to bring in a heaping plate of *Sayadiah* on the first day these offerings materialized, adamant not to accept charity under any circumstances. Over my loud objections, she relented.

"*Haram* to leave food on the floor like that," she said to justify the quick reversal.

I wanted to remind her that we ate all our meals on the floor every day, and she never considered that a sin before, but I restrained myself. To my utter chagrin, she shoved the aromatic fish-over-rice dish in the refrigerator and forbade my brother's and I from consuming it.

That evening, Yasser came home almost crumbling from exhaustion, his shirt stained with sweat under his armpits, the ends of his shirt dangled out of his jeans. When he removed his shoes, his socks smelled extra foul. We had not seen him in two days.

Mother ordered Yasser to bathe before dinner, heated the fish dish, and placed it on the floor before us. “One should never reject God’s bounty,” she declared with a scowl.

From then on, she accepted the rich offerings at our door as part of an undeclared agreement with the neighbors. Yasser provided protection. In return, they showed appreciation and extended payments for his services with whatever they could contribute. I didn’t know if any handed him money, but I wouldn’t rule it out.

The missing men all returned on the same day, but no one dared talk about it.

“He just showed up at the store,” Wael said about his work neighbor. “Looking like a ghost, refusing to say where he was.”

“*Khalass*!” Yasser silenced Wael with the single word that halted any discussion or action and left no room for further comments or objections. Wael shut up at once. Nabil raised both eyebrows. Mother took Fayzeh to visit her friend, Um Faheem. I shook head-to-toe for a very long time.

With limited supplies and access to what was needed, power repairs took forever. Twenty-two days of blackout were an eternity for the sick who depended on lifesaving home equipment and for bread earners whose livelihoods had to be put on hold. Abu Nidal performed his magic and a small number of diesel generators appeared. Electricity slowly returned to pockets in our sector as people who could afford generators extended cables to their neighbors who lacked the funds. Yasser secured an impressive generator for our quarter.

The day the generator kicked in, my mother went door-to-door. I thought she was checking on neighbors, but when she returned with an extremely satisfied look on her face, I had to ask.

"What did you do?"

"I told everyone to stop sending food. *Khalass*!" She swiped her palms together. "Yasser did his job. I've always been able to feed my family."

Amidst the disarray and hubbub, work on recovering our internet service had to wait. I was stuck, hesitant to seek internet access in other areas of the camp and incur Abu Nidal's wrath. I worried my group of young readers would think I had abandoned them and dispatched Ghazi to assure the children—and specifically Jannat—that I would soon return. I sent works by other poets, some more contemporary, and stressed to my little spy that he should continue collecting information about Khaled.

Ghazi had matured tenfold in the past months. For boys like him, the amount of exposures to cruelty measured age, not the passing of months and years. He no longer belittled my walk or the way I talked, he offered respect. I accepted his courtesy and gave him the appreciation he deserved by naming him my Lieutenant.

He returned with a letter from Jannat tucked between the two loaned books. With the sheet of paper folded in half, I could see it contained more than just one line. I slipped into the bathroom and almost ripped it open. Jannat had written three verses this time:

O soft, gentle breeze, do carry my heartfelt greetings,
To the one who can bring life and hope to my soul

Even by wafting a greeting from far away
Will life ever bring us together again?
How I would love to be with you,
Even for a brief moment
Royal blood courses in your veins; so unique
As if God created you of musk,
And the rest of mankind, of mud.

I immediately recognized ibn Zaydun's Ode of Lamentable Separation. Of both poets, I had not anticipated Jannat choosing from the male's collection. My pupil couldn't have switched gender roles. Ibn Zaydun spoke to Wallada in this poem; a man addressing a woman, not the other way around. If she meant to direct her missive to me, she would have used the female's perspective and words. Besides, the creation parallel here missed the mark, it was entirely reversed in my case. No, I could not possibly be the one intended in her message, nor the previous one.

At best, Jannat was imprinting on the teacher who had opened for her a new world through literature. I had once been at the intellectual point where she recently landed. My mind and soul experienced a similar metamorphosis. I recognized, understood, and admired her startling transformation.

I folded Jannat's missive and looked outside my window across the alley. Colorful pieces of clothing hung to dry on wires outside Ameena's shuttered window. How I wished she would open the panes and wave me over. Alone in my eternal spot, I basked in Jannat's verse choices and their possible implications, yet a compelling urge to talk to my Ameena literally shook me. Taking several steadying breaths, I closed my eyes to summon her challenging face and silently spoke my mind:

My dear Ameena, you were wrong. Wallada did not whisper in my pupil's ear. If the poet had in yours, then pray tell me with which words. And where, in God's massive universe, do *I* stand with you?

Had that obnoxious Swede managed to wiggle his way into your heart and infest your mind? I suspect the doctor, with his poor grasp on the Arabic language, couldn't read, let alone appreciate or share a single poetic expression! So, what if you admire his commitment to the Palestinian cause? Love requires—no, demands—more than admiration. Trust me. I know. True love demands perseverance and unwavering dedication. I willfully continue to endure your celestial existence in my sphere, your lack of clarity, your current absence, your steadfast friendship, and also your sympathy. I even brave the wisp of hope and lustrous veils of optimism you keep breathing into my life.

My sweet Ameena, you will soon learn that Younis couldn't be the upright, sturdy tree with deep roots you wish him to be, but nothing more than a leaf, twirling around a resplendent sunflower. He cannot withstand the violent winds of our existence and will be blown far, far away.

CHAPTER TWENTY-FIVE

My thoughts swung like a pendulum between Ameena and Jannat for days on end. The explosion completely severed my connection to Ameena and I sulked in misery. Burying my anguish in books did nothing but intensify my need to see her face, hear her voice. My longing for Ameena's cleansing timbre differed from my desire to enjoy Jannat's quaint murmur. The two compulsions existed on different levels—a hanker for Jannat's voice bore skin deep, while a desperate hunger for Ameena's scoured me to the bone.

I transformed into an able, refined person when I spoke with Ameena and became a vibrant, sensual man in Jannat's presence. I wasn't conflicted. I existed in both forms, a fact brought to light by Jannat's introduction into my life. Could Ameena recognize that virile side of me? Could she accept it?

Lust. A word I never thought I would use in the same sentence while thinking about Ameena.

Damn you, Jannat. Again. For sharpening the pangs of this earthly vivification. I was no different from the rest of mankind. Mud constituted my essence, but perhaps my patch was extra pliable and mushy.

In a generous and considerate move, Yasser offered me his phone to send Ameena a text message explaining the power and internet problems.

"I know," she wrote back. "Everyone okay, right?"

"Yes."

She responded with a brown thumbs'-up emoji. That was it. Her lone pictograph drove me crazy yet silenced me and made me wish I hadn't put Yasser through the expense. She must have known about the power outage and other details from her father. Did she even miss our talks? Miss me?

During the blackout, Turtleneck stayed away from the camp. I couldn't ask him about Ameena. I never brought up her name whenever he visited. But desperation was a menacing force. I was willing to trample my pride and enquire about her the next time he graced us with his insufferable presence.

I never had the chance. The Swede left the country without stopping at our house. I was disappointed to miss the opportunity to bask in his admission of failure. He couldn't secure a plausible path for my resettlement in Sweden as he had promised to win Ameena's favor. I rejoiced in the notion that his preordained defeat meant that she would no longer be bound to him. The same circumstances which kept me captive in the refugee camp had conspired to free my Ameena of Doctor Turtleneck. How I wished I could witness the means she would use to destroy the man!

I followed the erratic efforts to reestablish internet connections after power was finally fully restored. The disconnect lingered longer than expected and people started to complain but no one dared move about without Abu Nidal's permission. The kingpin had different priorities to address. Security and restoring order took precedent. I think he intentionally kept our area without coverage so he could control communications and uncover those who colluded with his rivals.

Our news sources about the outside world came through newspapers and television again. As if our situation weren't dreadful enough, reports that Lebanese police in Beirut had captured an organ-trafficking ring hit our streets. The atrocious crime became the talk of the town, so to speak, and kept people from complaining about their internet for a while.

Nabil barged into *Ustath* Ihsan's bookshop one day and dragged me out, saying he had important news to discuss. We went to a café, which everyone dubbed "Internet Café" because five desk-top computers drew a loyal following. Without live internet, the snug place now served as a simple tearoom. Floral sheets covered monitors on Formica tables.

"It's her brother!" Nabil exclaimed soon as we sat down. "Abdullah Squared is *Madame*'s brother. Some legal trouble keeps him away from her house. That's why his sister goes to see him in that apartment. She wears a disguise to shield her husband from possible implications." Nabil smacked my knee. "I told you there is a simple and innocent explanation."

I rubbed my knee. That was simple? And what was innocent about Fayzeh working for a wanted man?

"What legal trouble?" I asked.

"No one admits to knowing." Nabil wiggled his eyebrows. "He might very well be another smuggler."

"Weapons? Drugs?"

"Something that has to do with hospitals."

"Medications? Equipment?" I typed fast, running out of patience.

Nabil shook his head. "I don't know. No one dared say anything else about him."

I scratched my head. Such incomplete intelligence. My brother could stand to learn a thing or two from Ghazi. I drummed my knuckles on the table. The monstrous ring snatching people and stealing their body parts lit up every neuron in my brain. I could not think of any act more sinister than that. I swallowed to shake the horrible notion off. The appalling ring was reported to operate in the heart of Beirut, never a mention of the *Jdeideh* neighborhood. Not a single news outlet pointed in that direction. Not wanting to disturb my brother further, I kept my abominable suspicions under wraps. After all, Fayzeh had been at her job for months and she was still intact.

"You know how these things go," Nabil said. "Sooner or later, Izzat will make enquiries through back channels, then bribe someone. Whatever charges against his brother-in-law will disappear."

"Your sources?"

"The mechanic who works on Izzat's Mercedes." Nabil patted his chest. "He's a fan of heavyweight wrestling. Mad Dog O'Malley and The Iron Sheik are his idols."

I arched an eyebrow.

"Ring-names," Nabil chuckled. "Anyway, we hit it off. I told the mechanic I can secure parts he needs under market value, and he can pocket the difference. Thank God for Yasser's link to Abu Nidal's network. Abdullah Squared used to take his BMW to this shop. My new pal hates the man's guts. Never paid him enough."

"Thank God for stingy men."

"For sure!" Laughing, Nabil smacked my knee again. "Now that we know what's going on, it's time to talk to Fayzeh."

"I've been monitoring her drawer. She hasn't added anything since the cufflinks."

"Good. Good. She must have returned them to *Madame* and this adventure is over."

"Or she noticed our surveillance and is using another hiding place."

"Why are you so skeptical? Why can't you accept that she might only be helping her employer?"

I offered no answer, just sighed. My sister was out of her depth, floundering in treacherous waters.

CHAPTER TWENTY-SIX

I awoke to horrible wheezing in the middle of the night. The hacking noise came from my left, where Mother slept. The streetlight outside my window fell short of reaching that far into the room and cloaked her in shadows. I crawled over, traced the back of her hand and arm. Her wheezing became quieter. She labored to breathe.

"Yassseeerrr!" I bellowed to wake up my brothers. It took me several seconds to jostle to my feet.

"Shut up," Wael moaned. "He's not home."

Nabil lifted on his elbows. "What's wrong?"

I reached the light switch. Mother's face was so swollen, I could hardly recognize her, puffed up eyes indistinguishable, lips purple. She clutched her thick throat with a swollen hand. I threw off her covers. Her legs extended straight, blotched red and doubled in size.

"Hosss . . . ppittt . . . alll!" I screamed.

Wael jumped into action and carried her downstairs, Nabil bolted after him. I grabbed my cane and stumbled outside as fast as I could manage. Wael ran down the alley with Mother in his arms, screaming, "Help! We need a car!"

Several neighbors spilled out. No one owned a car. Yasser was the only person who had access to one. I banged my cane on Abu Nidal's front door. No one answered. I turned to find Ameena's mother talking to Nabil down the alley with a phone to her ear.

"He's not home!" Nabil shouted.

I hobbled after my brothers, cursing every foul word my mind retained.

A young man revved his motorcycle and motioned for Wael to sit behind him. They wedged Mother on Wael's lap and took off in the direction of the UNRWA clinic, the closest medical facility. Nabil darted after the motorbike, leaving me behind. Two men held me by the arms and sprinted after him. We made it to the clinic ten excruciating minutes later.

An orderly led me into a room where Mother lay on a table motionless. A plastic tube protruded from her throat. Cradling her face, Nabil touched his forehead to hers. Wael hugged her waist and rested his cheek against her bosom. The fluorescent light in the ceiling hummed as loud as their weeping.

I strained to hear my mother's breathing rhythm, focused on her chest under Wael's big head to detect movement.

"Mmooo . . . vve!" I shoved Wael off, then Nabil to give her room.

"Nooo!" Wael wailed and clung tighter. Nabil straightened but didn't budge. He stood still, smoothing back Mother's gray-streaked hair.

Someone patted my shoulder. "All signs point to anaphylaxis," the man in a white coat spoke with a soft voice. "A severe allergic reaction."

I pointed a quivering finger at the tube in her throat. Why was it not attached to a breathing machine or an oxygen tank?

"We did everything we could to open her airways."

I shuffled closer, touched my mother's cheek with the back of my hand. Lukewarm. Damp.

"From the condition of her skin and color," the doctor said behind me. "The way it escalated, I can confidently guess the allergen was topical."

Wael lifted his head. "What are you saying?"

"She touched a poisonous substance. Not in food or drink. It went directly through the skin. Probably accumulated over a short period for the critical amount."

I moved a hand to her cold, bloated feet, heels smooth and waxy. "Ccrr . . . Ccr ..." I swallowed then tried again, "Ccrreeemm?"

"Most likely. Yes, it could be a cream. Powerful antioxidants in cheap ointments expire and turn poisonous to some people."

Mother blurred in and out before my eyes. Slow at first, then faster her body pulsed. I gripped the edge of the cold table.

"I don't understand," Nabil's guttural voice jolted me.

"I can't tell for sure." The doctor dropped his voice lower, slowing his words. "Without an autopsy."

My legs gave out. I dropped to my knees.

"Take your time with her." The doctor withdrew to the door. "*Al-baqa' lillah.*"

Spasms threw me to the cold floor. My brothers and other hands tried to contain me as I convulsed and twisted. I don't recall what everyone said or did. All I remember was the doctor's condolences ringing in my ears; *only God remains.*

What about me?

I was the one left behind untamed with rampant, putrefying wrath.

CHAPTER TWENTY-SEVEN

April painted everything with yellow hues. Pollen adrift in the air tinged my sisters' black dresses and white scarves. I focused on that image to remain steady during the burial and three days of mourning that followed.

An imam orated chapters from the Qur'an in a melodious, orotund voice as people flooded the tent set up at the end of our alley, the same tent which held Maryam's wedding ceremony.

The butcher, Abu Ali, and his wife delivered trays of rice cooked with lamb every day to feed the crowds. I knew Mother was on good terms with her neighbors but was surprised to see so many people show up. The horrendous circumstances of her death created waves of gossip and opened many eyes to the dangers of the expired products in circulation.

Abu Nidal paid all expenses. Everyone proclaimed he showed tremendous compassion and unprecedented generosity. I believe he wanted to atone for his inability to prevent poisonous goods from trickling into the areas he controlled.

I couldn't look at wailing Um Faheem, nor accept her sorrow. She should be among the dead. If it weren't for her *fantastic* cream, Mother would still be alive. For the sake of my sisters, I held my suspicions, swallowed bitter resentment, and carried on. Shaking hands, accepting hugs, eating bland lamb, sleeping and waking to Fayzeh's sobs, Nabil's silent tears, Wael's heavy sighs, and Yasser slamming doors. Maryam took refuge with her husband and son.

I drank pots of thick coffee, stayed awake nights, then collapsed into mid-day stupors. I limped onward yet failed to dislodge from my misery. The one person I needed by my side wasn't there.

Ameena called Yasser's phone the morning we placed my mother in the ground.

"She's scheduled to arrive at the end of the month," Yasser quipped as he handed me the phone.

"Waseem . . . Waseem . . . Waseem," Ameena kept repeating my name, her voice catching in her throat. Several heartbeats of silence followed—mine, hers . . . no difference.

"*Abooh*," she then whispered into the phone, said nothing else. She didn't need to. The simple utterance transported her across vast lands and seas, planted her next to me, and pressed her healing hands to my bleeding heart.

The fourth day after the funeral, we dismantled the tent and stayed home. Maryam draped a bed sheet over the television, as if shrouding it would somehow award respect to Mother's spirit. Recordings of Qur'an recitations played from my brothers' phones well into the night. I wrapped Mother's Palestinian tile in one of her colorful scarves, tucked it inside a pillowcase, and placed it next to my father's bundle in my drawer. The glued tile was mine. None of my siblings objected to my ownership. Their bewilderment at why I thought the broken square was so valuable showed in their drawn faces. I couldn't put into words the avalanche of feelings I suffered whenever I glanced at that piece of history. I no longer distinguished its designs, cracks, or colors. My mother's wistful, sad eyes dominated my view.

Once I had begun to think clearly, I gave the tube of poison to Ghazi to track where and how it came into our neighbor's possession. He learned that a beautician sold the lotion to Um Faheem. The woman operated a makeshift salon in her home and regularly stocked it with supplies from the southern region of the camp. Having no qualms whatsoever, I passed the news to Yasser. Knowing my brother would deliver the information to his mentor, I waited for Abu Nidal's harsh, puissant whip to crack and maim.

For days, Yasser rarely spoke and bottled up his fury at ignorant beauticians, greedy smugglers, and Abu Nidal's delayed retaliation. Above all, I knew Yasser was angry at himself for not being there when Mother needed him. Outrage radiated from his eyes the instant he woke up, and the rustling and turning at night indicated he hardly slept at all.

Wael spent most of his time outside work at Wardah's place. I envied his sanctuary.

My sisters quietly divided Mother's meager belongings among them—a Citizen watch, her wedding band, a dainty necklace, and the pair of windmill earrings I had brought from Holland. Maryam donated some of Mother's clothes to needy widows. My brothers pooled money to spend on orphans, inviting prayers for mercy on her soul. I asked *Ustath* Ihsan to take most of my books to an UNRWA school, dispatched a few to Jannat as well. I owned nothing else to appropriate on my mother's behalf.

I went through the customary motions of charity out of social compliance, not conviction. Mother didn't need our help to send her to a better place. Her spirit settled in a heaven of her choice the instant she left our world.

If heaven is not a concept, if it is materialized by a physical place, then I imagine Mother's celestial body is now enjoying oranges in *Yaffa*. Her entire life, she yearned to escape the camp and return home to Palestine. The simple desire for a taste kept her going for fifty-four years in a world devoid of hope, strangled by deprivation. *Yaffa* oranges were not her favorite fruit by choice, they were her elixir of life.

~

Ghazi knocked on the door in the early morning, face drawn, his typically unruly hair combed back and sleek with oil. I smelled the hint of olives.

"*Al-baqa' lillah*," he mumbled condolences.

I forced a tight smile. The boy made an effort to look presentable for this solemn occasion, he showed even greater maturity than I gave him credit for.

He handed me a double folded piece of paper. "From Sister Jannat."

I dropped the smile. He must have been frequenting the mosque. Referring to Jannat as a sister supposedly reflected respect. Religious men used the term with non-relative females. Everyone became related in their eyes, as if such a bond would regulate behavior among strangers and instill a measure of kindness.

Jannat, my sister! I couldn't swallow the notion. An image of her wearing a nun's habit flashed in my head. I shuddered. Not that kind of sister, either. I grabbed the paper and shook the messenger's hand.

I held on to the letter and waited until everyone went to work, but Wael wouldn't leave. He sat with his head bowed, listening to the consolatory voice of *Shaiekh* Abdulbaset reciting from the Qur'an. I identified the reciter's mesmerizing voice as my brothers favored his outstanding intonation over that of other renowned *sheikhs*. Since Mother's funeral, Wael had broadcasted recitations of the entire Qur'an by Abdulbaset from his phone.

I cleared my throat to get his attention. He hugged his knees and gently rocked back and forth, ignoring me. Never had I seen my somewhat aloof brother in this vulnerable state. I tucked Jannat's letter under my cushion and forced myself to be patient. Wael seemed in need of solace. Short of crawling over to give him a warm hug, I had no clue what else to do other than grant him peace and quiet. I leaned my back against the wall and listened with him.

Abdulbaset started to recite *Ar-Rahman* sura. Though I never learned in childhood any parts of the Qur'an by heart, as most boys and girls did, I recognized the repetitive, questioning verses in The All-Merciful chapter: "*Which, then, of your Lord's blessings do you both deny?*"

I counted. The refrain repeated thirty-one times in the seventy-eight verse sura. And after each time we heard it, Wael would sigh the same answer, "Not any of them."

I watched him closely, moist eyes staring ahead, low voice laced with a mild quiver, rocking movement escalating in speed. He truly believed his outspoken admittance.

Faith, I wish I could commandeer a speck of his. My soul would gain some respite from the violent storm raging inside. After our mother's tragic death, my brother would not deny her atrocious death as a blessing bestowed.

I continued to listen. The last verses in the sura detailed the delights that await the pious in paradise. Guilt compounded my fury. Here I sat, simmering in indignation because I couldn't accept my brother's positive attitude, while the All Merciful informed me, through Abdulbaset's entrancing voice, of the pleasures Mother would enjoy in paradise. No mention of *Yaffa* oranges, but so much more. I earnestly labored to believe the Godly promise.

Wael finally abandoned the room, leaving an enormous, unfamiliar gap in my chest. Like the zucchini Mother cored before stuffing them with meat and rice, witnessing Wael's acceptance of her departure left me hollowed, confused, and feeling more alone than ever.

I opened Jannat's letter in the hopes of ushering pleasant sensations. My dear pupil did not disappoint. Her selection came from the work of a more recent poet, Elia Abu Madi. I had sent her the Lebanese-American's collection to broaden her experience and steer her poetic journey toward modern times. She couldn't have picked a more uplifting stanza:

> *Love, and by dawn the whole cosmos will fill your dwelling, hate, and by evening the whole universe will become a dark prison.*
>
> *If only the desert could love, each grain of sand would blossom, and every mirage would be a pool of water.*
>
> *A cup without wine is nothing but glass, and man without love is nothing but skin and bones.*

I dropped my eyelids and with them, the words descended to fill that chasm in my chest. I had never thought of myself more than pale skin and gnarled bones. But I had considered myself a *man with love* since forever. Having devoured myriads of books and more literary content than I could count, it took Jannat's timely, perceptive quotes to make me evaluate my passion and examine the nature of love that swelled in my heart.

CHAPTER TWENTY-EIGHT

Fayzeh took three weeks off to manage the household, but within a couple of days I wished she would go back to work. Her boorish demeanor provided a startling contrast to Maryam's benevolent attitude. Fayzeh stomped around as if she were the queen of a castle, snapping fingers and orders while complaining about everything we did, or rather failed to do. Then at the end of the day, like clockwork, her royal highness would break down and cry herself to sleep. Her selfish nature led me to believe that on top of mourning a mother, pangs of dejection tugged at the strings of her heart. Khaled was a no-show. The man she fancied never came to offer condolences.

My brothers tip-toed around her, but impatient mutterings and rolled eyes betrayed their exasperation. Her barbed tongue grated on Yasser's nerves, in particular. He would stare daggers at the queen when she wasn't aware, as if searching for reasons to explain this arrogant behavior.

It seemed to me my sister had forgotten how to live with us. Having spent considerable time in *Madame*'s circle, she no longer tolerated the realities of our life in the camp—eking out a dreary existence on a daily basis suddenly affronted her senses. She complained of foul smells drifting from our alley and often demanded I close windows before the donkey-drawn vegetable cart arrived. Her majesty would pinch her nose each time one of us used the bathroom since we left a mess and failed to make our waste smell like jasmine. She scoffed at me, showing utter disgust toward the short plastic chair with a hole in its seat, which I placed over our squat latrine whenever I needed to go, as if it hadn't been there all her life.

Laundry was an awful all-day affair. Scarce water, dripping faucets, and low pressure prevented her from operating the washing machine she had bought months ago, which Mother never used and turned into storage space. Forced to boil whites, soak and scrub my brother's oil-smudged work clothes, my sister's whining rose a notch with each piece she wrung and hung to dry. Her eminence ridiculed Maryam for using cloth diapers, dismissing the fact that disposable ones were an expensive luxury for a young family trying to save for their child's education.

Fayzeh's list of grievances went on and on, as if she had forgotten what it was like before she answered nature's calling on sitting toilets in *Madame*'s fancy house. Or how she used to help Mother hand-wash clothes as fast as possible on the days water reached our rusty pipes uninterrupted. Or that at especially difficult times, our main meal depended on whether the faithful donkey trudged down our alley. To top it all off, Fayzeh injected some English and French words in her speech to show off her newfound refinement. Whenever she mentioned Khaled, she would use "Chef" for his occupational pursuits instead of *Tabbakh*, only she mispronounced the word as *Sheif*. It drove me crazy not to be able to properly enunciate the word and correct her mistake. My brothers adopted her mangled title for the chef-in-training. I endured the assault of *Sheif Khaled* on my hearing faculties each time his name came up by gritting my teeth.

My pondering didn't last. Ghazi whistled his familiar signal on an early morning thick with fog. I trudged my way to our meeting spot behind the barber shop.

"Not easy to chase, you know. They are clever but not as smart as I am." Ghazi snapped his fingers. "I tracked all the pieces down on the list you gave me."

I clapped several times to show confidence in his abilities and resourcefulness. Though the boy had experienced a growth spurt that brought him closer to my eye level, I wanted to make sure he heard my clear appreciation of his fine detective work in case he couldn't see the expression on my face in the midst of swirling fog.

Ghazi handed me a piece of paper. "Who bought each item and for how much."

My damp, anxious fingers left smudges on the paper. The boy-man had delivered the most disturbing intelligence blurb about my sister that I didn't know how to process. The list of names and numbers confirmed that Fayzeh and her beloved Khaled had sold the items in her stash.

"And there's this too." Ghazi produced a letter from Jannat.

I pocketed the missive and shook his hand to dismiss him. Pushing Fayzeh's woes to the back of my mind, I focused on Jannat's note as I headed home but had to postpone reading it until I slipped under the covers at night. To escape my brother's gut-wrenching sighs, restless rustles, and Fayzeh's sobbing, I opened the letter and squinted against the semi-lit space by my window. This time, Jannat had used red ink:

When night falls, anticipate me visiting you,
For I believe night is the best keeper of secrets.
I feel a love for you that if the sun had it,

It would not shine, nor the moon rise,
nor the stars begin their nightly journey.

Wallada! This was part of Wallada's famous, public confession to ibn Zaydun. I sent a mental salute to Ameena's literary prowess. Jannat connected with Wallada at last.

Smudges at the top and bottom of the page diverted my attention. I tilted the sheet of paper further toward the streetlight. Faint pencil marks spelled my name at the top.

This letter was specifically addressed to me! My name etched right there on the very first line followed by a comma, and Jannat had signed it at the end. Never before in her letters had she done either.

What was that small blob under her name? I lifted the paper to examine it as a radiologist would an X-ray image. It looked like the faint trace of a little heart left behind after an attempt to erase it.

A bolt of enlightenment drenched me with cold sweat. This was no sympathy letter, nor an expression of simple infatuation, not even a customary student's admiration of her tutor. This was a declaration of a person suffering from the fever of . . . dare I say it?

Love!

Wait, wait a second. *I* was the enraptured soul who deemed Ameena a descendant of royal blood as ibn Zaydun declared of his love interest. *I* set Ameena apart from all other mundane females, saw her as a goddess and craved her company even for a brief moment. *I* held a torch in my heart for her which dwarfed an entire galaxy akin to Wallada's eloquent statement. *I* was the one crazy in love with Ameena.

And Jannat felt love for me? When did this happen? How? And if true, was her revelation supposed to cheer me up at this darkest time in my life? Could she not see who I am? What was wrong with this woman?

What was wrong with me?

CHAPTER TWENTY-NINE

The following evening, only Yasser and I were home to suffer Fayzeh's theatrics. Her incessant sniveling and huffing drove me to the edge of insanity. I could take her nasal cadence and brusque manner no longer.

"Shushsh!" I snapped.

"You shut up!" she bellowed. "My sweet mother died and abandoned me!"

Yasser lowered his phone for a moment. "She was our mother, too."

"As if he cares," Fayzeh snarled, pointing at me. "He hasn't shed a single tear."

Her words stung like a hornet, but that was when I took notice of how others would come to view my reaction. Keeping on top of cascading events had forced me to suppress my emotions, lock them in a vault so I could plow forward. She was right. I hadn't cried. Not even once.

"Stop this nonsense," Yasser growled and returned to texting.

Fayzeh's shoe sailed over my shoulder. "He's heartless!"

Yasser dropped his phone and stretched to his full height. "I said stop this nonsense, right now."

Stunned by my sister's blindside attack, I wished Wael or Nabil were there. The way Yasser advanced toward her was alarming. I had never seen him take that menacing stance against any of us.

Fayzeh stood before him, shifted back her shoulders, and lifted her chin in defiance. She opened her mouth again.

"Shushsh," I muttered to silence her. If she had an ounce of intelligence, she would remain quiet to deflect Yasser's ire. To my dismay, she looked at me, eyes narrowed to slits.

"Your protector is gone, Waseem. She's dead!" Fayzeh turned to face Yasser. "I will never wash this animal's feet again."

"*Khalass*!" Yasser barked before his slap dropped our sister to a heap on the floor.

He raised his hand once more.

I threw myself on top of Fayzeh and absorbed the second blow but failed to muffle her screams. Nabil barged into the house. He grabbed Yasser and manhandled him outside. Fayzeh shoved me away. She ran into the bathroom. Before the door closed, she hissed, "Soon I'll be rid of you. All of you. Just wait and see."

Nabil called Wael, brought him up to speed on what had transpired, and urged him to keep Yasser away from home for the rest of the night. I took Nabil to the roof and left our sister alone to nurse her wounded pride.

"What's wrong with Yasser?" Nabil helped me sit on a concrete block anchoring an aluminum sheet. "He's never been violent with us. And to lash-out at poor Fayzeh? I don't understand what's happening to our family."

The screen on my tablet glowed extra bright under the starless skies as I typed, "He blames himself."

"For what?"

"Mother's death."

"For that expired cream?" Nabil crouched before me. "Uh-uh, Yasser's too smart to bear that burden. He knows his boss can't completely block goods leaking into his territory from other parts of the camp. Not everyone is loyal to Abu Nidal. Hawks of Freedom are spreading their wings for more area control. Wait," Nabil clutched my knee. "Do *you* blame Yasser?"

"Nnooo." I firmly shook my head. I wanted to say I blamed Um Faheem for being generous with her lotion but decided to shift the focus of our conversation. "Yasser knows something terrible about Fayzeh."

A creature scurried behind Nabil, most likely a rat. My brother sprang up and clapped his hands to scare the rodent away. "What's the problem now?"

"Don't you find it strange Abu Nidal hasn't done anything in retaliation for the explosion?"

"*Aah*," Nabil nodded. "What does that have to do with our sister?"

"She's involved. Yasser is in a tough spot with his boss. He's covering for her."

"No, no, no. Now you're making wild claims. Way too paranoid." Lifting one foot onto an adjacent block, Nabil rested an elbow on his raised knee. "Tell me, how could she be involved?"

"Khaled. I've learned things."

A child bawled from a distance, a baby followed with heart-wrenching cries, then another joined the chorus.

"Come out with it, Waseem. Don't drip like the bathroom broken faucet."

"The Hawks of Freedom tried to recruit him. That's why he left for Beirut. To escape their clutches."

"I see."

"I think they used his parents as leverage, pressured him to conspire against Abu Nidal. And Fayzeh could be tainted as his accomplice."

"I think you've read too many spy novels."

"I don't believe Khaled delivered all that was asked of him."

"He's smart enough, I admit."

"The Hawks must have used someone else to orchestrate the blackout. Someone knowledgeable enough of the system."

"That's reasonable. I'm not agreeing with your crazy theory, but for the sake of argument, Fayzeh wouldn't have been able to convey detailed information to make the explosion as effective as it was." Nabil leaned close. "Waseem, if you discovered efforts to recruit Khaled, then Yasser must know, too. Our sister might be in grave danger."

"Exactly."

"Abu Nidal is going to discover everything and target Fayzeh?"

"Just by her association with a perceived traitor."

"Abu Nidal will strike back with a vengeance. And soon. Yasser is trying to shield Fayzeh before the doors of hell burst open. I still don't understand why he tried to beat her."

"His nerves are shattered."

Nabil stomped down his foot. "Not an excuse, brother!"

"Just an explanation."

The crying children went quiet at once, as if they were in the same house and their mother was able to comfort them.

"And what about you?" Nabil cupped my shoulder. "Why did she turn on you?"

I lifted my gaze to the flashing lights of a passing plane. I couldn't possibly tell my sensitive brother that our sister accused me of being indifferent to Mother's death. He would resent her for it. My world had collapsed when Mother passed. Fayzeh expected—wanted—me to fall apart, but as the bard T.S. Eliot write in *The Hollow Men*: *This is the way the world ends, not with a bang, but a whimper.*

I sighed and quickly typed, "She always hated washing my feet."

Nabil blew a long breath. "She never understood."

"Wwhaatt?" I asked.

"Mother knew the sort of person her daughter became. Fayzeh always resented your . . . presence. Ever since she was little. I'm sure you remember her many thoughtless acts?"

"Not much," I lied. Growing up, Fayzeh was worse than mean. Barring her forced foot massages, she had mostly skirted around me to ignore and avoid touching me.

Nabil tilted his head sideways. "Harsh words? Called you vile names?"

I shrugged. Nothing I hadn't heard on the streets. She was a woman now. Childhood transgressions belonged in the past.

The rat and his family pitter-pattered across tin sheets behind Nabil. My brother didn't flinch.

"Mother shielded you as much as she could," he said. "She hoped forcing Fayzeh to wash your feet would humble and soften her, temper her haughty attitude. Remember when we were children, how every morning Mother would give us a hug at the door before we left for school or work?"

I swallowed to dislodge the lump in my throat. I could admit that I always yearned for the simple ritual to include me, but what good would it do to bring it up?

I nodded.

"Mother would whisper in our ear that even though we all came from her womb, God chose your broken body to house her soul. It took me a long time to understand what she meant." Nabil kneeled before me. "Know what The Messenger said about where heaven lies?"

I stared at him, working hard to follow his logic. People were fond of repeating the specific words about heaven attributed to prophet Mohammad and inscribing them in art. Girls embroidered them onto pillows and hanging tapestry. Boys spray-painted or brushed the phrase on walls, doodled it on big rocks, engraved it on tree trunks. Every which way one turned in the camp; the saying would pop-up to keep hope alive and help nurture children into principled adults.

I took my time to type, "Heaven lies beneath the feet of mothers."

Nabil circled my ankles. "And yours, my good brother. And yours."

CHAPTER THIRTY

The next day, Fayzeh went to work, Yasser disappeared, and the internet came alive. I wanted to go to the nargileh lounge to video call Ameena but found a way to resist the impulse. Abu Nidal would strike within days, if not hours. The small window to do anything productive was closing fast.

I stuffed most of Fayzeh's belongings in my suitcase and asked Nabil to take me to *Madame*'s house. We huddled in the back of a beaten taxi with the valise wedged between us. Pop songs shrieked from the radio, which was in dire need of new speakers. I tolerated the auditory assault of static and crackle, as it provided good cover for our conversation. Darting and swiveling through heavy traffic, the driver jerked the car and made sudden stops then bolted as if the wheels caught fire. It was difficult to type with the tablet dangling on my chest. I unhooked its straps to secure a good grip.

Nabil slid closer. "What's your plan?"

I had stayed up all night contemplating and searching for solutions to Fayzeh's predicament. A crude plot had emerged at the crack of dawn. There was no time to perfect it.

"Disclose, threaten, and demand."

"*Ya Allah*! Extortion?" Nabil said under his breath. "Forget it. Don't tell me."

"Did you bring money?"

Nabil sighed. "Every lira I have. I was saving for Wael's wedding, you know." He shook his head. "Apparently our brother will have to wait."

"Exchange to Euros while I talk to *Madame*."

"Not dollars?"

"Must have Euros."

"Fine, fine." Nabil patted the suitcase. "You're thinking about hiding Fayzeh? For how long?"

"Not hide."

"What, then?"

"Now you want to know?"

"*Aah, aah*." He glanced at the driver. "Quickly before we arrive."

"Tell *Madame* what we know about her brother."

"Well, of course," Nabil muttered under his breath.

I shot him a warning stare, but his eyes were riveted on my tablet screen. I continued to type, "Threaten to alert authorities, neighbors, social media, anyone."

"This is bad. Very bad."

"Demand she helps Fayzeh out of Lebanon."

"What?" He snatched the tablet and re-read my words, then shoved it back. "Out of the country? Where? How?"

That part was still fuzzy, but I didn't want to present shortcomings to my anxious brother. I schemed as I wrote, "I'm hoping *Madame* is in good standing with her husband."

"Broad assumption."

I knew that, didn't need Nabil to tell me. I ignored him. "Husband trades furniture. Ships containers through the harbor. His reach is far."

Nabil rubbed his stubble-covered chin. "*Aah*, so?"

"Fayzeh can be stowed away on one of his ships heading for Cyprus or Italy. She'll apply for asylum or whatever."

"You serious?"

"At least she'll be safe. Lots of people have done it."

"You're going to . . . smuggle her out?"

"Khaled, too. I'm sure he doesn't want me to expose him to Abu Nidal. She will not travel alone."

"*Ya Allah*! *Ya Sattar*!" Nabil muttered, closed his eyes, and pinched the bridge of his nose. He continued to pray. "*Ya Hafeeth*! *Ya Lateef*! *Ya Mueen*!"

I listened to his calls for protection and help from the Almighty and considered repeating them. My half-baked plan was nothing close to being safe, nor guaranteed. It depended on *Madame*'s full cooperation and fear of exposure to her refined society. It didn't matter what sort of crime her brother was accused of; it would prove devastating if gossip revealed that a woman in her station harbored the criminal from the law. Such malicious slander would soil her reputation and cast dark shadows onto her big-shot husband's business dealings.

The plan also relied on how much *Madame* appreciated a faithful maid who helped cover for her, on Fayzeh's willingness to leave, and on Khaled's eagerness to flee. I curled my fingers into a fist. There were too many holes in my design and no time to fill them.

I glanced at Nabil. We would need more than prayers if Abdullah were one of the sinister gangsters trading in body parts, one who managed to elude capture with his sister's help. I could be delivering Fayzeh's head and healthy organs to a murderous thug on a silver platter. My entire body shuddered. I tucked my hands under my thighs to hold it together.

If I had concrete proof of Abdullah's association, I would expose the bastard in the blink of an eye. After I ensure Fayzeh's escape. A number of freight ships go through the harbor on a daily basis. I could tap merchants not associated with *Madame*'s husband, brother, or Abu Nidal to push my scheme onward. But with no large sums of money at my fingertips, I needed time to search for leverage and entice another shady merchant. I had not a minute to spare, no trustworthy emissaries outside the camp, and no credible method to confirm or unearth sensitive information. Nor could I further involve Nabil or Ghazi in any shape or form.

A truck overloaded with men perched atop large black sacks made a right turn ahead of us. Only a miracle could explain how the lopsided load failed to topple the vehicle over. Perhaps the time had come for me to believe in miracles.

My temples throbbed with the need to find other ways to ascertain Abdullah's illegal activities, to corroborate my suspicions with hard evidence. Once my sister was safe, I would anonymously leak discovered intelligence about him to the proper authorities or to Abu Nidal. As far as I knew, the kingpin smuggled merchandise into our camp to circumvent shortages of almost everything essential to ease people's lives. Ameena's father would never stand for the atrocities committed by the captured gang in Beirut. Or would he?

I shook my head, banishing any doubt from my racing mind. Abu Nidal would do the right thing. He formed ties with powerful entities in the city. Would he call in some favors if he learned about the escape of an alleged gang member?

There was a flip side to this embroilment. Abdullah could be smuggling vital medical equipment to underserved communities. Uncovering his clandestine work could cause devastating ramifications for medical care throughout the country, not just inside refugee camps.

A car horn blared from behind and snapped Nabil out of his chanting. "How are you going to convince Fayzeh to do this, huh?"

"Nnott . . . mmeee." I poked his chest. "Yyouu."

"What!!" He finally exploded.

"She won't listen to me. Only you."

"I very much doubt that."

"It's not hard. After what Yasser did, she'll want to leave. Start a new life with Khaled."

Nabil rolled down his window and stuck out his face. "I can't believe this. I just can't."

A red Fiat whizzed dangerously close by. He sat back. "And Khaled? Why are you so sure he would go along?"

"The things we found in Fayzeh's drawer?"

"*Aah*?"

"She kept them for him then sold them. He's the thief."

"You can't know that for sure."

"I can. I know where each item was sold, to whom, and for how much."

"You scare me sometimes, you know that?"

I shrugged.

"Look, you can't banish our sister, send her off on a dangerous path for simply helping her man steal things."

"Khaled wants to buy passage on a smuggler's small boat to Cyprus."

"*Ya Allah*!" Nabil massaged his temples. "Please don't tell me Fayzeh plans to . . . elope with him."

"It's possible. I'm offering a safer trip on a big ship. He won't refuse."

"Offering? You're blackmailing him. The man is screwed, stuck between a wall and a rock no matter what he does. Either we—well, you—hand him over to Abu Nidal for possible—and I say possible—involvement in the explosion, or he falls in the Hawks' nest. And we're not even sure he actually did anything. I've gotten to know him. *Sheif* Khaled is a good man."

I gritted my teeth; a Pavlovian response to hearing the distorted word. "Suspicions alone would be the end of him in this cutthroat syndicate. I'm doing him a favor. Fayzeh comes first."

"*Aah*, right," Nabil huffed. "How did you learn about the boat to Cyprus?"

"Sources."

We stopped at a traffic light and the taxi driver turned down the shrieking radio only to yell and honk at the driver of the car to our left. I stopped typing and decided to keep my answer vague so Nabil wouldn't offer more questions. Ghazi's involvement to bring forth this information was too valuable to expose, even to my trusted brother.

"I'll do it." Nabil turned sideways to face me, giving his back to the driver who kept ogling me in his rearview mirror. "I will accompany Fayzeh on her . . . journey."

"Nnoo!"

"Our sister needs us. We can't leave her under the mercy of Khaled, so far away from family. What if he mistreats her?"

"You just said he is a good man?!" I shook my head and continued to type, but Nabil stilled my hand, locked his gaze with mine.

"It's my chance to get out, too. Try a different life. The life I can't . . . dare to dream of here. Be . . . *me*."

The way he spoke, starting with a normal voice then dropping to a near whisper on the last sentence delivered a punishing blow to the pit of my stomach. I couldn't breathe, couldn't pretend misunderstanding, couldn't ignore his anguish. My gentle, intelligent brother craved to drop his macho shield. He looked me in the eye and abandoned his obnoxious talk about ultra-masculine wrestlers whenever a guarded moment such as this one arrived.

Should I give him the opportunity to express his deepest desires? Grant him the comfort of confession and clear acknowledgement? It was the least I could offer. My hand trembled as I hastened to write an encouraging response, but the taxi took off with a jerk causing the tablet to slip from my fingers and for Nabil to sit back. My insides twisted into a merciless knot as complicated as his difficult existence. I gave my brother's shoulder a gentle squeeze to show willingness to listen.

"Maybe I'll finally have a chance to attend an international wrestling match. Watch the action in person." Nabil forced a chuckle. I could tell because it sounded similar to the one he had forged during our bath time long ago, when he confessed his jealousy of women. He might as well have dumped a bucket of cold water over my head to accompany his fake laugh right here inside this taxi.

"Turn left," he instructed the driver. "Waseem, if *Madame* goes along with your twisted scheme, she could refuse to include me." Looking outside his open window, Nabil's voice returned to its normal pitch. "She doesn't know me."

"Yesss!" The single word confirmation was all I could produce. The perfect moment for our sensitive conversation passed. My brother put up his shield. Never before in my life had I so truly hated my inability to speak. I feared Nabil followed the advice of Mark Twain: *Never tell the truth to people who are not worthy of it.*

Nabil considered me unworthy of his revelations. Exactly how and when I failed to provide my dear brother with a haven for his truth, I could not recall and, no matter how much I wanted to, I could not think of a single idea on how to establish such a safe space.

The car cruised at a steady speed. I nudged Nabil with my elbow to turn his attention to my tablet. "I will find a way for you!"

His lips formed a sad smile, the kind that broke the heart. "I'll talk to *Madame*. It's easier and faster than you typing. I might be able to prevent her from throwing us to the dogs."

"I'll do it." I wiggled my eyebrows to inject some levity into our dejected, dreadful mood. "Women are usually reluctant to dismiss a handsome, crippled man."

"Man?" Nabil cocked an eyebrow. "Devil is more like it."

I refastened the straps to my tablet and swallowed the insult. Last night, my brother had elevated me to the station of a saint, and now he pitched me down to Satan's caste.

I gave Nabil a thumbs-up, identifying more with my current position, for what is a devil if not an opportunistic manipulator?

Madame turned out to be a reasonable, shrewd woman once I showed her the picture of Abdullah Squared entering and leaving the apartment. I didn't need to explain much after she studied my eyes and realized I wasn't bluffing. She summoned Fayzeh and Khaled into the spacious room with gilded furniture and presented them with an offer they couldn't refuse. In three days' time, a merchandise ship laden with shipping containers would sail to Cyprus.

I knew the stealth move was possible but was nonetheless surprised to discover how casually *Madame* accepted my threat and how easy she made the surreptitious process sound. She even gave money to keep them afloat for a few months, far more than the cash Nabil carried. I decided to keep our family's funds. Wael would have his wedding, after all.

Nabil didn't mention his desire to escape with the couple. Perhaps he changed his mind. Unsure how to feel about that, I kept my hands still on my screen until *Madame* decreed Fayzeh and Khaled would hide in Abdullah's apartment for when the time came to sneak them out.

"No. Not acceptable," I typed and yelled at once, vehemently rejecting the stupid idea. I couldn't risk my sister losing a kidney or any of her organs, nor have her eggs harvested, while she lay drugged in that suspicious place if my unfounded allegations about Abdullah's sinister trading somehow turned out to be true. *Sheif* Khaled could lose a limb or an eye, for all I cared, but Fayzeh not even a toenail.

Nabil elbowed me. I ignored him and forgave his ignorance. "Both will stay here as usual with other workers. But out of sight."

"*Aah*, right," Nabil hastened to confirm my order. "Better to keep things in this house running as normally as possible and not draw undo attention. Wouldn't you agree, *Madame*?"

She nodded and extended her hand in agreement.

Nabil almost ripped her arm off with his eager handshake. "Three days. Not long at all."

I had never seen a man faint. Khaled came close when he learned he would flee the Hawks' talons and avoid Abu Nidal's scourge. He slumped into a chair and held his head between both hands, muttering fervent thanks to the Almighty. I like to imagine he was also thanking me.

During the meeting, my sister and I never spoke. After *Madame* enumerated details, Fayzeh kissed her employer's hand and engulfed Nabil in a long, silent hug. She neglected to acknowledge that I was the orchestrator of her escape to a better life. I didn't care. All that mattered was that my sister would be safe.

Nabil's voice cracked when he bade her goodbye. He managed a tearful promise to visit during the time she would be in hiding and fetch the rest of her things. As we walked out, Nabil grabbed Khaled's hand, tugged him close and whispered something.

"Of course, I'm honored," Khaled said in a gruff voice. "I'll wait for you tomorrow morning."

In the taxi home, I asked Nabil, "What did you want from Khaled?"

"To write his book on Fayzeh. We should get them married as soon as possible."

I clapped my hands. I hadn't thought of that. From despair, Nabil had scooped up a suitor for our sister. A smile found its way to my lips. I had set an example, taught my brother a valuable skill.

"And to tell him I would be joining them in the last minute," Nabil added. "Now Khaled knows I will be watching him should he decide to misbehave."

My smile turned into a frown. I struggled to type, "*Madame* doesn't know!!!"

"She doesn't need to. It's a big ship. I'll find a spot. And if I can't, I'll know the process and try for another ship later." He patted my hand. "You've done well, big brother. Time to let me take over."

CHAPTER THIRTY-ONE

The taxi abandoned us near the entrance of the camp. We continued on foot. At the gates, armed men carrying automatic rifles and chains of ammunition across their chests—heavier than the usual arsenal—tripled in number. Heightened security meant we were heading for serious trouble. A burly guard stopped Nabil for a brusque frisk. He hesitated to pat my waist as I hissed, growled, and flipped him a solid finger. He spat and stepped aside to let us pass. Nabil bowed his head, sighed each breath, and repeatedly lagged behind. I nudged him with my cane several times. Approaching our alley, he stopped and clutched my arm.

"What do we tell Yasser?"

"The truth. But no details."

"How's that?"

"She's safe and far away. That's all he needs to know."

Nabil suddenly straightened, opened his eyes wide, and mumbled, "Behind you. Heading this way."

I turned to see Yasser hurrying toward us, the look on his face unreadable.

"You all right?" He asked me first, then turned to Nabil. "Where were you, *ya khara*?"

Nabil stumbled back a step at the vulgarity. Yasser barely spoke to us, and when he did, he never used derogatory language.

"Errann . . . ddss," I answered on behalf of stunned Nabil. "Wwhyyy?"

"Go straight home. Wait with Wael until you hear from me. I told Maryam and Farook to stay at their place." Yasser looked over his shoulders. "I can't find Fayzeh."

"We just left her," Nabil whispered.

"Beirut?" Yasser whispered back. "Work?"

We nodded.

"*Kis ikht halshaghleh,*" Yasser spewed the vile words, spit between his legs. "*Ma'almi* is about to slam sky to earth. I must see to it that Fayzeh—"

"She's safe," I raised my tablet to interrupt him. "Don't worry."

"You think you know what's going on? If I don't find her," he slammed his chest, "we're all screwed!"

"Do what you have to do. She's in hiding."

"Where?" Yasser clutched a fistful of Nabil's shirt instead of mine. "How?"

"We took care of everything." Nabil raised open palms in surrender. "No one will find her. Trust us."

Yasser worked his clenched jaw. His phone dinged from his pocket. He released Nabil with a slight shove. "I have to go. Details later." Glancing at the phone, he started to back away. "Ameena called my number earlier today, tried to reach you, Waseem. *Ma'almi* is keeping her away a while longer." Yasser turned to sprint ahead of us.

"Ssee yyou hommme," I said to Nabil and limped in the direction of the nearest place with internet connection. I couldn't wait to cleanse my soul with Ameena's sublime voice and ethereal face.

Nabil fell into step. "Yasser said we should go straight home." He circled my arm and tugged. "I know you want to call her, but we should heed our brother's warning. I've never seen him this riled up before."

I freed my arm and limped faster.

"Be reasonable. Think." Nabil passed me to walk backward. "Her father wants her to stay away. Whatever he has planned is going to be scary. Yasser even kept Wael home rather than have him go to Wardah's. Yasser wants us together for best protection." Hands stretched to his sides, my brother blocked my path, forcing me to stop. "*Yalla*, let's go home. Call her tomorrow after Abu Nidal's storm blows over."

"Nnoo." I tried to escape. Close to losing balance, I struck his legs with my cane. He clamped both hands on my arms.

"Don't be stubborn and foolish. Look around you. Shops closed . . . streets deserted. I'm telling you, it's too dangerous."

I glanced around. Streets were barren, as if everyone went to Friday prayer, only it was Tuesday. People had been warned and hid behind closed doors. I relented and allowed Nabil to escort me home.

I hunkered with my brothers and waited to hear from Yasser. We took turns peeking out the window. A pin drop could be heard. Nothing moved, save shadows of ravens circling the sky.

Time crawled until it was my turn to monitor the alley again. I spotted a man zigzagging his way in the distance, flattening his back against the walls as he edged down the alley. Why did I recognize him? Where had I seen him before? I pressed my forehead against the glass and squinted to focus. Yes, same broad shoulders and dark glasses. This suspicious man with a bulge under his jacket had accompanied Ameena and her father to the airport before we left for Holland. He stopped at a corner and beckoned with a hand holding a pistol to someone on the other side. Or was it a group of men? Abu Nidal's guerrilla army protecting him from the Hawks? If fighting erupted, no one in our neighborhood would be safe. My brothers and I sat like lambs awaiting slaughter. And where was Yasser?

As the sun hid behind the building to our left, strange noise roiled in the distance. Rapid thwacking rose louder and louder, as if a charging herd of elephants descended from the sky and were charging our neighborhood. Tree leaves, newspaper sheets, and plastic trash bags rolled and bounced around in our alley. A giant shadow swept Abu Nidal's shuttered windows. I looked up to see a helicopter pass, then another hover overhead.

Nabil pulled me back from the quivering glass pane. "What's happening?"

"I see the Lebanese flag painted on their tails," Wael shouted as he craned his neck and flattened his cheek against the window. "They must be canvassing the camp."

We exchanged glances. Who were they looking for?

Nabil punched numbers on his cellphone. "Hope Yasser is okay."

"Don't." Wael snatched the phone. "You need to calm down. He's busy dealing with all this crazy shit. Leave him alone."

"You're right, you're right." Nabil interlocked his fingers on top of his head and paced the room. "*Ya Allah. Ya Rahman.*"

"Pile cushions against window." I typed fast. "Push dresser to block door."

Wael jumped to work, while Nabil stood watching. "Why?" He asked, as if his mind refused to accept what could happen.

"*Yalla!*" Wael shouted to nudge Nabil off his stunned pedestal and help him with the heavy dresser.

Excruciating minutes ticked as we listened to the helicopters chuff above, slicing through the charged atmosphere and jolting our insides until their thrumming started to abate.

Gunfire popped in the distance several times. When we could no longer hear any raucous clamor, Wael called Maryam and Wardah. Both families were fine. Nabil shoved the dresser and went to check on the neighbors, urging them to stay indoors. He returned, repositioned the door block, and drove us crazy with his pacing and chanting while we waited for news.

I peeked from the uncovered corners of my window. Darkness shrouded everything. I heard Yasser's footsteps on the stairs before my brothers noticed. I motioned for them to move the dresser and clear the door.

"What? No!" Wael and Nabil whispered together.

I clapped my hands to rush them. "Yassserrr!"

They sprinted to slide the dresser aside.

As soon as Yasser entered, he threw himself on his back and folded his arms over his forehead, shielding his face, wheezing and coughing. We gathered around him and gave him a chance to catch his breath. His sleeves were ripped, fingers blotched with black smudge. I smelled remnants of something highly acidic, like vinegar, only much stronger. Was he exposed to tear gas? I fetched a soaked towel from the kitchen and placed it in his hands. He squeezed out water and rubbed his face. I ran my eyes over his body head-to-toe, checking for blood. Nothing.

"It's over," he said to the ceiling.

Nabil knelt by his side. "What happened?"

"*Ma'almi* set a trap. The Lebanese Security Forces captured the Hawks leader and most of his pack. Caught off guard while they were moving contraband."

"Weapons?" Wael asked.

"Heavy stuff, RPGs, AKs, and a large cache of narcotics. They'll go to prison for a very long time." Yasser sat up and tossed the towel to a corner. "It's almost over."

"Almost?" The question came from Nabil and Wael at the same time.

"A handful of thugs slipped away. Sooner or later, we'll find them. Until then, we need to stay vigilant." Yasser pulled out a black revolver from his back belt, emptied its chamber, and set everything on the dresser. A spent shell fell to the rug and rolled behind one of the dresser's stubby legs. Since none of my brothers paid it any attention, I assumed I was the only one who heard its muffled thud. I snatched it and hid it in my pocket.

Nabil squeezed Yasser's shoulder. "Brother, please tell me you didn't use this pistol."

Shrugging off his shirt, Yasser's lips formed a lopsided grin. "Didn't need to."

My brothers threw their arms around him, patting his back and cheering. Over their shoulders, Yasser's serious gaze met mine. He winked.

I winked back, if you call batting both eyes in dread a wink.

"Waseem! Finally. Quick, guess where I am." Ameena's enchanting face filled the screen of my tablet. She pressed her lips together in an obvious attempt to hold back a smile. Innocent mischief added extra luster to her sparkling, dark irises.

I had rushed to the nargileh place in the morning, then cooled my heels and waited until the owner opened its doors. My hands trembled as I initiated the video call—not the usual lurches and jerks—but an emotional treble, the kind that excitement and longing inflicted.

"Wwherrr?" I asked.

"Oh, try." She gave her smile full rein. "You'll never guess."

I scratched my head. If that was the case, then why bother? I decided to play the game anyway. Behind her, I could only see a white curtain.

"Bbeddd rrooomm."

"Yes, yes." She clapped her hands.

Now, I was very excited, but I didn't expect her to be as well. She fidgeted, bringing her face too close to the camera of her phone. She had answered the call with her usual demeanor, as if we had coffee together yesterday. No awkward questions on how I've been or any of the usual chitchat people used to bridge the passage of time and a divide in distance. She went straight to the point. I sighed with contentment. My Ameena hadn't changed.

"Now guess where this bedroom is." She pointed behind her. "See this curtain?"

I nodded.

"I'm going to open it and flip the camera so you can see outside."

The bedroom zoomed across my screen as she moved—too quick to distinguish anything. She pulled back the curtain to a view of a grassy area stretching toward a vast body of water in the distance, a calm sea. My heart drummed fast. I had seen that particular vibrant color of blue before. Ameena was not in Amsterdam, nor anywhere near gloomy Holland.

She angled her phone to the right. "Do you see that tower in the distance?"

I focused on the peaked top of a limestone structure and cleared my dry throat. "Yyesss."

She flipped the camera, and her face filled my view again. Tears swelled in her eyes. "Waseem, that's the Clock Tower of *Yaffa*. I'm in Palestine."

It took me seconds to process what she said. She made it to Palestine? To my mother's hometown? I gripped my tablet as it stood stable on a table and slid it closer. "Showww mmeee aagga . . . innn."

"Sure." Ameena wiped running tears with the tips of her fingers before the Mediterranean shoreline and the tower filled my view once more. A group of women jogged along a neat path. Several families ate at picnic tables and benches. Bikers meandered between lush trees and radiant flowerbeds.

"As soon as I arrived," Ameena said. "I walked around the old city and tried to visit my grandfather's house. It was easy to find near the center. I knocked on the big wooden door with interlocking framed squares, the same door my grandfather cut and carved with his hands. He used to tell me about it all the time when I was little, even described the details on its round, brass, double handles. An Israeli family lives there now. I talked to them in English, of course. They had American accents. I told them I'm the Palestinian granddaughter of the man who built the house for our family and I just wanted to see it. They wouldn't let me in, Waseem. My heart burned. I stood outside for hours, snapped pictures."

She blew a long breath, sounding deflated. "I had to leave in the end, walked around, took more pictures and recorded videos everywhere I went. I'll send anything I've collected so you can download and see them anytime you want."

I oscillated side-to-side, as if in a trance. Beastly sounds came from my throat, abrasive and offensive. I couldn't stop, couldn't say anything, couldn't see more details. Tears ran and gathered on my chin, then dripped onto my hands. Mucus oozed from my nostrils and soaked my moist sleeve. I wasn't crying. I was sobbing.

"Oh, Waseem, how I wish you were here," she crooned. "I can't wait to tell you about this dream trip. When Baba asked me to postpone, and my stay in Holland was about to end, I had to try to come here before my UN passport expired. It wasn't easy by any meaning of the word. Israeli officers at the airport examined my blue book, questioned me over four hours. They asked why I came, where I'm staying, if I have relatives here, things like that." She moved her phone camera to the right in slow motion.

A boy ran alongside his father, launching a red kite until it soared in the sunlight.

"I told them I don't have family left in Palestine, but of course they already knew that, so I said I'm visiting an old friend. It feels that way, Waseem. I feel I know every fragment, every hand-span of this land. Each Palestinian man, woman, and child I came across is a relative, an old-time friend, or acquaintance. Like I've always been here and belong here. The officers asked for the friend's name and whereabouts." She chuckled, causing the images on my screen to bounce. "You'd be proud of my performance. I came prepared. I stayed calm and focused, gave them info on a relative of Younis and kept repeating my answers until they wished me a pleasant stay behind forced smiles. Oh, Waseem, everything here is so beautiful *and* painful at the same time. If only you could savor the breeze, smell the sea, touch the sand, taste the —"

"Orrraangge!" The word rolled off my quivering lips.

"Oranges? Sure, I'll sneak a few in my luggage for you. I'm booked for Saturday, the thirteenth of July. My flight arrives late, so I'll come over Sunday." She started to turn the phone, and I quickly killed my camera. I didn't want her to witness me start to crumble.

"What happened? I can't see you."

"Cc . . . cconn . . . tionnn," I mumbled.

"Connection was excellent a second ago. Hang up and I'll call."

"Nnoo tti . . . mmme."

"Oh, you need to go. Okay. Call again tomorrow same time, but if we can't connect," tilting her head, she waved, "see you soon."

I remained in my seat for a long time after our call ended. Patrons in the lounge came and went. Spoons clanged against tea glasses. Nargileh smoke swirled, and flavors changed around me. I just sat there, shedding hot tears, examining photos, playing and replaying the videos she'd sent.

CHAPTER THIRTY-TWO

As much as I wanted to talk to Ameena every day, I refrained from calling her. Like a dramatic teenager, I lost it at the slightest sentimental remembrance and succumbed to a vast sense of loneliness. I bawled my heart out a disconcerting number of times when no one was around.

Something inexplicable stopped me from visiting Jannat as well. I continued to send books to the entire student group and more poetry diwans with Ghazi. I didn't stop to discern my aversion and convinced myself I was doing Jannat a favor. Her hinted feverish attachment to me would soon pass once she graduated from her current education level, with a mind further enlightened and eyes open wider to truly see me. Like a heavy, burdensome sack, she would drop her crush in favor of a sound, handsome fellow who was bound to make an appearance in her life.

I learned little of the social structure in Jannat's sector of the camp. Were there no eligible bachelors in her circle? I couldn't be the one man with whom she enjoyed regular encounters. Her father's insistence that she chaperone our club gatherings indicated he was the conservative type. But I hardly saw or talked to the cobbler after our initial meeting. Was it possible he considered me a good prospect for his lovely, intelligent, secluded daughter and encouraged our interactions by this setup?

Perhaps I was not as hideous looking as I thought. I should borrow Jannat's invisible spectacles when I examined myself in the mirror next time. Did Ameena possess the same eyewear?

Darwin's theory about survival of the fittest must be faulty. Some women looked beyond the physical and were attracted by high intellect. Judging from the stupid mayhem some handsome men had committed throughout history, the human race, otherwise, would have gone extinct ages ago.

I knew nothing for certain. But once alone at night I lay captive to the brutally honest, devilish mini-me wagging a finger by my right shoulder, forced to acknowledge the twisted reasons behind my evasive behavior. I was accustomed to having the strings of my heart resonate under Ameena's fingers. Despite my earthly attraction to Jannat, I feared a new cadence would disrupt our unique symphony. Pure egotistical reasons drove me to ignore Jannat's overtures. I wasn't sparing her the agony of a broken heart. I was preserving mine for Ameena, and only Ameena.

Does selfishness constitute the essence of love?

My entire life I stuck to Ameena, glued myself to her, and she allowed it, encouraged and graciously embraced my attachment and friendship. Ameena bore through my multi-layered mask and dealt with me as an equal. But would she welcome a hint of romantic inclinations? Or would she be taken off-guard once I mustered the courage to express my true feelings as I had been when Jannat subtly confessed hers?

Did I really, honestly, wholeheartedly, want to know?

I followed the news with a hawk's sharp eyes and a moth's superior hearing. Numerous outlets assured the public that law forces had ensnared all members of the evil organ trafficking gang, uncovering trade trails all over the world. My suspicious mind refused to grant me peace. I had firsthand experience of how determined men could circumvent the law and evade capture. The Hawks of Freedom and Abu Nidal demonstrated stark examples.

I headed to the UNRWA clinic in the early morning hours to search for the nurse who helped prepare me during Vincent's visit. Master of his domain, Mayor Abdo knew everything about everyone. If any whispers of rumors circled the medical arena, he would detect them. I banked on that recollection and pressed onward. I needed to discover Abdullah's true pursuits before I left Fayzeh's fate in his sister's hands. I should have talked to Abdo before I rushed to put Fayzeh on the launch pad.

But here I stood, my hand paused before sending her off, reaching out to the Mayor at the very last minute. I had failed my brother. Would I fail my sister, too?

With no one at the front desk, I eased through the entrance. Patients scattered in all directions, infants and children cried as if performing a symphony composed with a haunting melancholy in mind. Walking down a baby blue hallway, the crisp smell of fresh paint mixed with the strong chemical odor of disinfectants overpowered me. I had to stop and lean against a wall until a wave of nausea passed.

Memories of this place, images of Mother's lifeless body lying on a table, kept flooding my mind. I looked around. Which room was it? I couldn't remember. It must have been one farthest from the entrance, for an eternity had stretched before I reached her. Shaking off the sickening clench gripping my insides, I pushed on looking for the X-ray room.

Time worked against me. One day left before Fayzeh's ship sailed. I still had the chance to pull her out if needed. She could hate me all she wanted, but at least she would do it with her entire body intact.

Creaking wheels sounded behind me. I turned to come face-to-face with dear Abdo and his silver-streaked beard pushing a vacant wheelchair.

"Hey, look at you!" He rounded the wheelchair and opened his arms wide. "You're a celebrity, my friend."

"Mmmayyorrr." I stepped into a manly embrace; back-slapping, awkward, and brief.

He stepped back, replacing his wide smile with a frown. "You forgot my name?"

I reached for my tablet. "I named you Mayor because you know everything here." I gripped his forearm and looked into his eyes. "Abbdddo."

"That's right!" He exploded with a loud chuckle. "So nice to see you standing before me at my eye level. I'm happy for you, heard so much about you after your return." He pulled me closer, pretending to whisper. "I told you Miss Ameena doesn't take no for an answer from anyone."

"Yesss."

Abdo tilted his head as if appraising my cane and nodded. "Nice! Suits you much better than that walker."

I acknowledged his compliment with a nod and a strong tap to the linoleum floor. As much as I wanted to chat and be polite, I couldn't waste any time. "I have a favor to ask you. A question. Urgent."

"I'm on my way to pick up a patient." He gestured at the wheelchair. "Have a seat and ask me anything you want, my friend."

Sliding onto the chair, I trapped my cane between my knees, typed fast and lifted the tablet for him to read. "There's a man named Abdullah Abdullah. Secretly trades in the medical industry, not sure what. Can you please find out for me?"

Abdo stopped before a vacant room and wheeled me inside. He shut the door. "I'm not going to ask why you want to know about *him* . . . or how you discovered his . . . *hobby*." Abdo whispered for real this time. "And I don't want to know, but you better stay clear of this man."

My heart jumped to my throat. I sprang to my feet faster than I could ever manage to before. "Wwhyyy?"

"Whatever you need, I can get it for you. He's unreachable and should remain so."

"Wwhyyy?"

Abdo clasped his hands together. "Because he is *necessary*. For many unfortunate people inside and outside the camps. Trust me on this, my friend."

"Wwhyyy?" I repeated, a bit louder this time. Necessary? For what, exactly? I needed confirmation. "Ppllee . . . sss?"

"See this?" Abdo hopped to an oxygen cylinder in a corner. "And this?" He caressed a blood pressure monitor dangling from a wall as if soothing a baby. "And this?" He tapped a machine connected to a face mask. "It's a *luxury* to have these here. But a lot of sick people need this equipment to survive and don't have access to it, couldn't afford to even if they could reach a hospital or a doctor. Other instruments needed for surgeries are dangerous and scarce." Abdo wagged his index finger in my face. "He is essential, I tell you, well-known and respected in the underground medical field."

Relief turned my bones to mush. I dropped onto the chair. True to his given title, this mayor knew everybody, ensuring Fayzeh's relatively safe escape.

~

By the end of May, Fayzeh was wed and on her way to Italy. Nabil handled everything in Beirut. We kept Wael and Maryam in the dark with the promise to inform them of Fayzeh's final whereabouts when the right time came. I insisted on keeping Yasser out of the loop to protect him. He agreed it was the smart thing to do. Since Yasser was Abu Nidal's right hand and direct informant, he managed to block intelligence about Fayzeh and Khaled from reaching his employer's ears. But we all knew the fragile dam could collapse any minute. If and when it did, Yasser possessed no knowledge of any details. The ploy would protect him from severe repercussions.

Wael and Wardah married in a big ceremony mid-June—two weeks following Fayzeh's union. It was Yasser's idea to expedite matters to release tensions and demonstrate to doubters that Abu Nidal's reign stood as strong and unchallenged as ever. During the celebrations in the familiar tent, Yasser and his posse carried holstered pistols on their hips in plain view and surveyed the grounds. They intimidated and cowed anyone who might be foolish enough to look the wrong way at Abu Nidal. No one reached that level of stupidity, so unpleasant incidents did not mar our happy occasion. Yasser seldom came home after that day, busy chasing fleeing Hawks' members.

I kept anticipating the moment when Nabil would follow up on his scheme to flee, but as the wheels of our difficult days turned, and he remained home, I convinced myself he'd abandoned the idea. Reality smacked me on the head to drop such conviction one night as I caught him stuffing papers and some personal belongings into a backpack. The following morning, he went to work and returned at the end of the day as usual, leading me to believe he postponed his escape. Perhaps he planned to wait until the danger of exposure passed before attempting to literally follow Fayzeh's footsteps. Or maybe he decided to remain by my side. Fearful it might be the former, I didn't poke or prod for answers.

Wael moved in with his in-laws, leaving me to depend on Nabil alone with day-to-day necessities as Yasser remained elusive. Nabil maintained our household, shopping, cleaning, quietly slipping into Fayzeh's role without the constant complaining and badgering. And when Maryam couldn't come over or send us a plate of whatever she cooked for her family, Nabil prepared our meals.

I came to the realization that my dependency, my complicated presence in Nabil's life, kept my eager-to-fly brother caged. *Me*, the one person in our family who suffered multiple forms of imprisonment. I needed to set Nabil free.

I set out to show him I was capable of taking care of myself, starting in the kitchen. It couldn't be that hard to make a sandwich or reheat Maryam's leftovers. The mundane tasks, however, proved extremely difficult with my stiff hands.

Mother must have been watching over me when I attempted to use the oven one afternoon before Nabil's return from work. Bent over the open oven door, I managed to turn the gas knob, but repeated efforts to strike a matchstick failed until finally one caught fire. Flames blast out of the oven into my face, and I lost my balance. If it weren't for my swift reaction to turn the knob and kill the gas, I would have burned down our entire building.

Nabil spent most of the night laughing at my singed eyebrows, thinking I had attempted to shave them off. I refused to correct his ridiculous notion. Why would I, or anyone want to do that? I never came near the oven or stove again.

I asked Maryam to leave out loaves of bread within my reach and ingredients to make sandwiches in the refrigerator—I could grasp the door handle easily enough—to give Nabil some free time off every now and then. A diet of cheese and olives, spreadable *labneh*, and creamy hummus worked wonders to alleviate some of my anger for being so inept. The guilt, though, remained steadfast. I failed Nabil. Again. Failed him on a grand scale.

CHAPTER THIRTY-THREE

As Sunday the thirteenth of July approached, I forced myself not to check the calendar, then avoided the clock, even abandoned my watch to the dark confines of the dresser drawer. Needing to control my excitement so as not to lose it in Ameena's presence, I planned to survey her house from the window and spot her leaving, which would give me time to steady my nerves and welcome her in a composed, mature manner.

The day arrived, and I agonized over what to wear over my best trousers. I couldn't decide between a white or blue shirt. I landed on white, as it went best with my father's gray necktie. A childish desire to flaunt my improved tie knotting skills drove me to spend precious time in front of the mirror. Nervousness and a rushed breakfast loosened my intestines, and I ended up spending a good part of the morning marooned and moaning on the latrine.

Ameena arrived early. I was not ready. I staggered out of the bathroom to see Nabil opening the door to greet her. I quickly pulled the bathroom door shut behind me.

"*Ahlan. Ahlan wa sahlan*," Nabil shook her hand. "It's wonderful to see you again."

"*Shukran*. I've heard so many things happened in my absence. Congratulations on Wael's marriage." She passed Nabil and stepped into full view.

A yellow, short-sleeved dress enrobed her to the knees, gathered at the waist under a brown sash, and gave her tan skin a magical glow. A matching ribbon collected her dark hair into a loose ponytail. Flat, leather sandals exposed a dainty anklet. The slight weight she had gained around her hips suited her, transformed her into the sublime goddess, Ishtar. I half-expected to see white lilies adorn her head and graceful doves flitting around her shoulders.

She placed a large white gift-bag on the dresser and stood, in all her stunning glory, before me. Raising both arms, she stepped into a full-body embrace. "Oh, Waseem. I'm so sorry about your mother."

With one hand still clutching the bathroom doorknob, I didn't know what to do with the other. Ameena was hugging me, never in this affectionate manner, certainly unlike her clumsy, reserved pats on my back when we had parted in Holland. She used to lock both arms around my shoulders during spastic episodes. But this closeness—this open show of affection—totally took me by surprise. She would never have dared such a display of intimacy before living in Europe. I was wrong earlier. Ameena *had* changed. And I savored her transformation.

Lifting my free hand to the small of her back, I kept my fingers curled into my palm as a token of respect. She smelled of springtime and sea air. I wanted to thank her, but in my shaken sentimental state, I feared to open my mouth, concerned I would nibble her soft neck.

Nabil wiggled his eyebrows behind Ameena's back. I glowered at him and dropped my hand. She released me and turned to him. "*Allah yirhamha. Khalto* was my second mother."

"*Allah yirhamna jamee'an*," Nabil repeated her prayers for mercy to include us all and grabbed his work clothes from a hook. "I must open the shop."

"Oh, don't let me keep you. I'll visit with Waseem. Catch up on things."

"Umm, see you later," my baffled brother mumbled and left us alone.

"I brought you something." She picked up the gift bag and sat on the floor. "Come, let me show you. Where's Fayzeh? I brought her a gift. Hopefully something she'll like."

I grabbed my tablet and eased onto the cushions across from Ameena. "Fayzeh traveling with her husband."

"What? She's married? When? To whom? What does he do? How come no one told me? Where are they? When can I see them?" Ameena fired her questions in a single breath. She tried to swat my tablet aside. "Oh, put this silly thing away and talk to me."

I shook my head and refused to set aside my communication tool. I needed to keep my hands busy, though my eyes riveted on the hearts stringed in her delicate anklet made it difficult to type quick answers to her rapid-fire inquiries.

"A month ago. Khaled. Chief. Germany. No plans to return soon."

She scowled. "He's a chief? Of what? A tribe? Oh God! Is he an old man?"

Confused, I looked at my screen. I had used Fayzeh's mangled title for Khaled's occupation, *Sheif.* But, with my stupid, jittery nerves, I mashed languages, replacing the letter *f* with *kh.* No wonder Ameena was lost.

Cursing Fayzeh for her lingering linguistic influence under my breath, I corrected the typo. "A chef. A cook. In a restaurant."

"Oh, I see." Ameena pointed at my tablet. "I hate conversing with this, but okay, tell me everything."

"It happened fast," I continued to add small lies to mitigate her prodding. "He had a job offer in Germany and an opportunity to migrate. We hurried everything so she could go with him."

"To Germany? He must be Lebanese. I mean holds the Lebanese passport, otherwise he wouldn't be able to go. Am I right?"

"Yyesss," I said, hesitant to stretch the lie, hating to deceive my faithful friend. But I had no choice. She was the one person who shouldn't know the truth about the possible betrayal of her childhood friend.

"Wait a minute, wait a minute." Ameena narrowed her eyes. "How could immigration papers work for Fayzeh so fast? A Palestinian refugee with a Laissez-Passer? Younis and I tried every imaginable idea for you. Not a single door opened."

My shoulders slumped. She wasn't going to let this go. "Fayzeh was granted a visa soon as she married. They will petition as a couple." I flicked my hand in the air to reflect innocent ignorance. "Something like that. It was all arranged through his work."

Ameena arched one eyebrow. "As a cook?"

Nodding, I held her gaze with tremendous difficulty. "Checheffff."

"He must be an *exceptional* chef." She wiggled ten fingers in my face. "With golden hands."

I couldn't contain laughter and tipped back. She saw right through my stupid farce. With all my spying and investigative skills, I was no James Bond when it came to spinning tales to this woman.

She grabbed my arms before I completely fell over and steadied me. "Once Fayzeh is settled, connect us. I'd love to hear all about her new life . . . in Germany." Smiling, she shook her head. "I have news to share. But first things first." She produced five oranges from the gift bag. "It was the end of season. I wish I could bring you more. They truly have a distinctive flavor. Brought a couple for my parents, too."

I scratched the peel and sniffed the mythic citrus fruit embedded in Mother's ever-present soul. The tart yet sweet fragrance imprinted on my conscience. I could never forget that fresh, succulent smell.

Ameena held an orange. "Want a taste?"

"Llatte . . . rrr," I said to stop her from digging her manicured nails into the peel. "Thaann—"

"Oh, Waseem, don't thank me. There's more." She arranged the oranges in a pile and pulled out a bundle wrapped in rainbow colors. "This took me a long time to find," she placed the gift in my lap, "then I literally stumbled upon it."

Quivering with excitement, I clawed away at the wrapping. A solid object peeked behind layers of bubble wrap, the shape of a palm-size triangle with rounded points. Removing plastic sheets one at a time, faded colors started to show, then dark lines. Water dripped onto the back of my hands. I wiped my cheeks, but there were no tears. I was drooling. I unwrapped the last sheet. A thick ceramic piece stared at me.

"It's one half," Ameena whispered. "I couldn't find the other."

Flipping the piece back and forth, I examined every detail, same geometric designs, same colors as my mother's tile. Rocking back and forth, I asked. "Wwherrr? Hhowww?"

"Where your grandmother's neighborhood used to stand. You showed me roughly where it was when you were in the hospital. On Google Maps."

I stared at her open-mouthed, rocking faster and faster, but I couldn't find words.

"The whole neighborhood was bull-dozed, flattened and replaced by a public beach." She clamped a hand on my shoulder and slowed me down. "Strolling on the sand by the water, I found parts of roofs, pottery, plates, so many chunks of beautiful tiles. Israelis used the rubble from Palestinian houses to fill the grounds. My foot struck this piece, and I couldn't believe my eyes." She enveloped me with open arms and careened with me, rocking, jerking, swaying every which way. Her warm lips grazed my ear as she whispered, "I so wished you were there with me."

Alone in our tiny room at the heart of the refugee camp, we danced, Ameena and I. We waltzed to the tortuous tune of painful memories and obliterated hopes.

~

The best days of my life followed. Four fleeting days, to be exact. Two more letters from Jannat arrived but sat unopened in my drawer.

In my dreams, I spent nights nestled in Ameena's arms with her gift tucked under my pillow. Carnal desires drenched me in sweat and ecstasy as I floated about in a euphoric sphere. I did not inhabit an athlete's idyllic body, nor did I serenade love poems and songs with eloquence and poise. Basking in the silvery aura of her radiant, full moon, I was myself, the physically impaired man who lacked the ability to articulate, strolling hand-in-hand with sensual Ameena on the beaches of *Yaffa*, flirting, kissing, caressing history, and creating a future for us in Palestine.

We shared a pot of strong Arabic coffee each afternoon before she went home from work, with Maryam and her baby always present. Ameena spilled details of her journey and time away. Sometimes, when she conversed with Maryam, I would listen, paying scant attention to their small talk, but instead following the melody of Ameena's voice, rising and dipping as if playing an instrument to a dramatic piece of music.

"*Ana Elbatta elbaladyyeh . . . Basbah fi batni elmaiyyeh,*" Ameena crooned to my nephew one day as she held his chubby hands and swung them left to right.

I smiled at her song and the image it evoked: graceful Ameena as a domesticated duck swimming in the middle of a lake. Far from it. I just couldn't conjure up the image.

"*Laqoonee etnain yahoodiyyeh . . . Qaloolee wein elhawiyyeh*," she continued to sing and swing. My lucky nephew babbled, drooled, and giggled along with her.

I met my sister's gaze as she raised her eyebrows. Obviously Ameena's carol surprised Maryam. Not me. Ameena chose that specific children's rhyme to reflect her experience in Palestine. Two Jewish men—actually, more than two—did intercept her to demand her identification papers.

"*Qolti lhum . . .*" She stopped, brought her face closer to the toddler's, and winked.

Maryam placed her hands behind her son to catch him when Ameena would reveal what she told the inquisitors with a release of his hands.

"*Ana . . . fidaiyyeh*! *Ana . . . fidaiyyeh*!" The women chanted together and laughed.

Great! Ameena and my sister announced to the future generation that they identified as freedom fighters. Though I laughed with them, a strange and uneasy feeling settled in my stomach. This was not a simple chanting of a nursery rhyme. This was a declaration of war.

"*Ya Zareef-eltool wakiff la qullak*," Ameena started another song, pulling the boy to his feet to follow the verse's command calling on the tall, legendary hero, Zareef-eltool. Every wedding and celebratory occasion recounted the nameless character's brave tales with this special melody, simply describing him as a man of nice height. For someone with stunted legs' growth as mine, I could see why this nickname was appealing. But so many real heroes could replace the mystic character in folk ballads.

Symbolism was necessary in teaching children about resistance, but why not use the names of actual freedom fighters who gave their lives to the cause? They had surely earned the honor. I shook my head.

Ameena stopped bouncing my nephew. "What?"

I raised my tablet. "An epic myth."

"He is not!" Maryam shielded the toddler's eyes, as if he could read my text. "Zareef-eltool saved countless lives, fought in almost every battle."

"Since when?"

"Since the beginning," Ameena answered. "Since we were forced from our homes and lands."

It was pointless. I knew the analogy, the weight of such a metaphor, but couldn't resist challenging Ameena. I don't know why. Perhaps I liked to see her riled up, cheeks turning pink, intelligent eyes flashing bolts of lightning. I missed our interactions, missed her. And maybe because I hated to think that she favored tall men.

"Shouldn't he be dead by now?" I typed.

"Don't you know?" Ameena twirled my nephew around and winked. "Palestinians never die."

That was it. With a simple, decades-old ballad, Ameena resurrected my dear mother. I sensed her presence around me, singing along with the women, twirling with her grandchild, planting blasted seeds of hope and charting dreams.

I think I heard my father's voice echo in the distance as well.

CHAPTER THIRTY-FOUR

On the fourth day, a slight catch in Ameena's tone raised some red flags. She was holding things back, important things. I vowed to prod for the mystery the following day, which was a Friday, the day I decided to resume my visits to the reading club and face Jannat.

I set out at my usual time with a spring under my feet, skipping onward in my own clumsy manner every few steps as I imagined a happy, carefree person would. Ameena had returned to me, and our bond was stronger than ever. She hadn't changed much. Hope still wafted through her astral composition, that ambrosial musk in ibn Zaydun's accolade.

I sniffed my armpit and almost lost balance. All right then, Ameena's scent had not transferred onto my skin, but it sure clung to my soul. Today would be a good day. I forced myself to slow down lest I arrive at Jannat's bruised from a mishap or sweating with repulsive odor.

I recalled her unopened letters, which I had skimmed before I departed. Guilt poisoned my usual anticipation and ruined my elation at the quotes she'd penned. Her excerpts exposed unmistakably tender feelings, though she continued to disguise them by writing then erasing my name. Her tell-tale signature hearts persisted as mere etched traces.

Rounding a corner, my feet dragged with a mind spiraling into conflicted notions.

Should I address her implied confession? Or should I continue to play the game of pretense and assume her poetic selections merely demonstrated a romantic taste? If I asked her to clarify the intentions behind her selected clauses, I'd have to articulate a gentle rejection—a task I never thought I'd need to perform. I would have to confess that my heart was entirely, solidly filled by love of another woman. But was that even accurate?

I arrived at my destination, and the Tigress let me in. She chattered about events that happened during my hiatus. I retained none of the information, anticipating the moment Jannat would join us. I received hugs, salutes, and elated high-fives from my precious cadre and refrained from asking about my trusted aide. Did she keep me waiting on purpose? Was this another game of hers? After a solid ten minutes of catching up with club members, I started to doubt she would appear at all. I turned to the Tigress, ready to type an inquiry about her sister when Jannat walked into the room. My fingers literally stopped, hovering over my tablet in midair.

"*Ahlan*, Waseemmmm," she sang, wearing a rich shade of fuchsia for her hijab.

"*Maa . . . rrrha . . . baa*," I mumbled and almost drooled. I felt vindicated yet exposed by her splendor. The color suited her so well, complementing her healthy, vibrant skin and highlighting captivating glossy lips. Dark kohl extenuated her banana-shaped, piercing eyes.

"We missed you around here," she said as she received embraces from several girls. "I heard about trouble in your area keeping you occupied." She waltzed around the room with small, confident steps to enforce her usual duties, sharing more hugs and repositioning cushions. "Our zoo is overjoyed its groundskeeper is back."

The children launched a frenzy of confirmations, using their assigned, feral voices. In my peripheral vision, a wolf trapped a trio of lambs in one of the corners. Jannat pretended to wrestle the wolf away from his poor prey and escorted him to a designated spot. She turned to face me, unveiled a dazzling smile, and locked her gaze with mine. "As am I." She took one step closer and added, "Waseemmmm."

A shiver ran down my spine and weakened my knees. I wobbled as if I were the flute she held to her moist lips, scattering my waning composure to a gentle breeze. This charming siren and intrepid sorceress knew her assets and how they affected me. Flattered to the bone, I did not mind the manipulation. I admired her more for it.

"So sorry about your mother," Jannat said, stressing each word. "*Allah yirhamha.*"

I nodded to accept her prayers of mercy. Children's prattle faded to the background, and I could hear every rustle of her clothing, feel every breath she exhaled.

"Thank you for the letters," I typed, not knowing how to proceed.

She touched the back of my hand to still my trembling fingers, the first intentional physical contact between us. She might as well have pushed a searing iron rod straight through to my groin. I shifted sideways, leaning closer, desiring more.

"Did my letters bring you some joy?" she asked, her soft voice low and intimate.

"Yesss," I whispered.

"Good. I took lots of time and care writing them to impress you." She pressed her cute lips together and released them with a pop, as if smacking the space separating us. "I just wanted you to know, so don't worry."

Worry? I was light years beyond worried. I was stunned, utterly lost. Did she just blow me a kiss? I fumbled with my tablet before I lifted it like a shield between us. "About what?"

I couldn't determine who was the cruelest actor in this crazy exchange. Her, for playing with my nerves as a cat toyed with a mouse. Or me, for demanding she provided clarity and defined her intentions. Come on, Jannat. Spell it out. In your own words this time.

I watched her like a hawk, expecting her to shield her eyes, dip her head, turn or move away to dodge my inquiry. But she did none of that.

Jannat grabbed my arm with both hands. "You are under no obligation. But you ought to know, Waseemmm." She slightly hunched her shoulders to meet me at eye-level. "You are loved and cherished . . . by me."

Somewhere behind me, bees buzzed, birds chirped, snakes hissed, cows mooed. At that pivotal moment, a single thought dominated my stupid, paralyzed mind. No longer a zebra, I was a lion on the verge of releasing a triumphant, exploding roar.

What came out of my throat, however, was a loud, earsplitting shrill.

Jannat jumped back.

The kids stopped their mischief.

A big woman barged in asking if everyone was all right.

"Oh, we were just clearing throats, getting ready to start reading aloud," Jannat addressed her concerned neighbor. She commandeered her toward the door. "Sorry about the noise. Won't happen again, I promise."

The interruption gave me a chance to collect my wits. By the time Jannat returned, I was already engaged, distributing new books to eager hands. The session ended without having another private talk, or rather I avoided several chances and kept my head down. When it was time to leave, Jannat's dejected expression nudged me to offer a sliver of chivalry. I turned to her at the door and whispered, "Mmosst unn . . . exppec . . . ttedd. Thaannnkk yyou."

Maybe I should have added something else, a confession of how much I admired her, or a declaration of the special person I thought she was. But all I could muster was my sincere appreciation for her love.

I was held captive, that was quite clear to me, my heart enslaved by Ameena. Or rather by my romantic idea of her, and not free to grant any bit of it to Jannat, no matter how much I desired to. And I did desire Jannat. I felt the attraction stimulate each nerve cell, infect every healthy gland, and cascade through all the muscle fibers of this body I inhabit.

As I dragged home, a lightbulb lit up in my head with the perceptive visionary words of Kafka: *Love has as few problems as a motorcar. The only problems are the driver, the passengers, and the road.*

I was the cartographer of my eternal fixation on Ameena. I alone created the map, etched every path, steep valley, and jagged peak. What sort of driver was I if I lacked the will to steer my own destiny? I was the jailer of my soul, not Ameena. Jannat could be the passenger holding the key that could ignite my engine to launch me to new destinations.

But only if I let her. Why would I? Ameena had returned to embrace me once more.

I arrived home strangely exhausted to find Maryam had sanitized everything with bleach before she fled the premises. The strong odor hit me in waves until nausea threatened to upend my stomach. I stuck my head out the window to find a cool breeze and coughed into my sleeve. A familiar tall man with an overstuffed backpack came down the alley. I leaned farther to take a better look at his face and almost fell over.

Younis approached Abu Nidal's door. The camp's beloved doctor had returned. I thought I was rid of him for good. But there he was, walking with unmistakable arrogance, striding into Ameena's house. Could he have finally found a way for me to leave this place? Or did he come here in an official capacity to treat more patients? Now that Ameena was back, Abu Nidal would not allow the man to dwell in their home as last time. People would talk. If the Swede had returned to fulfill a medical mission, which I would sincerely admire, he should have arranged for different accommodations. The audacity of the man, to show up at Ameena's home like that was despicable.

Lost in my thoughts, I failed to notice Nabil and Yasser enter our building. They startled me when they walked into the room. Exchanging strange glances, they motioned for me to take a seat.

Nabil squatted beside me. He coughed, "We heard news."

"I just found out about it," Yasser said, his tone taut, almost grim.

I briefly scrunched my eyes. *Please fate, spare my sister.* "Ffaayzzzeh?"

"She made it to Cyprus, soon to arrive in Italy." Nabil patted my knee. "She's fine."

I opened my mouth, but Nabil quickly said as if he read my mind, "Maryam and the baby are fine. Wael, too. This is not about family."

Yasser heaved a heavy sigh. "I don't know how to tell you this, but—"

A loud shrill pierced the atmosphere, a high-pitched *zaghrouta* started just as the first began to fade, then another launched until a series of joyous, colloquial announcements filled the alley. I went to the window to see what the celebrations were about. My brothers flanked me.

The jubilee came from Ameena's house. Abu Nidal walked out with a Kalashnikov raised above his head. Smiling, he emptied his weapon in the air. We jumped away from the window, but these were not warning shots.

Yasser circled my shoulders. "Ameena just got engaged."

CHAPTER THIRTY-FIVE

I am not one man. I am Mr. Darcy, Heathcliff, and the Count of Monte Cristo rolled into one. My noble, all-consuming obsession with Ameena turned savage and succumbed to the tyranny of vengeance. A burdened wheat stalk, I bowed under her sultry sun with the words of the Iraqi poet, Ahmad Matar, pulsating in my mind: *But in the hour of its bowing, it hides the seeds of its survival, concealing in the earth's womb a coming of revolution.*

I shunned Ameena's efforts to reach me, locked myself at home, closed my window and rejected her calls. My siblings helped at first, then tried to trick me into seeing her, accused me of being childish, vindictive, and, as Yasser eloquently put it, delusional. I didn't care. Gone was the time when I cared for my image in her eyes. The cherished periods of respect and adoration were dead and gone.

Yes, I decreed. Selfishness embodied love.

All thoughts of Jannat vanished from the crevasses of my implacable mind along with any tenderness they had evoked. I intentionally revved the engine to my motorcar and drove it over the cliff of reason. Pangs of regret for abandoning sweet Jannat failed to fetter my anger, and I sank deeper into the viscid quicksand of retaliation.

For days and nights lasting many lifetimes, I devised schemes and charted plans to dispose of Ameena's beau. The best idea revolved around a tip sent through my spies to the right person. All I needed was a small lie and a half-truth, a hint that Doctor Turtleneck was somehow involved in the recent violent turn of events. By all appearances, he left the camp at the most opportune time and returned after the dust settled.

I could easily have asked one of my boys to slip something incriminating in the doctor's pockets or backpack while he conducted examinations all over the camp, a piece of paper with a name and possible whereabouts of a runaway Hawk. My minions could then spread rumors that the doctor mended broken wings of his future father-in-law's enemies while in hiding. One day, while eavesdropping on Yasser's phone conversation with his boss, I learned of two names, prepared the damning note in English, dictated it to be handwritten by Lieutenant Ghazi, and hid it in my pillowcase until the right time arrived to launch my revenge.

Isolated inside my hateful cocoon, I finally lived up to the name my looks inspired. Ugliness molded my appearance when I was in the womb. Despite everything my beautiful mother did to mask it, hideousness steeped to perfection inside me and bubbled through the pores of my skin to reveal my true nature. Even my sporadic coughs turned stubborn, started to produce green phlegm.

I was my mother's Waseem no longer. I was Quasimodo's evil twin, a hunchbacked creature full of self-loathing and animosity toward any smiling unfortunate who crossed my path.

And toward Ameena?

Never. Never toward her.

If she had been cold-hearted and aloof as Dickens's Estella, the hurt would have been easier to endure. But true to the meaning of her name, Ameena held my trust all those years and was the one woman I called a faithful friend. She was no more than a girl clawing her way out of our cumulative misery, while retaining as much dignity as possible. With all her intelligence and might, she tried to pull me out with her. She simply failed. The fault of elevating her to a goddess was mine, all mine. I was the fool with great expectations, a dreamer who built castles in the sky and dared to desire a better life. My mother's hopefulness crept up on me, snuck under my skin, and infected my mind.

Adding insult to injury, Jannat had stormed my world, fed and further cultivated my delusions of normalcy. And what did I do? I failed to recognize her as the bountiful gift that fate had delivered to my fingertips. I could have placed my hand on hers and accepted her generous heart, but I willfully abandoned her to chase moot realities. I embraced Don Quixote's refusal to see the windmills for what they were, and Younis became the giant I dared to fight.

Friday prayer time, I sat alone at home, hatching more plans to eliminate the infiltrator. A verse from the poem *Araka Assiya al-Dam'a* by the tenth century poet Abu Firas al-Hamdani echoed in my head and drove my sinister schemes: *O thou art playing with a promise to be with me, of which my demise is closer than seeing you, so be it, perish all the waters if I die of thirst.*

Parched for some semblance of normal life with my Ameena, I wished all men—namely Younis—to be forever deprived of a single drop of possibility.

I felt an affinity to the Abbasid era prince, court poet, and fighter against the Byzantine Empire. He was captured and imprisoned in Constantinople for several years, where he wrote his most famous work, the collection of poems titled *al-Rumiyyat*. Though it may be understood that he versified about romance and ardor, the poems actually portray his devotion and love for country. *Arak Assiya al-Dam'a* was the one poem that pushed his cousin and ruler of Upper Mesopotamia to ransom and secure the poet's release. He enjoyed freedom for two short years before that ruler's successor had him killed.

Fine, fine. I am no poet, nor was I born of noble blood, and I certainly was not a soldier in any army. But I was a prisoner. Remained to be one. Ameena ransomed my soul, released my mind from the confines of a twisted body and a deprived existence, only to slam the sharp edge of a guillotine down my neck.

What good do I gain from being free if she deserted me?

A stupid dove smacked into my closed window and lay dazed on the sill. I opened one pane and flicked it off, not waiting to see if it took flight. Before I closed the window, a pebble sailed into the room and landed by my feet. I stuck my head out.

Ameena stood below, hands on her hips, wearing a dull green T-shirt over faded jeans.

I quickly pulled back.

Another pebble jumped into my lap.

I shut the window, drew the curtain closed.

A rock smashed the glass and settled on my cushion. I couldn't believe my eyes. She broke our window. Shards fell against the wall behind the curtain.

"That's it, Waseem!" Ameena yelled. "I've had it with your stubbornness. Come out and talk to me right now or I'll . . . I'll—"

I peeked from behind the curtain. "Orrr wwhaaattt?"

Rearing back, she hurled a rock. It grazed my shoulder, but I could swear she was aiming for my head. Another projectile flew in, followed by a bigger one. "The alley is full of ammunition, Waseem."

"Cccrra . . . aazzy!" I yelled down.

"That's right!" She lifted a thick stick onto one shoulder and marched toward the entrance of my building. "Now, I'm coming up and you better open the door."

Pushing sharp pieces of glass aside with my cane, I made it to the door and opened it. Ameena had both arms raised, poised to strike. What she held was no stick. It was a sledgehammer.

"Oh! You stopped acting stupid." She balanced her bludgeon against the wall and elbowed me out of her way into the room. "We're making progress."

I slammed the door shut, determined not to talk. She could deliver what she was so determined to say and leave. She had always hated my typing instead of speaking. If I didn't reach for my tablet, my silence would drive her insane, and I would extract a small measure of satisfaction.

"Where is it?" Ameena looked around.

I arched an eyebrow.

"It's time you tell me what's going on. There it is." Taking my tablet off the dresser, she pushed it into my hands. "Here, if you'd rather use it. I don't want any misunderstandings between us." She picked up a cushion, flipped it upside down, and patted it to remove any broken glass, then plopped down. "Have Yasser fix the window."

I met her unapologetic, daring gaze. She must have straightened her hair in a salon or something because her curls were gone. Dark locks framed her furious face, lifeless and unnatural.

"Come on, Waseem." She winked. "You've wasted too much time already."

I lost gumption. Who was I fooling? One wink from Ameena drained any willpower I had to remain silent, which was one of the reasons I didn't want to see her in the first place. I knew that would happen. Sighing, I typed and lifted the tablet so she could read, "I hate your hair."

"Me, too." She flicked insipid strands behind her shoulders. "I had to please Mama. She thinks it's a nice look for the wedding."

Like the strike of a matchstick, she ignited my ire with the casual mention of her impending marriage.

"When?"

"Are you going to stay over there?"

"Yes. When?"

"Yasser didn't tell you?"

"No. When?"

"Not even Maryam? Neighbo—"

I swaggered forward intent on intimidation. The corner of the blasted rug tripped me, and I landed on both knees. My tablet slid across the room. "Wwheennn?" I groaned.

"Next Thursday." She reached for my hand, but I refused and adjusted my position to sit as far away from her as possible. "Mama has gone overboard with preparations. I'm giving her what she wants, a massive party, *dabkeh* dancers, a live band, and a supposedly well-known singer from *Saida*, Zain El-Abideen. I never heard of him, but she doesn't care." Ameena rolled her eyes. "You'll see what I'm talking about. She invited half the camp."

I clenched my jaw, fighting to stay stable. She expected me to go to her wedding? Why not wobble on the dance floor, too? Flail around like a fish out of water, grab the microphone and scream my heart out? I could do it. No one was courageous enough to intervene before I made a spectacle. Oh, the things I could do to create lasting memories. Yes, I would definitely go.

"I'm moving to Sweden, Waseem. I'm finally out of here. Can you believe it?"

I shook my head in denial.

"As soon as I acquire residency status and can travel, I'll visit as often as I can." She bowed to look at her clasped hands and whispered, "I tried, Waseem. I really tried to find a way out for you. Younis did, too. You must know that." She lifted her head. "We'll keep trying. I'm not leaving you behind, I promise."

I met her gaze, wistful, honest. How could I *not* love Ameena? It was impossible. Do I love her enough to let her go? How could I release what I never possessed? Am I honorable enough to wish her happiness? Why should I when each breath I took without her lacerated my heart?

I pointed at the window. "Lo . . . vve himmm?"

"I do," she said unabashed, without the slightest hesitation.

The muscles in my legs tightened. Tension raced through my body until it seized my lungs. I brought my knees to my chest and wrapped my arms around them in an attempt to arrest the trembling.

"Waseem, you know what's most important?"

Again, I shook my head, not wanting to hear repugnance lacing my voice.

"He loves me more than I ever dreamt possible."

I am not magnanimous, never have been and never will be. I decided right then and there not to attend her wedding with clear intentions to inflict pain. If anything, she would spend her ceremony searching for me, wondering, expecting my arrival. Knowing that I would disturb her special day suited my very core. A rejected heart—my heart—shrank to the size where a mere speck of decency found no room.

If she truly knew me, she would expect my acrimony. She would understand it, accept it. If she really cared, as a loyal *friend* should, and if she genuinely cherished our friendship, she would forget about me. Better yet, she would teach herself to hate me and move on with her new life.

CHAPTER THIRTY-SIX

I roamed the streets most afternoons in a hopeless attempt to dampen my outrage. Squeezing between people busy eking out a living in the dirty, narrow pathways did not salve my wounds. I must have projected my boiling anger into a ferocious, threatening visage as I moved in vigorous, clumsy trots. Women skirted around me, many changed directions lest they hazard an encounter with the irate Waseem. Men I knew flicked their heads in distant guarded greetings. Individuals I did not recognize pressed their backs to dingy walls to allow me more room as I stumped the grounds.

I heard mothers and daughters whisper as I passed, confirming that the rumor mill speculated on reasons behind my obvious fury to no certainty. Nobody was able to pry into my personal affairs. I smiled to myself. The beauty of being an oddity rested within itself. Common folk couldn't begin to fathom the depths of my feelings if I kept them ignorant of my thoughts and motivations.

On Wednesday, the day before Ameena's wedding, I literally stumbled into my lieutenant when rounding a corner. Ghazi helped me regain my balance then did a swift turn, ready to skip ahead. I grabbed his arm to stop him.

He yelped in pain. He kept his hooded head down.

I let go. My grip was not that hard. The boy was hurt.

"Wwaattt happi . . . nneddd?"

He shrugged and tugged on the long sleeve of his hoodie to avoid eye contact. "I tripped over a fruit crate."

I growled a guttural, menacing warning.

He lifted his head, dwarfed by a hoodie at least three sizes too large for him. I could see his neck and upper shoulder from the drooping wide collar. Red lines zig-zagged his pale skin—fresh marks—as if he had been whipped by a thin rope just moments earlier.

I struggled to maintain composure and saluted my lieutenant, granting him the dignity of respecting the lie. He returned the salute with difficulty and slipped away. I kept watching his gaunt body drowning in that sweater move down the alley until he disappeared from sight. I bolted toward his home.

The chance to unleash my bottled wrath onto Ghazi's abusive father gave me speed and laser-sharp focus. I saw no one, heard nothing on the way as I charged with my slick cane aflame in my hand. I arrived to a somewhat quiet alley. Good. Every neighbor would hear his screams.

The ugly black door stood ajar. I kicked hard to fling it against the wall.

"Who's there?" Ghazi's father yelled from inside. "That you, boy? How dare you leave without my permission."

About to advance into the dim dungeon, I heard someone call my name. I turned to see no other than Younis standing behind me.

He shook his head. "Don't do it."

I planted my feet apart and lifted my ebony weapon to ward him off. "Yesss," I hissed.

"Come here *ya khara*!" the man shouted from inside. "I want to finish what your brainless mother interrupted."

Furious, my muscles threatened to spasm. I flexed my arms to stave off convulsions.

The tall Swede balled his fists and took a step closer. "I want to help." Unusually clad in a black T-shirt over dark jeans, he projected an intimidating aura.

I scowled. Mr. Turtleneck, the camp's beloved doctor, my personal nemesis, wanted to help me beat the monster who hurt my boy. The hatred toward Ameena's intended that rocked my world and rotted my core reached its full capacity. There he stood, angry and resolute, compelling me to admire his gumption. What sick twist of fate had befallen me?

My grip on the cane started to wane. I strengthened my hold for fear my stance might reflect the slither of admiration forcing itself through thick, calloused layers of repugnance.

"I just treated one of the boys who live here," Younis whispered. "His mother brought him to me. The poor boy was in so much pain but wouldn't say what happened. Gave him my sweater to cover the wounds. I know what caused that kind of injury." Younis glanced over his shoulder. "I saw him talking to you. I'm guessing you're aware of his situation?"

"Yesss."

"Let's teach the son-of-a-bitch inside a lesson he'll never forget."

I truly hated this guy but found myself nodding and tapping my cane in affirmation.

"Allow me to do the talking. You do what you need to do, just don't leave permanent damage." Younis winced. "I'm a doctor. I took an oath to do no harm, but someone has to protect this child and his siblings." He gestured for me to follow him. "There's no official authority here to report domestic violence. It's up to you and me to administer justice."

I marched behind Younis, loathing him to levels I never thought possible. Frustration poured gasoline on the blazing fire consuming my conflicted emotions. But without hesitation, I charged into the room a scant second after him.

Ghazi's father sat on the floor, his back to a wall. Skinny legs extended straight and both hands raised in defense. Younis stood over him, fists pumping by his sides.

"You know who we are?" he asked in a threatening tone.

"*Dactor*!" The man's mumble accompanied a bewildered half-smile. He darted his beady eyes to me. "Waseem?"

I advanced, looked around the room and found a leather belt dangling from a nail in a corner. I snatched the belt and flicked it to crack the stifling, still air.

"What do you want?" Ghazi's father croaked, trepidation mixed with confusion in his voice.

"Waseem is Ghazi's friend," my accomplice stated in an unmistakable, menacing inflection.

The look on the father's face instantly flipped to one full of fear. If I weren't totally focused on the task at hand, I would have awarded Turtleneck a touché. The doctor knew how to deliver a message.

"We're here to even the score, asshole!" Younis grabbed the man by the collar of his stained shirt and lifted his shoulders clear off the wall.

"Wait! Wait! What? No!" The Worst Father of the Year babbled and clawed at Younis's hands. "Ghazi . . . my son. Only a mis . . . understanding," he gulped between words.

I thrust the tip of my cane between his ribs and leaned for him to feel stabbing pressure biting into his flesh. I had forgotten about the iPad dangling on my chest, and it smacked his forehead. I flogged the space by his ear once and barely missed his earlobe. Seeing sheer panic, I did it again, dangerously close to losing my balance and toppling over my target.

"Listen here," Younis threatened. "We are watching you. If you as much lay a finger on any of the children or their mother again, you will not see us coming. Understand?"

The man bobbed his head.

Younis shoved him against the wall, then released his grip.

I pulled back and endeavored to keep a straight face. That was it? He wasn't going to smack him or thrash him around? Issue more threats? Blinded by his quest, this outsider had overlooked a harsh reality of our camp. In our lawless enclave, there was one authority to which one could report crimes and assure a painful retaliation—many times disproportional, but I didn't care in this case. Ghazi's beating merited brutal retribution.

I fumbled with my tablet, typed with satisfaction, and shoved it in his abuser's face, "I will inform Abu Nidal."

"That's right!" Younis threw his arm around my shoulder. "If you dare to cross the line, Waseem will not hesitate to inform my father-in-law."

I twitched to flick the doctor's arm off. His self-aggrandizing proclamation cut me to the quick.

God! I absolutely, genuinely, and wholeheartedly detest this man.

CHAPTER THIRTY-SEVEN

"Men are so stupid!" Maryam declared from the ironing board Thursday morning. "Because of your stubbornness, Wael and Nabil refuse to go to the wedding."

Watching my nephew's sticky hands try to catch a red fish swimming across my tablet screen, I stressed, "Yaasserrr. Yyouu. Goinn . . . ingg."

"Ameena is like a sister to me. As dear as Fayzeh. You robbed me of the chance to be with Fayzeh when she married. Now, I will not abandon Ameena no matter what you say." Maryam took a sip of water and spit-sprayed it over a shirt. "Yasser has no choice but to go. He has a job to do, *alhamdullilah*. Look at how he's handling all of this. He desired to marry Ameena, remember?"

I wanted to offer that he probably still does but thought best not to interrupt Maryam's tirade. A series of coughs masked my frustration.

"You never get sick, so don't hide behind that fake cough."

I wasn't faking the hacks, damn it. I reached for that glass of water Maryam was using and soothed my throat.

"We both know you have no defense. Seeing Ameena in love with Younis is much harder on Yasser than you, losing a friend. He is taking it as a man, moving on and wishing her well. But you, you—" Maryam slammed the iron down on a shirt cuff, "—are stupid. You intimidate your brothers to miss out on the wedding of a decade. Did it occur to you that it might be Nabil's best chance to find a suitable wife?"

I had not expected my brothers' loyalty to reach this level, to skip the wedding for my sake, but I loved their unspoken support. I opened my mouth to explain that I didn't ask them to boycott the ceremony, but she didn't give me the opportunity to utter a syllable.

"And you are refusing to celebrate the most important event in your best friend's life, the woman who moved heaven and earth to arrange the overseas medical treatment that changed *your* life. Why, *aah*? Why?"

Lost for words, the plight of the red fish crossing my tablet suddenly became compelling.

"She's always been there for you." Maryam balanced the iron on its base and lifted the steaming shirt to examine it. "If you think you are punishing her because she's leaving and you're stuck here, then you are not just stupid, you are mean and . . . and cruel." Maryam draped the shirt on a hanger to join two others on the doorknob. "You, big brother, are selfish and weak."

My blessed nephew came to my rescue by yelling louder than his mother. Maryam unplugged the iron and lifted him into her arms. "Listen, Waseem. I'm going home to get ready. If you still possess an atom of our dear mother's soul, you'll put on one of those shirts, make yourself presentable, and go. Mama would have rushed there, gushing with joy to wish Ameena well."

I stared at the closed door after Maryam's departure, burning holes in the scratched wood. Did she have to bring Mother into this? My sister assumed I was dejected because I was losing a *friend*. Of course, she would think that. The other possibility was too remote for her to consider, the fact that I was losing the love of my life was beyond far-fetched. I was no more than a stupid spiteful man in Maryam's eyes.

When would Ameena see me as such? Why had she never discovered my genuine character? Ever since childhood, she had put me on a strange pedestal, forced me to be someone I wasn't, even strived to physically change me, helped me obtain an education and experience a glorious world beyond the horizons of the refugee camp. All for what? If she recognized what I was truly capable of, she would kick me off her glorified podium and finally set me free from the constraints her love imposed. Whoever said that love freed the soul had never been enslaved by Ameena's irons.

I plucked a shirt off a hanger and donned it. I would grant Maryam her wish, and represent our mother at the wedding. But I would not shake hands to congratulate the happy couple, nor would I stay quiet. Rummaging for Father's necktie in my keepsake bundle, I saw Mother's floral scarf folded under the note I had prepared to incriminate Doctor Turtleneck. My hand trembled as I rubbed the soft material between my fingers. Indeed, I would make an appearance and not hold anything back.

I made a splash entry as I limped into the party tent with Mother's colorful scarf wrapped around my neck. People dressed in their finest looked at my fashion statement with raised eyebrows and sneers—a vast array of people, standing, sitting, eating, dancing. Ameena's mother and a good number of women boasted traditionally embroidered *tobes*, others paraded in sleek evening gowns. Some men wore three-piece suits, but more opted for open-collar shirts. Bodies blocked every direction I turned. I couldn't proceed past the first couple of packed tables adorned with white tablecloths and vases filled with red roses. I imagined smashing those centerpieces with my cane. If Ameena's mother saw her daughter through my eyes, she would have filled the vases with vibrant sunflowers. It would definitely save her some serious money.

Soon, Yasser pushed through the crowd and escorted me to a row of chairs close to a square, linoleum dance floor. Several women pointed at my neckwear and whispered to each other. I took my seat. The man to my right glowered and moved down the row, leaving three chairs between us.

"Glad you came to your senses," Yasser shouted over the din. "I'll call our brothers to join us." He patted my shoulder and mumbled, "Good man," before he left me alone.

I hid my wry smile behind a closed fist. What I was about to do would shred Yasser's statement. My eyes darted to my target.

On a raised dais at the far end of the dance floor, Ameena lounged next to her groom, seated on huge throne-like chairs with gilded crowns. Like the crystal chandelier adorning one of the Rijksmuseum's halls, Ameena bedazzled in a radiant gown. I closed my eyes for a moment but still basked in her luminescence. Animated, talking to women and accepting hugs, she frequently pointed, waved, and whispered to the grinning, pompous penguin by her side. Though I couldn't distinguish the expression in her eyes from such distance, I could tell she was happy; her resplendent, poignant smile was impossible to misinterpret.

An over enthusiastic drummer beat his instrument with such vigor that I thought he stood right behind me, about to smack my head with his sticks. I turned to find the band stationed at the opposite end of the tent. A young singer in a shiny suit caroled into the microphone, earning every lira of his fees. The floor under my feet pulsed with the beat. I scanned the throng packing the dance floor.

Tall and lanky, flailing like a scarecrow in the wind, *Ustath* Ihsan danced with a beautiful young woman, most likely one of his daughters. Attired in a stunning royal blue dress, Maryam twirled about, holding hands with her husband and propping up their baby on her hip. Men, women, and children filled the dance area, heads bobbing, arms pumping, legs stomping, long hair and hijabs whiplashing delighted, glistening faces.

I tried to imagine Jannat among the hordes of people. Given the chance to unleash her provocative, poetic spirit, she could become the seductive, enchanting dancer women love to gossip about. But Jannat wasn't here. She languished in a past as distant as my mother's womb. I was not reborn into Jannat's caring hands. This time I was sure I did her a favor by staying away. She deserved a man with a tender heart and sound personality. And I stood here, watching Ameena's every move, counting each blink and wink, forever damaged.

Was it Voltaire who said *love is a canvas furnished by nature and embroidered by imagination*? Tapping my cane to the maddening beats, my stubborn needle pulled frayed threads and sank them into the old, tattered tarp of Ameena and I. Sweet Jannat should fold her blank canvas and tuck it away in a safe place until the right man, a good man, delivered the golden silk she deserved.

The festive atmosphere spread as a virus to infect hearts and feet. Ameena's wedding couldn't be more exuberant. She always carried the nurturing sun wherever she went, and now, her warm aura enraptured everyone. Including me. Despite all the animosity I had packed under my ribs, my lips stretched into a smile against my will.

Close to the buffet counters, Abu Nidal bustled between tables filled with men dressed in dark suits. Cigarette smoke shrouded some faces, but the way he doted on them, laughing and slapping hands, told me they were important figures.

A cough singed my lungs from all that tobacco smoke swirling around. I caressed the note in the pocket of my trousers and snaked my way in Abu Nidal's direction. I had left my tablet at home, but I wouldn't need to spell much once I gave him the note. He would call on Yasser for help, and I would translate the note, describe how a pupil of mine found the piece of paper after it fell from the groom's backpack during one of his rounds.

Of course, I would not divulge the boy's name, nor the neighborhood where Younis supposedly conducted his medical treatments. A straight and simple explanation would suffice to plant seeds of doubt in Abu Nidal's mind and raise suspicions about his son-in-law's loyalties. He could call off the whole marriage affair to investigate the allegations and give me back my Ameena.

A young man, decked in a *kufiyah* and the traditional, long shirt, *qimbaz*, over black trousers, pranced by me, leading his *dabkeh* group to commandeer the dance floor. They erupted with cheers and whistles. Drums beat louder and faster. Swirling a white handkerchief above his head, Abu Nidal leapt to join the group in black leather boots, stomping and capering.

I edged to a sturdy post to observe. Let the man enjoy the moment before I soured his mood.

Lifting the hem of her dress with one hand and hoisting her son in the other, Maryam approached. "Isn't she gorgeous? Look how beautiful, how happy she is. They're going to Paris for the honeymoon. She is so lucky!" My sister rubbed my arm. "Aren't you glad you came?"

The boy wiggled and screamed, cutting me off before I could respond with a blood-curdling scream of my own. Muscles controlling my lungs contracted with sharp pain, as if my rib cage collapsed onto them. I rubbed my chest and stretched my neck, laboring to breathe.

"Oh, you're emotional. We all are." Maryam patted my back. "Ameena deserves the best life could give."

My eyes stung as if Maryam's words exploded with tear gas. My delusional hopes for a quasi-normal relationship with Ameena ran deep. What could I ever offer her? Other than total devotion, nothing whatsoever. She had always yearned to escape the camp. Not only would Younis extract her from this bleak existence and grant her this fondest wish, he would also place the world at her feet, provide unfettered travels to anywhere her heart desired—even to Palestine. And she loved *him*.

Farook joined us. He pointed at Mother's scarf. "You sure like to draw attention."

"Leave him alone. He's here. That's what matters." Maryam fanned her face. "Oh, our little man needs to be changed." She handed the boy to his father and shuffled away. Dangling his son at arm's length, Farook followed her wake.

The *dabkeh* group leader and his ensemble lifted the groom off his chair, carried him onto their shoulders to the polished floor, and forced him to dance. Younis in his stiff tuxedo waddled in place, just like an Emperor penguin. I heard laughter from all directions. I wasn't the only one amused by this moron.

"Why don't you show us your moves, then?"

Ameena startled me with her goading invitation. Too preoccupied by the spectacle before me, I hadn't sensed her approach. Leaning heavily on my cane, I turned to face her.

"Come," she extended her hand. "Dance with me, Waseem."

I shook my head in disbelief. As I planned to paint her groom with the darkest of shades and accuse him of treason, she mocked me? Bad timing, Ameena. Bad timing.

She batted long eyelashes—longer than naturally possible—and stepped closer. "Is that *khalto*'s scarf?"

I nodded and choked back a groan. What else could I do? She stood so close, reminding me of the special bond she shared with my mother. If I had an ounce of courage, I would graze her cheek with mine, kiss her full lips, and throw every sacred taboo to the wind.

She touched Mother's scarf. "What a wonderful tribute to her memory. Thank you, Waseem, for wearing it and gracing my wedding with her presence." Taking my hands in hers, she tugged me off the post and let my cane crash. "I'd like to dance, but I don't want to draw attention away from Younis." She smacked her lips together. "I'm trying hard not to laugh. At least he's making an effort. And you must stop calling him Turtleneck from now on." She tilted her head and winked, a move that always shot a bolt of joy straight through my rotten heart. "Oh, Waseem, my dear, dear friend . . . I want you to know he is good for me."

She began to sway to the music. My body followed her moves. Her sun-kissed, flowery scent, her delightful voice, her frankness and inviting openness cast a spell on me. I locked my gaze on hers and lost any will to sabotage her future. Jealousy which had entombed my soul with bitterness shattered into pathetic pieces. The world, the crowds, dancers, music, lights, all reduced to nothingness. I bowed to the bewitching essence of Ameena.

Oh, Ameena. If only you allowed me to wallow in darkness. If only you didn't help pave a path to educate me. I wish I never read all those books which shaped the world's conscience and awakened mine. If only I remained ignorant of the all-encompassing stories, epic tales, and piercing poetry that inspired humanity and invigorated the man in me. What good had come from all this collected knowledge? How could I reveal the depth of my emotions? What language would I use? Which words and expressions would convey my feelings with clarity to caress your heart?

At that pendulous moment, the lines of the Syrian poet Nizar Qabbani filled my mind: *When a man is in love, how can he use old words? Should a woman desiring her lover lie down with grammarians and linguists? I said nothing to the woman I loved but gathered love's adjectives into a suitcase and fled from all languages.*

I surrendered, raised the white flag, and caved. I said nothing, did nothing but teeter and totter in her arms. The note remained hidden in my pocket.

Too soon, the moment of bliss ended. Abu Nidal elbowed me aside, grabbed Ameena's hand, and whisked her into the throng of oblivious dancers.

I watched her join hands with Younis to stomp the floor with unabashed glee, pulverizing my entire world with each step. I reached my fill, grabbed my cane, and fled the tent.

Up to this day, I never saw her again.

TWO YEARS LATER

CHAPTER THIRTY-EIGHT

I walked into the office and went straight to the point. "What do you think?"

In her mid-fifties and looking twenty years younger, Birgitta leaned back behind a pine desk. "Sorry to keep you waiting, Ameena. My client is oh," she slapped fingers together, "*för pratsam*."

"Sorry?"

"Ah, too talkative, wouldn't stop."

"No problem." I waved a dismissive hand to hurry things along. "So? Be honest."

"I like it." She motioned for me to take a seat. "I like it a lot."

I plopped into one of the leather armchairs facing the desk. "You think your colleague will be interested?"

"Lucas is focused on non-fiction, so this fits his interests. I sent it to him, already. We'll see what he says. And we could tempt him."

"How?" I crossed my legs, hoping to project poise and composure. In truth, I was dying to get the story into a renowned literary agent's hands. I had an obligation to fulfill, a feverish calling I couldn't explain, not to my husband, nor to his aunt,

Birgitta, who had become like a mother figure from the day I arrived in Sweden.

"We could entice Lucas," Birgitta removed her spectacles, "by offering the truth."

"I read and emailed you the file—as is—I didn't mess with it."

"*Lilla gumman*, that's not what I'm talking about."

"You know how it's been for me since I moved here, Birgitta," I said, heartened by the endearing term she always used with me. "All the language classes and constant training? Unable to see my parents, waiting for my residency papers? And finally starting my dream job at the regional office. I mean, it's been an emotional roller coaster. Younis has been understanding, totally supportive, but he's a stranger to everything I grew up with."

"My nephew is trying his best."

"Oh, I know he is. It's just that I . . . miss my friend." Too agitated to sit still, I left my chair to pace the room, dropping my nonchalant façade. "Waseem stopped talking to me. He totally cut me off. I tried to reach out to his sister, any of his brothers. Nothing. Complete silence. My parents offer tidbits of news but don't provide details. Then I received Waseem's iPad in the mail with a note from Yasser to return it to Rasheed in The Hague."

Birgitta picked up a black ballpoint pen and twirled it between her fingers like a baton. "Wait a minute, Rasheed went through his files and discovered the story? I find that odd, almost unethical for a professor who values personal ownership and copyrights. It's unprofessional at best."

"Oh, no. Sorry, I didn't explain." I flicked hair out of my eyes. "Rasheed's the one who purchased and set up the iPad for Waseem when we were living with his family, remember? Waseem never changed the password. The tablet is registered under Rasheed's account, so he has access to everything."

"Still, it doesn't give him the right to share and publish personal files of Waseem's. We'll have a big legal problem on our hands, invasion of privacy issues if Lucas wants the manuscript." Birgitta sighed, repeatedly clicked her pen. "Ameena, we can't possibly push this project forward."

"But I have rights to the story. Didn't I tell you?"

She dropped the pen and rubbed her temples. "*Lilla gumman*, you told me lots of things, my head is spinning."

"Look, I spoke to Rasheed. Before he donated the iPad to another vocally challenged person, he had to clean it up, you know before he restored default settings? That's when he found a note from Waseem directing him to the file, entrusting him to send it to me to do whatever I want with the story." I rolled my hand toward the door. "And I want it out there, for all the world to read and learn."

Birgitta arched an eyebrow. "You have that note?"

"Yes, yes." I breathed fast, as if I were a corralled horse running in circles.

"The note spells your name? In print?"

"Rasheed secured hard copies of everything, including that note. So, don't worry, that's not the problem." I stopped before the window to stare at my reflection in the glass pane. Shoulders slumped, face drown, I looked miserable, felt worst, and barely held it together. "You know how hard it was for me to read through his narrative? I had no idea Waseem was writing a tribute to our relationship, or that he . . . he ever viewed me as more than a friend."

Birgitta rounded the desk and approached me with arms wide-open. "I understand. I can't imagine."

I stepped into her comforting embrace and dumped my frustrations onto her dainty shoulders. "Why did I fail to see it? How could I have been so blind, so disconnected, so callous to not sense how he felt about me?" I pulled back and drew a steadying breath. "I am *not* Heathcliff's Catherine."

"Of course, you aren't," Birgitta confirmed without skipping a beat. "But surely you sensed *something*, Ameena. You are a strong, smart woman with a kind heart."

"I . . . I knew he favored me. And I liked spending time with him. I mean, growing up, he was . . . safe to be with. We depended on each other. I saw him as another part of me, the masculine side, you know?"

Birgitta arched a single eyebrow.

"Every woman has a hidden side. Please don't tell me you have no idea what I'm talking about. I'm not crazy and I don't have a split personality. Don't we all have others inside us?"

"*Ja, ja*," she mumbled, "I think I know what you mean."

"Waseem is my *other*. He thought he vicariously lived through me, but it's the other way around." My heart went insane behind my ribs. I overlapped my hands over my chest to tame its manic rhythm. "I wouldn't have made it out of the camp, wouldn't have come this far, if it weren't for his existence in my life. Oh, God! I used him!" My heart pushed its way up to my throat, and I doubled over with the weight of this selfish realization.

"Here," Birgitta slipped a wastebasket before me.

I wish my heart spewed out. Emptying the contents of my stomach, I wanted to rid my body of the pain. "I *used* Waseem. Used him my entire life, believing I was a good friend, a good person for sticking by his side."

Birgitta rubbed my back and handed me a wad of tissues. "How can you think that?"

I snapped my head up. "I felt . . . good around him."

"And you awakened his passions, helped him flourish, and live a fulfilling life. Read his testimony again, *lilla gumman*. You granted him enduring, loyal friendship, without questions, qualms, or any expectations. That's a rare, extremely valuable virtue. Most people go through their entire lives without receiving such a special gift. They fall in and out of love, then move on but don't sustain a divine, endearing bond with another human being."

"I loved him," I whispered. "Still do."

"Should I be worried about my nephew?"

"Oh, God, no. Younis understands. I love Waseem not . . . not in the romantic way he craved, but he holds a special place in my heart."

"Waseem knows that, Ameena. I think he truly does." Birgitta steered me toward a cluttered sofa, shoved aside binders before we sat together. "Why do you think he sent you the story? It's his way of telling you he understands. Yasser wouldn't have sent the iPad without his brother's permission. From everything I've learned about Waseem's nature, through his own words, I'm convinced he knows exactly what he's doing." She kissed my forehead. "My dear Ameena, Waseem meant for you to learn he accepts reality now."

I shook my head, tears running down my cheeks. "He didn't send his story directly to me. Why this roundabout way? And why wait this long?"

Birgitta patted my hand. "If I'm to guess, I'd say he finally had an epiphany, he reached the point of understanding and forgiveness."

"No. His silence so far, bringing Rasheed into the picture, saying I can do whatever I want with his story, all of it is . . . vengeful. It's not forgiving, nor understanding. He meant to hurt me, to prolong my pain."

"Oh, *lilla gumman*, I don't think that's the case." Birgitta lifted my quivering chin. "Why do you feel that way?"

I locked my gaze on a point in space beyond her shoulder, distinguishing no details, yet seeing things with glaring clarity. "Because that's what I would do," I whispered. "I must go to him. Now that I finally have my Swedish passport and borders have opened after travel restrictions of the pandemic, I'm taking the rest of the month off to fly home."

"What about Younis? Will he travel with you?"

"He can't leave the hospital, not until the summer. But I'm not waiting. I miss my parents. I never thought I'd say it, but I miss everything and seeing everyone in our neighborhood. Isn't that strange?" I blew my nose. "Of course, not the smells of donkey poop and piles of garbage, or cigarette and nargileh smoke everywhere, but I long to . . . oh, I don't know, wake up in my room to busy sounds in the camp, hear *athan* resonate from mosque minarets, drink coffee with my mother . . . laugh with Waseem."

"*Hemlängtan.*"

"That's being homesick, right?"

Birgitta nodded. "*Ja, j*a. It's not strange at all. Tell you what," she rose to her feet, "I'll clear my calendar and go with you."

I looked up at the kind woman, elegant in a pants suit, green eyes as generous and giving as a flowing river. "Really? You're willing to travel to Lebanon?"

"To your refugee camp. I want to meet this Waseem character. Discover his definition of the truth."

"What do you mean?"

"He starts his story by declaring deception. If we get his story published, don't you think readers would want to know where the truth lies? I know I do." She returned to her desk. "And I bet Lucas is going to ask a ton of questions."

I followed her. "What sort of questions?"

"For one, what happened to Waseem after you moved away? Did he ever earn his online diploma? Does he still mentor children in the camp? With his cunning and scheming, I sort of picture him running the camp with his army of informants."

"Mama hardly ever sees him. But that means nothing, because she barely leaves the house and she's fallen into the habit of beautifying things whenever I ask about anything in the camp. She's accustomed to hiding reality. Baba keeps reassuring me that Waseem is fine."

Birgitta steepled her fingers. "If Rasheed has his iPad, what is Waseem using for communication? Did he get another device? Or can he finally put pen to paper? Maybe he received speech therapy and can converse and be clearly understood. And poor Jannat. What happened with her? I'm dying to know. Oh, and the sister, Fayzeh. Did she settle in Italy? Or is it Germany? Is she have in contact with him? Did Nabil manage to escape the camp?" Birgitta rearranged a stack of folders in a pile. "Far too many questions to be answered."

"So, you're serious about going?" I placed both palms flat on the desk. "When should I book our flights?"

The phone rang.

Birgitta held up her index figure and answered the call, nodded as she listened then said, "Well, I knew you would, Lucas." She turned to her computer screen and clicked the mouse. "I'm looking into it right now." Covering the phone's mouthpiece with her hand, she raised questioning eyes to me. "Can you do the thirteenth through the twentieth?"

I bobbed my head. I'd waited two long years, agonizing, worrying. I could hold on for ten more days to see Waseem and set things right between us.

CHAPTER THIRTY-NINE

In all my years at the camp, I never entered it in the dead of night. Cloaked in darkness and eerily quiet tenement buildings loomed frighteningly in some of the sectors we passed. I kept glancing at Birgitta in the backseat of my father's car, trying to gauge her reaction. The woman took in our daunting surroundings with fortitude, saying nothing. Baba personally drove us from the airport. When I asked why he didn't send Yasser, he annoyingly shook his head and uttered his simple refusal, "*Laa*."

The day I turned seven, I learned never to repeat a question to Baba. If he wanted me to know something, he would tell me. That was how my mother had explained it after he yelled and stormed out of the house when I nagged him to attend my birthday party. Those days of innocence and naivety were an illusion, a brutal mirage. In my mid-twenties now, I lugged a battered soul as heavy as the weathered vegetable cart that used to creak down our alley. Oblivious to Waseem's feelings for me, I felt as dense and fatigued as the donkey dragging it.

Anxious and sleep deprived, I kept my conversation with my father in Arabic brief so Birgitta would not feel slighted. Tilting my head back, I closed my eyes. Baba took the hint and let me rest for the final leg of my journey.

Ever since I read Waseem's revelations, my chest had adopted his laden heart. I lied to Birgitta, earlier. He didn't have a special place in my heart, he entirely occupied it—my other heart, the one which I possessed no awareness of and was always there—secretly beating to keep me alive. Not the heart with which I loved Younis, a kind husband I so cherished and admired.

My feelings toward Waseem ascended to a higher plane, beyond the physical. Was it possible for the body to house one heart, and another soul? That was the best scenario to explain my situation.

Waseem was not just a friend, nor was he my soulmate. People talk about soulmates as if they were a blessed reality, perhaps so for most. But Waseem and I are not most people. He is unique. His soul spoke to mine in a language others have yet to discover.

Since I learned of his true sentiment, every node in my brain released memories of us together, sucking on lollipops, scheming, chasing bald men, stealing books, reading, laughing, sharing, crying in pain, visiting museums and red-light districts, and devouring forbidden fruits of knowledge.

Waseem was wrong. I did not show him the world. Because of his depravity and courage, he forced me to knock down doors to procure medical treatments and allow his mind to flourish with the gifts of education. He launched me out of the camp on a mission to trigger his release. I returned to our cage determined to set him free.

How could I face him? How could I ease his burden without giving him hope for a relationship which would never come to be? How to restore our ambrosial bond? How not to disappoint? How to heal? Our souls were forever interlocked in steel restraints. The harder one of us tugged, the deeper the links dug into our conscience.

~

Breakfast at our house was a spectacle. Mother cooked every Arabic dish under the sun and forced Birgitta to sample everything. She even hand-fed her several bites. In addition to the *zaatar manaeesh*, hummus, falafel and *foul* spread, Mama prepared my absolute favorite; eggs with *halloum* cheese fried in local clarified butter. Sipping hot mint tea afterward, contentment settled my nerves. Though stuffed, I felt lighter, younger, myself once more.

Washing dishes, I glanced at Waseem's window—closed, but the curtains were drawn back. It was warm enough to enjoy a cool breeze, the late spring morning begged for open windows. At ten, he couldn't be still asleep.

"Your mother is a hoot," Birgitta said from behind. "I don't understand a thing she says, but she keeps talking as if Arabic is my mother-tongue. I like her."

"Did she show you her needle work in the sewing room yet?"

"She showed me the needles," Birgitta laughed. "I think that's where we're heading next." She touched my shoulder. "*Lilla gumman*, are you going to see him now?"

Drying my hands, I nodded. "It's past time I do."

"I'll wait here, keep company with your mother." Birgitta gave me a quick hug. "I can't wait until I meet him. But you set the pace."

I didn't have the chance to unpack, so I pulled the least wrinkled shirt I had over a pair of jeans and gathered my hair into a ponytail. Checking the mirror, I undid the ribbon to release my curls. Waseem liked my hair loose. A carefree look might help put him at ease and break the ice. I thought I had my nerves in check, but a sudden urge sent me running to the bathroom to retch my mother's delicious breakfast. Literally lighter, I washed, decided against keeping my hair down and restored my ponytail. I tucked Waseem's iPad under my arm and crossed the alley.

Yasser met me with a frown halfway up the stairs, then quickly switched to a weird, lopsided smile. "Ameena?"

How could he be surprised to see me? Even if Baba had kept him in the dark, with Mama's gossip mill running rampant, the entire camp learned of my arrival by now. I skipped up, focused on my mission. "I'm not talking to you."

"It's good to see you. You look lovely."

"Nice try." Unable to resist chastising him for the lack of communications the past two years, I wagged my finger. "Don't think flattery is going to work. Like I said, I'm not talking to you. Is he awake?"

"Ameena, listen." Yasser spread out his arms, blocking my ascent. "There's something you need to know."

"What is it?" I giggled my nervousness. Up close, Yasser's tight smile hid little of the panic in his eyes.

"Waseem has a . . . very bad cold. Maybe you should visit later when Maryam is here, or uh . . . other family members."

"I'm not on speaking terms with Maryam, either." I moved up another step. "Not a word from her since I left, and she's supposed to be my good friend."

"Please, Ameena."

"Oh, I'll play nice." I winked and attempted to pass Yasser. He shifted his weight to prevent my advance.

Another nervous giggle escaped my throat. "What's going on?"

"He really suffered a lot. You don't understand."

"Well, if you or any of your siblings answered my calls, I'd understand exactly what he went through. Now, will you move out of my way?"

"We did what he asked of us. He didn't want you to—"

"What? Worry?" I cut him off. "Good. Because I'm not worried. Not anymore. I'm angry. At all of you. And him, God, I'm so mad at him." Fed up with Yasser's delaying tactics, I shoved his chest with the iPad and climbed past him.

"He won't speak, Ameena." Yasser followed me.

"I brought his precious tablet. He can use it if he insists on being stubborn." I hesitated a fraction of a second with my hand on the doorknob. Taking a steadying breath, I walked into the room.

Nothing, nothing on God's earth, prepared me for what I faced.

Under the closed window, Waseem lay flat on his back under a thick blanket, his eyes closed. An oxygen mask connected to a tall cylinder covered his nose and mouth. His hands overlapped on his chest atop the covers, the color of his skin ashen and pale, as if he had never been exposed to the sun a day in his life. His body was so frail, it barely raised the blanket. This couldn't be Waseem, the vibrant, cunning friend I so needed to make amends with and restore into my life.

"He won't speak because he can't," Yasser whispered. "He hasn't said a word in days."

Waseem hovered midair before my eyes. I blinked. Hot tears ran down my face. He alighted and settled on the cushions. "Why?" I clutched my convulsing throat. "When?"

"Pneumonia."

"From Covid?"

"We think it was influenza. Waseem continued to go out in the biting cold to teach those kids and . . . well, we don't know if the original infection was Corona or not. Testing is rare in the camp, if available at all."

Yasser's heavy sigh pushed my feet a step farther into the room.

"He wouldn't rest, working like a mad man, hardly eating or sleeping, lugging books around on a cart as if the earth's rotation depended on his delivery. He put up several portable libraries in different sectors of the camp. Every month, he and his uh . . . helpers would move the carts to another alley so more children could have access. He wouldn't stop, wouldn't slow down no matter what we said, until the infection turned into pneumonia."

Yasser's voice hummed in my ear. Every word he uttered buzzed like a hornets' nest.

"When my brother couldn't bounce back," Yasser continued the assault, "he made me promise to guarantee his mission continues on and instructed me to send you his tablet after he's . . . gone. But I thought . . . I shouldn't wait, maybe you'd want to . . . say goodbye. His body lost the fight late winter. He's been uninterested in his surroundings ever since. On good days, he sometimes wakes in the afternoon when uh . . . other relatives are here. You should come back then?"

"Waseem, I'm here," I whispered.

"He was hospitalized in *Saida*. Your father paid for everything, but the doctors said to bring him home. Nothing could be done except keep him comfortable. We are praying. It's all in *Allah*'s hands, of course . . ."

I took my shoes off, careful not to make too much noise. Yasser kept talking behind me, but he might as well had been quiet. I stopped listening. I placed the tablet on the dresser as softly as I could manage and tip-toed closer. Under the mask, he was clean-shaven, his hair neat and combed. The top button of his ironed pajama shirt clasped.

"I'm here. Your Ameena." I didn't know if I said the words aloud. I couldn't hear my voice. What foolishness.

"Waseeeeem!" I yelled at the top of my lungs.

His eyelids didn't flutter. Not even once.

I dropped to my knees, held one of his paper-thin hands and closed my eyes. He smelled of chamomile and mint. "*Aboooh,*" I murmured.

Fingers twitched in mine. A weak pinch.

"Oh, Waseem! My dear, dear friend."

His hand slipped from my grasp onto the checkered covers. Did my crying weaken my hold? Or was his move intentional? I lifted both his hands, kissed the back of them, excited, delirious with hope.

"*Abooh. Abooh, Abooh!*" I sang my hymn.

In that small room in the middle of our refugee camp, logic completely deserted me. I imagined if I repeated our catchword long enough, he would respond. I had so much to say, to explain, to deliver, but my tongue found no more words.

I don't know how long I stayed like that, rocking, chanting. I sensed someone's hands on my shoulders. It could have been Yasser, or Maryam, or even my mother. Whoever it was, pulled me to my feet, dragged me home, and tucked me into bed.

CHAPTER FORTY

I opened my eyes to Baba's voice softly chanting my name.

"It's time you stop this nonsense." He sat on my bed, smoothed my hair. "I'll call your husband and drag him here if you keep on like this."

Like what? I looked past him toward my mother standing by the door holding a tray.

"Get up, Ameena. Eat." Baba waved her closer.

"Your favorite, eggs and *halloum*," Mama said, her tone sweet, but exaggerated.

I immediately regressed to a ten-year-old. What on earth was going on? Baba almost never came into my room. In fact, I couldn't recall a single incident when he had. Pulling up on elbows to rest my back on the headboard, my joints creaked, and my body ached all over.

Baba handed me a glass of orange juice. "*Yalla*, drink." He switched places with my mother.

I took a sip and cleared my throat. "Am I sick?"

"You've been sleeping for two days, *habibti*." Mama fed me a bite of pita bread dripping with egg yolk. "The doctor said not to worry. Your body needed rest."

I chewed fast. "I slept that long?"

"Yes, *habibti*." She shoved another bite into my mouth. "Exhaustion from long hours on the plane."

Knowing full well traveling wasn't the culprit, I held my tongue and accepted one more mouthful offered by my smiling mother—master in concealing facts. She must have also known the cause of my withdrawal.

I nodded. "Yes, long flight." Bits of food came flying out of my mouth. Mama dabbed her face with a tissue.

"You're going to be fine," Baba decreed from the door and stepped aside for Birgitta to enter before he left us women alone.

"*Lilla gumman*, you had us all worried."

"What happened, exactly?"

Birgitta pulled back the curtains to a sunny day. "Well, after you came back from visiting Wasee—"

Mama sucked a sharp, audible breath. Birgitta flinched, then continued to say, "—visiting your friend, you sort of passed out."

The room started spinning. I briefly closed my eyes to stop the dizziness. Even though my mother didn't understand English, she latched on to Waseem's name and clearly didn't want Birgitta to finish uttering it. She hid his condition from me, thinking I was too fragile to handle the news or fretting I would sabotage my residency chances in Sweden if I left before receiving official papers. Mama knew I would have come running had I known Waseem was so sick. She realized how much he meant to me and deliberately kept me in the dark. I grabbed the plate from her hands and smiled an apology to hide my irritation. "I can feed myself, Mama."

Waseem, my beautiful, sensitive, intelligent, misunderstood, non-responsive Waseem. He lived in one world, craved another, and thrived in mythic realms offered by novels, poetry, and plays.

If I possessed half of his intelligence, if I could recall a quote that captured the clandestine quality of his beauty, I would. My head pounding, nothing came to me except lyrics of a song: *This world was never meant for one as beautiful as you.*

I rubbed my forehead. "You know what, Mama? I'm dying for caffeine."

"I'll make us a strong pot of coffee with lots of cardamom." She eased off the bed and headed to the door. "Eat more eggs, *habibti*." She turned to Birgitta and mimed sipping from a cup. "*Ahweh*?"

"Ah, *na'am. Shukran*," Birgitta accepted and thanked her in perfect Arabic.

After Mother left, I placed the plate on the nightstand and raised my eyebrows at Birgitta. "You're speaking Arabic, now? Are you sure I wasn't asleep for two months?"

"I had to learn some words to get by." She sat beside me on the bed. "Your parents were going out of their minds. If it weren't for an experienced nurse from the UNRWA clinic, they would have followed their doctor's advice and moved you to a hospital in the city."

"Oh, no."

"The nurse convinced them to wait twenty-four hours. Said you were in shock . . . we all know why."

"Have you seen him, Birgitta?"

"Not yet. I didn't feel right visiting without you. Maryam came to check on you. We talked. Her English is fairly good, by the way. She was very concerned."

"Maryam is a dear friend. We were—are—like sisters. Fayzeh, too. I bet they're also keeping her unaware of his illness."

"Let's not talk about Fayzeh, now." Birgitta averted her eyes. "You need your rest."

I clutched her arm. "I've been asleep. Fully rested, I assure you. What about Fayzeh? Did she come with Maryam? Is she here in the camp?"

"No, Ameena. She's not." Birgitta tried to leave.

I tightened my hold. "What did Maryam tell you about her sister?"

Dropping back, Birgitta cocked her head. "I'm sure your parents will tell you when the time is right. I shouldn't—"

"It's bad, isn't it?" I interrupted. "Haven't you noticed? My parents believe in hiding truths. Everyone does around here."

"I believe people obscure their dire reality to preserve some level of . . . hope."

"My parents think I'm dainty and weak. They didn't inform me of Waseem's deteriorating health, remember? God only knows what else they're keeping from me."

"They dearly love you, Ameena!"

"Of course, they do. And I love them so much. But that's how things have been in this house all my life." Desperate for information, I released Birgitta's arm and sprang up in bed to sit with my back straight, ushering strength to seem stable, at ease. I took a couple of bites for added measure. "Tell me, please."

Birgitta pulled in a long breath. "Fayzeh made it to Cyprus, and her brother, Nabil, followed her a couple of months later. But her husband, what's his name?"

"Khaled."

"His asylum plea was denied. Nabil's too. They were to be deported back here. So, both men got on one of those small human trafficking boats to Italy."

"Oh, God! Far too many risk that horror out of desperation."

"And far too many don't make it. *Lilla gumman*, their boat capsized. Everyone aboard drowned."

"*Ya Allah*!" I choked on a scream. "No, no, not Nabil."

"I'm so sorry. I shouldn't have told you."

"I want to know." I stared at my shaking hands. Why was I shocked? I dealt with refugees and asylum seekers in my line of work, heard their horrors and shared their pain. Happy endings didn't occur often to people from our world. Nabil and Khaled turned out not to be exceptions. I slumped under the covers. This was all too much. I should escape back to sleep.

"Are you okay?" Birgitta asked, panic in her voice.

"I'm just . . . sad."

Birgitta tried to hug me, but I scrambled out of bed, held on to the nightstand until the floor under my feet steadied. "What time is it?"

"Three-fifteen."

"Maybe Waseem is awake, now. Yasser said sometimes he's alert in the afternoon. I must go to him."

"You will." She eased me back under the covers.

"I . . . need to go, Birgitta. Need to explain things."

"All in good time. Now, you must rest, regain your strength."

Mother came in with the coffee tray. She filled short cups to the brim, served Birgitta and handed me a cup dripping on its saucer. Knowing I would learn nothing new in a conversation about Fayzeh or Waseem with my mother, I did what I had always done with her: divert the conversation to a mundane topic. I licked the spilled coffee and examined the red and white design on the saucer. I motioned for Birgitta to check hers.

"Where did you buy this set from, Mama?"

"Yasser brought it just the other day. A gift from one of your father's friends. He did the man a favor or something."

"The art is similar to a—" I pressed my lips together to stop a sob, "—design of a Palestinian *tobe*."

"It's a new trend, incorporating traditional Palestinian embroidery designs into things other than cloth."

Birgitta flipped her saucer back and forth. "Don't you have something similar, Ameena?"

I shook my head. "The blue and white decorated plates I brought from Palestine are of the famous *Khalil* ceramics."

"Ah, from Hebron?" Birgitta asked.

My mother smacked the mattress. "*Khalil. Khalil.*" She wagged her finger at Birgitta. "No Hebron. *Khalil.* Tell her, Ameena. In this house, we say the Palestinian name of the city. The world has forgotten us, but we will never forget where we come from."

Catching on without me having to explain, Birgitta quickly apologized. "*Asifah. Khalil,*" she corrected, scraping her throat with obvious exaggeration to produce the *kh* sound.

Mother nodded and turned to me. "You can have this whole set, *habibti*. Yasser will bring me another. And even if he can't, I have so many, not exactly the same but really nice, some still in boxes."

"*Shukran*, Mama. I like these, but I prefer the ancestral ceramic patterns." I burned the roof of my mouth on a sip, trying hard to keep from wailing. We should be talking about Waseem's illness, Nabil's death, I thought. But here we sat, drinking coffee and discussing folkloric art as if we were relaxed women in a Swedish cafe sharing small talk on a casual day. So many questions swam in my head, but none reached my lips. I had sincere doubts my mother would answer any with full truths.

"People claim you should cut back on coffee to prepare your womb for a baby, but that's nonsense." Mama broke the heavy silence.

"What are you talking about, Mama?"

"You've been married for two years. Your father and I can't wait much longer to have a grandchild, Ameena. It's time you start the process. But don't worry. I drank two whole pots every day before and during my pregnancy with you, even while I was breastfeeding, and look how you turned out." She pinched my cheek. "Perfect!"

Too spent to argue, I let her bask in her proud moment, however detached from my reality and mistimed. What kind of madness was this? We sipped coffee, me gazing out the window in a twisted bundle of emotions, Birgitta leaning against the footboard, and Mama cradling my free hand, rubbing and twisting the wedding band around my finger. I recalled Waseem's frail hands in mine. Through the fog swirling in my brain, something about the feel of his knuckles nagged at me, but I couldn't pinpoint what it was.

Harvesting the energy surge induced by caffeine, I left the bed and approached my window. Cup and saucer rattled with each step. Thick brown liquid splashed my fingers. Behind me, Mama droned on about her embroidery accomplishments to Birgitta. I lost count of how many shawls and tablecloths she had shown her.

Bustling neighbors crowded our alley. Boys and some girls kicked a deflated ball up and down the narrow area, barely missing the magazine stand outside Mr. Ihsan's bookshop. Other girls clutching rag dolls huddled by a smeared wall. I looked for our faithful donkey then realized the hour was too late for his arrival. The shouting and yelling going on between men harmonized with the mosque's *athan* calling for afternoon prayers. Someone around must be frying garlic as the strong odor wafted straight up my nose. I sagged against the windowsill, sensing tension ebb from my body and beaten soul. This was home.

A woman came down the alley pushing a small carriage. I immediately recognized its mismatched, clunky wheels as they struggled around chunks of the broken pavement. The way she moved caused her blue-covered head to bob in a peculiar way. As if perched on short sticks, she walked in small, careful steps.

I balanced my cup and saucer on the windowsill and tilted sideways to take a better look.

Approaching, the woman lifted her face toward me. Kohl-framed, downturned eyelids. Banana eyes! Could this be Waseem's Jannat?

I waved a shaky hand in greeting. Did she recognize me?

The woman hesitated a second, barely broke her lips into a smile then waved back. Under the afternoon sun, a piece of jewelry on her hand sparkled, and I squinted against its glare. She lifted a green and red bundle out of the carriage, held it against her chest and unwrapped the colorful blanket to reveal a chubby baby's face. Holding its little hand, she kissed and pointed it toward me. I blew a soft kiss on my palm before she disappeared through the entrance to the building across.

Ten meters away from me, Waseem lay in pressed pajamas, freshly shaven and bathed in aromatic, nourishing soap. Touches indicating the tender care of a loving woman.

I swayed in my spot. The thing that nagged at me when I had cradled Waseem's hands and the sparkle on the woman's finger tried to come together in my fuzzy head.

The window across opened. The top silhouette of the woman in blue hijab appeared behind it. Her soft weeping reached me in waves and drenched my entire body with sweat.

Maddening seconds ticked.

Mama's voice faded. Birgitta's single syllable responses disappeared. Air stopped ruffling my hair. The glaring sun sought refuge behind a lonely cloud.

Eyes riveted on Waseem's window, the world—my world—plunged into darkness.

Yasser poked his head out, looked down and locked eyes with mine. He beckoned me with his hand then went back inside.

A frightening flare ignited in my head, powerful enough to bring the sun out of hiding. I swayed in my spot. Those mismatched wheels on the stroller, a clever way to repurpose Waseem's treasured walker. That woman and child. Yasser had mentioned other family members. Could they be *his* family? And he wanted me to meet them?

Clutching the drapes, I closed my eyes and took a steadying breath. If that was indeed Jannat, how could Yasser reach this level of selfish disregard to his brother's feelings? There was no imaginable way for him *not* to know about Waseem's infatuation with her.

A man's rich voice reciting the Qur'an blared and resounded through the alley. The porcelain set by my hand crashed and shattered into countless pieces.

Birgitta squatted to collect scattered shards. "Careful! I'll get the broom."

Mama held me by the shoulders and guided me in a wide semi-circle back to bed away from the debris. "*Allah yirhamoh*," she mumbled.

I stared at my mother, distinguishing none of her aged features, struggling to comprehend her prayer for mercy.

"Waseem is in a better place now, I'm sure of it. This is life, Ameena. We are all prisoners until death frees us."

Death? *Death*?! I blinked and brought my mother's face into focus, finding her summary of life's circle elegantly simple, yet painfully poignant. She didn't want Birgitta to utter his name moments before, but now that she thought he had died, she disclosed it. Waseem could not have departed this world. I had yet to tell him how much I cherished his existence in mine.

"I could not . . . set him . . . free," I croaked between sniffles.

"He is, now," Mama whispered.

I shook my head. "Not dead."

"Can't you hear the Qur'an from over there?"

I ran the sleeve of my nightgown across my face to wipe it dry. "They keep recitations going to accompany prayers for his recovery, that's all."

"Yes, I know. Much louder, now. And what about that crying? I'm telling you, *habibti*. Waseem's soul has been released."

I snapped my eyes toward the window with a belated epiphany. Words of my favorite poet, Mahmoud Darwish finally descended on me: *We are all captives, even if our wheat grows over the fences, and swallows rise from our broken chains, we are captives of what we love, what we desire, and what we are.*

I rubbed my chest, sensing—hearing—my rib cage collapse and crush my lungs. All my life, I had strived to find ways to unlock Waseem's many cells. Despite each key cut or duplicated, I remained blind and deaf to the cruel reality glaring in my face.

I was Waseem's true jailer. And he would forever be mine.

I shuffled to the window and slammed it shut to silence all noise. Sounds, smells, and childhood experiences, my jumbled road to education and strife to maturity, even my love to Younis, were all tied to Waseem. He was the home I was sick for.

"Oh, Mama, if only you knew."

"Know what?"

"I am the one held captive."

"Until you birth your own child, yes." Mama patted my belly. "When it happens, *inshallah*, you'll feel differently. I know what you're going through."

I chewed my lower lip to stop from screaming. I could explain what I meant to the woman who birthed me, but would she understand or even acknowledge my predicament? Mama must have known, or at the very least expected, that my relationship with Waseem had developed into a unique, unbreakable, special bond. Yet, she never said anything to address it all my years of existence. She had even encouraged it in her not-so-subtle way of avoidance. Now, she continued to disregard it.

"Do you really know how I feel, Mama?"

She tilted her head, a kind, warm look in her glistening eyes. "A mother always senses her child's emotions, remember that." She cradled my cheek. "This pain, Ameena? It doesn't need to pass. Learn to live with it. For people like us, loss is our lasting companion."

"Oh, Mama!" I broke down in her arms. The truths she uttered confounded my imprisonment.

"You will have new life growing inside you soon, I pray. Give it a chance, grant your child a better future. It's your obligation, Ameena, and your father and I deserve it. We must focus on tomorrow, keep going forward."

I shivered under the weight of past generations forcing their will into my empty womb. Ever since I was born, I had never stopped seeking a better life, plotting, dreaming, hoping. But at this precarious instant, I needed a reprieve, time to concentrate on the present, on Waseem. My mother's warm nest fell short from providing comfort. I felt deserted, alone in my misery and utterly defeated.

"I hope your first born will be a girl and turns out exactly like you."

I lifted my head. "I want a boy."

"That will make your father happy." Mama sighed. "Younis too, no doubt. Me, I'd prefer a girl. All children are priceless gifts, but having a daughter is something special." She held my face between both palms. "May *Allah* grant you what you want, *habibti*. But remember, having a healthy child should be the ultimate wish."

Why was my mother babbling about babies? Her conversational evasion tactics shot beyond the familiar norm. Standing before her at this crucial moment *not* talking about Waseem alienated me further. Disoriented and nearing numbness, I looked around. There was my bed, the bright reading lamp on my beaten-up nightstand, that sagging bookcase with my beloved collection in the corner beside my closet. And there stood Birgitta at my door with a lost look on her face, not understanding a word of our bizarre conversation, for sure. Did I reflect the same confused expression? Everything in my surroundings fit into place, yet I . . . did not.

"I'm going to pray for a boy," I said with determination. I think I stopped crying as my voice sounded strong. "And I shall name him Waseem."

A shrill of a *zaghrouta* penetrated the closed windowpanes. I shuddered as if an arrow aimed straight at my forehead struck with full force. Lightheaded and somehow suspended in space, I wiggled out of my mother's grasp and bolted out the door. Barefoot, I crushed dirt and pebbles away from my childhood room and the madness it afflicted. Shouting and yelling went on behind me, but I didn't risk a glimpse so as not to lose a single precious second. With only my nightgown on, I imagined I shed patches of the white fabric off with each step before I reached Waseem completely naked, unburdened, reborn anew into his safe kingdom.

Another *zaghrouta* echoed in the stairwell as I skipped up the stairs. I wasn't sure where it came from, but it certainly filled my ears. I barged into his room and stood breathless. Panting. Trembling. I distinguished none of the surroundings, no one else in the room. As if I had tunnel vision, everything plunged into darkness except my beloved friend sitting propped up on pillows.

"Waseem!" I screeched.

He winced. "I . . . hearrr . . . youu," he said in a distorted voice, hoarse and barely audible.

"I'm here." I sprinted forward and dropped to my knees. "I would've come sooner had I known you were sick. No one told me. I got on a plane as soon as I received your story."

He flicked his eyes over my left shoulder to someone behind me. The quick move reflected disappointment, or perhaps waning anger. I couldn't tell and didn't want to waste time nor care to discover to whom it was directed. I had so much to convey. "If only I could find a way to explain. I tried to reach out to you, Waseem. I really tried." Rough, cracking sobs broke from my constricting throat. "I'm so very, very sorry for all the pain I've caused."

Swimming eyes focused on mine, he whispered, "I . . . knnoww."

The turbulent emotional rocket that had launched me into his realm immediately crashed aflame with his calm admission. He knew. He understood. Of course, he did. He designed this outcome with his tormenting journal of our lives and stubborn silence the past two years. Waseem had meticulously kneaded me into this agonizing guilt. I nodded with strange serenity. Good for you, Waseem. You've exacted your revenge.

"We are even, now," I admitted.

He shook his head. "Allwwayysss . . . hhavve . . . bbeeennn!"

A loud *zaghrouta* rang around again. It came from over his head. The prism of light illuminating him widened to reveal the woman with the blue hijab cradling the baby. The joyous shrill came from her. She bent over to put an oxygen mask over Waseem's nose and mouth and waited for him to inhale before removing it.

"Mmyy . . . wwiffe."

"Jannat." I barely glanced at her small face and reached out to pat the baby's thigh. "And this is *your* baby," I breathed out the words, hardly hearing my voice over the incessant thumping in my ears.

"Mmy . . . ssonnn." Waseem hacked a guttural cough. "Hhealll . . . thyy."

"He's perfect." I overlapped my hands over my extremely loud heart. "What's his name?"

Waseem wiggled his eyebrows, slanting his lips into a mischievous smile.

Oh! That move, that simple, boyish smirk I had longed for, wrapped its electrifying probes around my heart and shocked it to normal rhythm. There sat *my* Waseem beside his wife and son in all his teasing, scheming, triumphant glory!

Jannat placed the oxygen mask over his face again. "It's sort of an unusual name," she said, or rather sang.

A hiccup mixed with a chuckle jumped out of me. Waseem's description of her distinctive voice was literal.

"Everyone tried to talk my husband out of it, but he insisted." She bounced the baby in her arms. "This is Zareef-eltool."

I dropped back onto my heels in surprise. My eyes returned to meet Waseem's; his eyebrows arched with a silent question. Painful convulsions churned and tittered in my tight chest, bubbled up my throat and exploded into a spasmodic laugh to blanket the small room and poured out the open window to pervade through our entire camp. The perpetual pessimist gave his offspring the most heroic name of all. It made little sense in this miserable world, but it did to me—to us.

THE END

ACKNOWLEDGMENTS

During the time span of developing this story, I have leaned extensively on the unconditional love of my family. The steadfast assurances of my mother, Nawal kept propelling me forward at critical moments. The amount of hope she stubbornly injected into this journey is impossible to quantify. The unwavering confidence of my husband, Saad helped me fulfill my dreams as a writer. By obliterating my doubts at crucial junctions while writing, he repeatedly demonstrated the exceptional man he truly is. My appreciation goes out to my lovely children, Leila and Bassel, who listened to me babble about a fictitious family. Their patience and gentle nudging helped me push through the emotional process of concluding this story.

I would like to give my sincere thanks to my agent, Susan Golomb, whose expertise and clear vision guided me to the bright light at the end of this tunnel. Special appreciation extends to my editor, Isaac Morris. From the instant he acquired the manuscript, to the day it came out as the book is it, he had been extremely supportive, detecting with sharp eyes angles and plot threads and suggesting pathways or expansions. My heartfelt thanks go to Stephan Zguta at Arcade Publishers as he saw this book's potential and to the publicity team, Rachel Marble and Janina Krayer.

The following persons have been instrumental with their backing, help, and encouragement. Their proficient critique and unbound generosity granted me priceless feedback as they offered their assessments with understanding and respect:

The late Roger Paulding for taking me under his wide instruction wing. Jane Marchant, a writer with tremendous talent and an invaluable friend. Bob Gregory, a generous individual with vast knowledge, who repeatedly lent me his expert ear. Luke Chauvin, who injected subtle humor in our discussions to lighten heavy loads when most needed. Trey Chambers, who provided a physical, intellectual, and emotional safe place for our critique circle. Raphael Sher, who's gentle heart opened my eyes to different possibilities while developing the plot. Sharon Dotson, who never ran out of optimism and reassurances. Paula Porter, who believed in me and never stopped. Loads of gratitude also go to Matt Chauvin, Marian Jacobs, and Emerald Gearing for their valuable insights.

Many thanks to the team at Art Omi Center in Columbia County, New York, where I spent a most fulfilling writers' residency to work on this book.

I will forever be grateful for the enriching presence of my cousin Ammourah in my life. He was the inspiration behind Waseem.

Above all, I bow in humility to the readers who found the time to consider my work and allowed me to enter their homes with my words. I am eternally grateful for such privilege and vow to work hard to continue to earn it.